Child of the Dead

Also by Don Coldsmith

Child
of the Dead

»»»»»»»»»»»»»»

DON COLDSMITH

Doubleday
NEW YORK   LONDON   TORONTO   SYDNEY   AUCKLAND

PUBLISHED BY DOUBLEDAY
a division of Bantam Doubleday Dell Publishing Group, Inc.
1540 Broadway, New York, New York 10036

DOUBLEDAY and the portrayal of an anchor with a dolphin
are trademarks of Doubleday, a division of
Bantam Doubleday Dell Publishing Group, Inc.

Library of Congress Cataloging-in-Publication Data

Coldsmith, Don, 1926–
    Child of the dead / Don Coldsmith.—1st ed.
        p.   cm.
    1. Indians of North America—Great Plains—Fiction.   2. Indian women—Great
    Plains—Fiction.   3. Orphans—Great Plains—Fiction.   I. Title.
    PS3553.O445C48   1995
    813′.54—dc20   94-25680
    CIP

ISBN 0-385-47029-0
February 1995
First Edition

10   9   8   7   6   5   4   3   2   1

To our friends Julienne and John Judd,
who will understand the intricacies
of these conflicting cultures

Introduction

In the eighteenth century, the coming of more Europeans into the Great Plains brought danger of a new kind . . . disease. The natives had little natural resistance against some of these, since they had never experienced them before. One of the most dreaded was small-pox, which decimated various Indian cultures as late as the 1860s. It may even have been used as a sort of bacteriological warfare somewhat later.

This is a fictional account of an accidental early epidemic among the People of the central prairie. The active Europeans in the area at that time were French traders. For this reason I have chosen to use the term *"poch."* This is an early French word for pocket, pouch, or pit, from which the English name of the disease derives: *pox.* It seemed to me that the first name used by the Plains Indians for the "spotted death" would be that used by the French: *poch.*

This is not primarily a story about smallpox, however. It, like others in this series, is a story about people. Cultures and their diverse problems come and go, but people remain people. They have hopes and dreams, happiness, disappointment, laughter and tears, love and loss, but a will to survive and search for something better.

DON COLDSMITH

Part One

Part One

1

»» »» »»

Running Deer watched the big lodges come down, one after another. It was always a time of mixed emotions, the day after the Sun Dance. Already, the Mountain band had finished their packing and departed. They were usually the first to go, because they had traveled farther to the reunion. The ragged line of people, horses, dogs, and pole-drags could still be seen to the northwest, their plume of dust growing smaller in the distance.

The Red Rocks, too, had traveled far from the southwest into the plains for the occasion. They, too, were nearly ready for the trail.

The Northern band, with their usual efficiency, would probably be the next to leave, she thought. That band, larger and with more political prestige, took great pride in such things.

Her own, the Southern band, was in no great hurry. The Sun Dance had been in their area this season, and they would travel only a few days to their summer range.

It was expected that the Eastern band, noted for foolish ways and inefficiency, would be the last to break camp. Was it not always so? Probably they would not be ready to leave until tomorrow. It was past noon now. Why, she wondered idly, did the Eastern band behave so?

They often showed resentment over the jokes and jibes of the other bands. Yet, they continued to behave in ways that made the jokes all too easy.

"He cannot help his foolishness," someone would say. "His grandmother was of the Eastern band, you know."

Running Deer was sure that they sometimes brought it on themselves. It must be a sad thing, she thought, to have no better way to gain attention than to behave foolishly. Ah, well . . .

Actually, her thoughts were sad anyway. Since she was a child, she had felt this time of sadness, a letdown after the Sun Dance. The festival itself was so exciting, so wonderful, that the day after its conclusion was an anticlimax. It always reminded her that she would not see friends and relatives of the other bands until next season's Moon of Roses. Some she would *never* see again for always. Cold Maker took his toll in lives during the Moon of Snows and the Moon of Hunger.

Deer shook her head, trying to clear it of such depressing thoughts. She wiped a tear from her left eye, hoping that no one had noticed, and turned her attention to packing.

Just to the east of the Southern band's camp, the people of the New band had struck their lodges and were preparing to travel. That was a thing which had happened only a few seasons ago. A band of strangers, with a completely different language, had joined the People. There had been some friction at first, but the new people had proved their friendship. There was even talk now of giving them a seat in the Council. The Big Council. Already, their leaders met in the councils of the Southern band.

She did not care. Let them do what they wished. Running Deer was no longer interested in politics. There was not much that interested her now, since the loss of her husband. She had not taken that well, she knew. She did not care about that, either. The opinions of others no longer mattered to her, because nothing did.

Theirs had been a good marriage. The best, actually. It had been a hard time for her when Walks in the Sun had gone with that ill-fated expedition to the south. But she had never lost faith. She had always known that he would return, even when others had given up hope. And he *had* come home, two seasons later.

She had welcomed him with open arms, secure in the knowledge of their love. It had been possible for her to survive that dreadful time

because of his position as a holy man of the People. Walks in the Sun
had been made to think that it was his duty to go with that exploring
party to give them guidance. She had been able to accept that, and
had rejoiced in his return.

Of course, she had been younger then. Considerably younger.
Deer could not have told now how many winters she had seen. She
had lost count. Not as many as wrinkled old Mare's Tooth, three
lodges down, but too many. Her children were grown and had lodges
of their own, and her grandchildren were quickly becoming tall. But
lately, she had lost interest even in her family. It was not so much her
age, she thought, but her bereavement. She had never managed to
recover from the death of her husband.

Walks in the Sun had been one of the most respected men in the
entire nation. Even the Real-chief, who was of the Northern band,
had sought advice from Sun. His status, his wisdom, his ability to
bring home the survivors of the expedition "too-far-south" . . . But
Deer, though she had taken great pride in all of this, had loved him
for his love. There was a strange mixture of feelings that had remained with her after his death. Pride in what he had been, in the
respect that the People had held for him. Even in the manner in
which he had died, for the good of the People, in a last selfless gesture, singing the Death Song. Her son, Singing Wolf, had told her
about that. He had witnessed it. Others congratulated her, and told
her how proud she should be . . .

They do not understand! she had told herself fiercely, many times
over the intervening years. Her feelings were mixed, but when it
came right down to it, she had to admit it. Walks in the Sun had made
a choice, one that must have been terrible for him. He had had to
choose between his love for her and his concern for the People. He
had chosen the People. He broke an ancient taboo knowingly, fully
aware that in doing so he would die. It made her furious, even now,
that there had been something more important to him than their love.
She almost hated him for that sometimes. Then she would be immediately filled with guilt and remorse for feeling that way. Many nights
she had spent alone in her lodge, crying over her loss. *Why, why did
you have to leave me?*

It had seemed to her that every attempt to comfort her made her
feel worse. Her friends told her how proud she should be. Her sons
and their wives had always seen that she lacked for nothing. Even

now, they were folding and rolling the cover of her modest lodge, preparing to travel. That made her feel old and helpless, too. Both of her sons' wives had asked her to live in their lodges, but she had refused. Partly, she hated to give up her independence. Partly, she was afraid that her occasional nighttime crying would be discovered. So, they helped her constantly, and the situation did not improve.

One thing had infuriated her, a short while after her husband's death. Someone had come to her lodge, knowing that her husband was dead, but seeking the power of his medicine.

"But did he not leave you his gift?" the man asked.

True, that sometimes happened. The gift of the healing spirits might be bestowed on the wife of a dying holy man. It could be accepted, and even gained strength sometimes through the use by a capable woman. Many wives, including Deer, were assistants to their husbands, and could easily repeat the rituals and chants. She could also refuse it, of course, and it would disappear.

To Running Deer, there had been no choice. To her, the thought of taking over his gift would have been to dishonor his memory. True, the widow of an owl prophet of the Northern band had done it quite successfully, but Deer could not. She had chased the erstwhile client from her lodge with a stick. He had retreated in astonishment, to tell everyone he knew about the strange behavior of the widow of Walks in the Sun.

Soon people began to avoid her. Her friends disappeared. Now, she knew, she was regarded as an unpleasant, crotchety old woman. She did not care, or at least pretended not to care. She knew that even her own grandchildren feared her a little. That was just as well. She was left in the solitude of her memories, little realizing that those memories which she called up were the *wrong* ones. She wallowed in pity for her loss, and in bitterness for the injustice of it all. She aged rapidly, and her former friends whispered of it.

It had been several years now, and her moods were no better. Worse, usually. She had gotten a mild lift from the Sun Dance, but the corresponding depression today, the day after, was worse than ever. If she could only cross over, be with her husband again . . . How could she accomplish it? She had thought many times of taking her life. Probably the only thing that had prevented it was the thought of her husband. It must be done in a way that would bring honor to his memory.

She had heard a story at this Sun Dance that would bear some consideration. An aging warrior of the Northern band had done it. During a late storm in the Moon of Hunger, food had become scarce. There was a very real danger that some would starve. This old fighter had tottered out into the teeth of the blizzard, stripped for battle and singing the challenge of the Death Song, as one would when facing an enemy in battle:

> "The grass and the sky go on forever,
> But today is a good day to die!"

He had been facing an enemy, the dreaded Cold Maker, spirit of all the dreadful chill which the People always expected in the moons of winter. In doing so, he may have saved the lives of some of the children.

Now, that sort of thing she could do. It would solve her own problems and bring further honor to her husband. Yes . . . she would say nothing, but treasure this idea in her mind. There would come a time when she would do it. Probably not until winter, for there would be no chance. Maybe not even this winter, but the chance would come, sometime. Then she would carry it off with defiance, with *honor*. Her former friends would be sorry.

"Mother?"

"Yes . . . yes, Wolf. What is it?"

She had been lost in thought, and had not even heard her son speak.

"I said, will you ride the pole-drag, or . . . ?"

"No!" She interrupted his question. "That is for the old and infirm, or tiny children. No, I will ride . . . Would you bring my gray mare?"

"Of course, Mother."

He went toward the horse herd, and encountered a family friend.

"What is the matter?" asked Bear's Tooth.

"I do not know . . . Nothing, maybe. But my mother . . . Did you notice, this morning? She seems almost happy."

"*Aiee!* That has been a long time coming!" said Bear's Tooth.

"Yes. But it is good, no?"

"I hope so . . ."

Wolf went on to the herd, and caught the mare with little difficulty. He was still surprised that his mother would choose to ride. He swung to the back of the gray . . . The animal had not been ridden for some time, and it would be good to take off the first skittishness before his mother tried to mount.

He slid to the ground before the nearly abandoned lodge site, and handed the rein to Running Deer.

"Did you think an old woman could not ride a fresh horse?" she chided him gently. "I was riding long before you were born, Wolf."

He was puzzled. It had been a long time since his mother had teased playfully like this. Not since his father's death, maybe. Still, he was uneasy. There was something here that he could not quite grasp.

Well, he would think on that later. Maybe, even, talk to his mother at greater length. For now, he must help with the preparation of his own lodge for travel. He joined his wife and began to load the rawhide packs on the pole-drag.

"What is it?" asked Rain.

"I am not sure," he answered slowly. "My mother . . . She seems almost *happy.*"

"*Aiee!* And this is a thing for worry?" she teased. "It is long in coming, Wolf."

"That is true," he agreed. "Well, we will see."

He could not shake the idea that something was being overlooked here. Something ominous.

2
» » »

The sway of the gray mare's gait was pleasant, rocking her into a relaxed mood. Running Deer could close her eyes, and dreamily pretend that she was a girl again.

She had loved to ride, and had even participated in a few hunts with the young men. She was proud of that. Still, having accomplished it—she had once even made a clean kill, unassisted—she had proved her worth. It had been pleasant to settle down with Walks in the Sun in their own lodge, to raise their family.

Just now, her daydreams carried her back to those times. She was young again, not the bitter old woman she had become. The mare was comfortable to ride. Deer could forget, or at least postpone the thought of how stiff she would be tomorrow. Well, so be it. If she did not feel like riding the mare, or even walking tomorrow, she would ride on the pole-drag behind one of the other horses. Her decision about what she would ultimately do with her life had given her a new outlook. She felt that for the first time in many seasons, she had taken control.

Yes, that was it! She now had few responsibilities. None, actually, because her grown children had seen to her every want. But today, she had the feeling that she had taken back her life. The decision that she would cross over in a grand suicide gesture pleased her. It must be at the proper time, of course, carefully staged. In her mind's eye she rehearsed what she would wear, how she would sing the Death Song. As bravely as any warrior ever did as he rode into a hopeless battle.

She must keep her intention secret, of course. Her family must not have the slightest hint that she had such a goal. They would probably try to prevent her from carrying out her plan. No, it would be her secret, hers alone.

In making her decision, she felt that she had now regained control of her life. It was a good feeling. She could now do as she wished, not as others thought she should. *I can do anything I want to,* she thought triumphantly. Hers was the privilege of age, to do as she chose.

Running Deer came very close to smiling as she rode, but was able to stifle the urge. To let the others see any hint of pleasure in her face would surely give them the idea that something was wrong. No, she must continue to be the bitter old woman that she had become, so that they would not suspect. That should not be difficult.

Dreamily, she drifted into the past. The rocking motion of the horse took her back to her childhood, her earliest memories. Like the other infants of the People, she had been entrusted to the care of a dependable old mare. Deer's mother, along with the other women, had often been occupied with the tasks of butchering and tanning skins, drying the meat of the buffalo hunts. The older children could help. Tiny infants could ride in the pack boards on their mothers' backs. The toddlers, however, would only be in the way.

She dimly remembered the strong hands of her father lifting her to the back of one of the horses and tying her in place. It was high, far above the ground, and Deer was proud, as he turned the mare out to graze. The People were horsemen, known for their skills. This too was a matter for pride, but was it any wonder? Most children of the People had learned to ride as she had, almost before they could walk.

"Are you all right, Mother?"

The voice of Singing Wolf brought her back to reality.

"What? Oh, yes, Wolf. I have been on a horse before . . . Before you were born!" she added tersely.

She could tell that her unused muscles were beginning to tighten, but she would never complain. She did hope that the leaders would not feel it necessary to cover too much distance today. It was apparent that her body would be stiff and sore, though she would not admit it, except to herself.

Actually, she was rather proud of the way in which she was able to ride today. The gray was an old family horse, steady and dependable. Her own grandchildren had been tied to the back of this mare as toddlers, just as she herself had been, on one of the mare's ancestors. *There is nothing new,* she thought.

An odd idea struck her. She would be stiff and uncomfortable, and could do a considerable amount of complaining about it. This would help her cling firmly to the image that she knew her family expected. In a way, she would have preferred to be considered a kind and gentle old woman, but it was probably too late for that. Everyone now expected her to be sour and bitter. Well, let them. She would see that they were not disappointed. But when the time came, they would be sorry . . .

Shadows were beginning to lengthen when the word was passed down the column that the scouts had selected a place for night camp. Deer remembered the spot. She had lived in these tallgrass hills, traveling and camping with her people, for some fifty summers. There would now be few camp sites that were not familiar to her.

This one was good. All were good, actually, after a day or a week of travel. But some, better than others, and this was one of the best. Clear, deep pools of cool water were strung along the sparkling creek like beads on a thong. White gravel bars, and plenty of grass for the horse herd.

The "wolf," the scout who had come back to the columns to report, now wheeled his horse and sprinted away. Bits of dirt and sod flew high in the air behind him. *Showing off,* Deer thought. *He knows that some girl is watching.* A few girls, of course, might be attracted by such antics. Most would be disgusted at the young man's pointless demands on the abilities of a good horse. Such useless expenditure of the animal's strength might someday be regretted. What if he did so and then encountered a life-threatening situation with an exhausted horse? The appreciative giggles of a couple of silly girls would mean little then. Deer consoled herself with the thought that any girl attracted by such stupidity would be no better than that young man deserved. She clucked her tongue in disapproval.

She, Running Deer, would certainly have taught any daughter of hers better than to be impressed by such antics. She and Sun had had a daughter, as she had always wished for one. It had been her first-born, a beautiful child. Little Bird had been just a toddler when her father went on the disastrous trip south. It was after he returned that illness struck down young Bird, taking her life in the Moon of Long Nights.

Deer had felt that somehow this was a trade. She had prayed so long and hard for her husband's safe return . . . That was granted, but in exchange . . . She wiped a tear away.

It had not been long before she realized that she was pregnant again. She gave birth to Singing Wolf, and then, much later, to Beaver Track. It was not that she was displeased with her sons, for she was very proud of them. Both were well thought of in the band. Well, in the whole nation, actually. Everyone knew the name of Singing Wolf, respected young holy man of the People.

Her other son, Beaver Track, though not quite so visible as Wolf, was known as a skilled tracker and hunter. She was equally proud of him.

Still, a daughter would have been a great comfort to her in these past few years . . . Another woman to talk to . . . Her sons' wives honored her, but it was not the same. By now, Bird would be grown, with her own lodge . . .

She wiped away another tear, hoping that no one noticed. Maybe if anyone had, they would only think that the wind had blown a bit of dust . . .

There was a shout from the head of the column, and she raised her eyes. A dark line of green snaked its way across the lighter green of the prairie grasses' lush growth. Deer followed the tree line with her eyes, tracing the course of the creek. Now the horses began to quicken their steps, scenting water ahead. She found it necessary to hold the gray mare to a walk. She did not care to subject her aging bones to a trot today. It was probably not the water that made the animals push forward, she realized. They were far from suffering with thirst. Probably the horses merely sensed the end of a day's travel by the attitude of the people. There were trees ahead, which probably meant a camping place, which meant that the animals would be relieved of their burdens. Naturally, they tried to push on, to achieve that.

Dogs ran ahead, too, to explore the area where they would spend the night. She could see the scouts now, against the dark green of the timbered strip. They beckoned the column in with hand signs, indicating the areas for camp and for the horse herd.

Stupid, she thought, watching the one who had run his horse needlessly. He was officiously directing those who approached. *Still trying to impress some girl.* It was perfectly obvious where they must camp, near the water and upstream from the horse herd. Any child would know that. She took great pains not to look at him as she turned upstream.

It occurred to her to wonder why she felt so. It was not really in her nature to resent foolish people. She had always been impatient with those who did not do their best, but this was different. *Maybe,* she thought, *I have come to hate everyone, not just the foolish.*

Then the guilt feelings returned, in the knowledge that Walks in the Sun would certainly not approve of such an attitude. He had been almost too much to live up to, in his wisdom and goodness. And for that, she almost hated him sometimes. Which, of course, made her feel guilt again. It was an endless circle.

Running Deer started to dismount, and Beaver Track came running to help her. Irritated by his attentiveness, she jerked her arm away and slid to the ground. A thousand needles seemed to jab at her feet and legs as the circulation started to return. *Aiee,* she *must* be getting old. But no, she recalled, dismounting after a long ride had always been so. Trying not to limp, she handed the rein to Beaver. "Here," she said, as she turned to remove the saddle, "hold her a moment . . . Then you can take her for me."

Deer turned and laid the padded saddle aside with her small pack. She averted her face, hoping that no one would see her wince with the stiffness in her knees. Well, it was good, anyway. Maybe she would ride again tomorrow. For now, she did not even want to think about it.

3
» » »

Deer was almost too stiff to move when she awoke the next morning, but she was determined not to show it. Stifling a groan, she rolled over and sat up, tossing aside her sleeping robe.

She had considered riding on the pole-drag this morning. *Travois*, the People were calling these devices now. They were trading with the French, the past decade or so, and the young people especially were beginning to use French words. Deer did not really approve. Why call her rawhide pack a *parfleche*, when "pack" told it all quite sufficiently?

"How are you feeling, Mother?" asked Singing Wolf.

If he had not asked, or if he had only said "good morning," she would probably have ridden the poles. His question struck her as overly concerned, however. A little demeaning . . . It irritated her that her son would talk down to her in this way. Her back stiffened.

"I am fine!" she snapped. "Where is Beaver Track?"

"Getting the horses. Did you want yours again?"

Deer would actually have been much more comfortable on the *travois*, or even walking, but this was not working out well. She was trapped into asserting herself.

"Of course," she said. "Why would I not?"

"Well, I . . . It is good, Mother," Wolf answered.

He turned away to help with the morning preparations to travel. Deer took a deep breath and let it out as a sigh. How had that happened? She could not back out now. She must ride the horse. Maybe a little exercise would help. She began to walk briskly, picking up a stick or two to toss on the morning fire. It hurt to bend, hurt her back and her legs. Once she wondered whether she could straighten again, but managed it, with a barely audible groan. She hoped that no one heard.

In a short while, her sore muscles were beginning to limber up a little. By the time the column was ready to move, Running Deer was able to mount with only a little help, and it was good. At least, it was satisfying.

The event that would affect the lives of them all took place that afternoon. There were those who said later that the young men who were acting as wolves had been negligent. Maybe they had. Yet, how were they to know? There was no smoke, no sign at all that a sizable camp was nestled in that ravine.

The first sign was the distant whinny of a horse. Instantly, the tired horses in the column pricked ears forward. Several gave answering calls. No one paid much attention. A stray horse, nothing more.

The wolves were instantly alert. Theirs was the responsibility to make sure. The People were on good terms with all of their neighbors just now, but it was always possible that outsiders might enter their territory. It would not do to be careless. A war party probing into a new area might inflict considerable damage.

One of the scouts reined his horse to the left to separate himself from the other, and they approached the crest of the little rise at the same time. Both stopped now, and sat, staring for a few moments. Then one wheeled his mount and came back toward the column at a full gallop.

"Stop!" he shouted ahead. "Something is wrong here. Where is Singing Wolf? Where is Broken Lance?"

In a matter of moments, the young holy man and the band chieftain had moved their horses forward to meet the frantic scout.

"What is it?" demanded Broken Lance.

The young wolf was visibly shaken, and for an instant could only point.

"A camp!" he mumbled finally. "A band . . . almost as large as ours. Maybe thirty lodges . . ."

"But what . . ." Singing Wolf started to say.

It was apparent that something was very wrong. There was no smoke, no noise, nothing at all to indicate a camp of this size. Just then, there was a slight shift in the breeze, and Singing Wolf caught a hint, a slight suggestion, of what might lie in the ravine beyond the rise. He knew, before the shaken scout spoke again, what he was about to say, because Wolf knew the smell of death.

"They are all dead!" blurted the young man.

"Let us stop where we are," Broken Lance said quickly. "No one goes in until we know more. Pass the word."

The scout turned to do so, and the chief turned to Singing Wolf.

"Holy man, will you see what you can tell? Choose who will go with you."

Singing Wolf nodded. "My brother, Beaver Track."

"It is good. I go, too," said Broken Lance. "That is enough."

It did not take long to ready themselves. Word passed quickly through the band as the three men rode forward. No one else was to approach until more could be learned about what lay in the ravine. There was some natural curiosity, of course. But anyone who tried to approach would be prevented from doing so. If the social pressure of custom failed, the rule would be enforced by warriors of the Bowstring Society, who rode slowly back and forth between the now halted column and the ravine ahead. Broken Lance was a member of that warrior society, and sometimes called on them to enforce the rulings of the council. Or in this case, his own ruling.

Singing Wolf realized that the old chief must consider this a very serious situation. Lance did not often call on the warrior society to enforce any ruling, especially his own. Broken Lance had always relied greatly on loyalty and good judgment among his followers. Wolf had long marveled at the way the chief could obtain the desired decisions from the council. Each participant usually seemed to feel that the final outcome had been his own idea.

The present situation had allowed no time for diplomacy. Lance had simply announced how it would be, and called on the Bowstrings to enforce it. By this abrupt decision, everyone realized that the un-planned halt was based on a matter of extreme importance.

Singing Wolf, as he rode forward beside the old chief, felt that the whole thing was unreal. It is not a usual thing to come upon an abandoned village. People of the prairie often move, yes. But they take their lodges with them. Sometimes, maybe, an old lodge skin might be left behind, as its owners assumed the use of the new.

However, that was not what the wolves had said. A whole village abandoned with the lodges intact? Not even abandoned, maybe. The smell of death was strong now. Could everyone have been killed by a war party? But the People would surely have heard of such a war in their territory, and they knew of no other tribe here, even. Not one of this description. Their allies the Head Splitters frequently camped in the area. But there had been Head Splitters at the Sun Dance. Since that nation had no Sun Dance of its own, there were usually quite a few who chose to participate in the ceremony of the People. They would have said something, would they not? If they had known . . . No, this was not likely a band of that nation.

Occasionally, a band of the Trader People would be encountered. They were usually welcome, because they had good things to trade. Exotic stone knives and arrow points made of flints of strange colors . . . pink, white, yellow, black . . . In recent years, even some metal knives and points. Strange food items, too, from faraway places. But when the Traders came through, everyone knew, because they traded with all.

There were others, sometimes. Cheyenne, the "finger-cutters" in hand-sign. Comanche, from the south, whose sign was like the motion of a snake. Surely, though, the presence of these groups would have been known. And, according to the wolves' description, this was not a war party, but a *village*, of skin lodges. That meant women and children.

Someone had asked if this might be a band of Shaved Heads from the east. Or Horn People, or even Kenzas from the northern range of the People. All of these groups were known to move out into the prairie sometimes for a summer buffalo hunt.

The wolves were indignant over this question.

"Do you think we would not know a hunting camp of Kenzas?" one snapped irritably. "These are skin lodges, like our own. This is the camp of a band much like ours!"

Broken Lance had stopped such argument with an impatient gesture, and the three had moved toward the rise.

Now, Singing Wolf could see the tips of the lodge poles ahead. They seemed to sprout from behind the ridge as the horsemen advanced up the slope. The smell of death was strong now. Wolf felt his neck hairs bristle. The strange thought crossed his mind that they were approaching the Other Side, with the spirit-world just beyond this ridge. But no, surely the death smell was a thing of *this* world, not of the other. But are they not all the same? Yet, surely the Other Side would not smell of death . . . Or *would* it? He wished that he could talk of this with his father.

It was almost a relief to see as they topped the rise that there were burial scaffolds in the ravine. Not in close proximity to the lodges, but a few bow shots' distance away, as it should be. Quite a number, though . . . A quick estimate of the number of lodges and of scaffolds showed that perhaps half the families of the band must be in mourning. A great tragedy of some sort . . .

They sat on the ridge, trying to understand. The well-ordered camp of lodges lay before them, with no sign of life. A breeze barely stirred an eagle feather hanging on a warrior's shield in front of one of the lodges. It took a moment for Wolf to realize that this should not be. If the warrior who owned the shield was alive, its presence said that he was at home. Yet there was no sign that any of these lodges was inhabited. No activity, no smoke from cooking fires, no sound. Only dead silence. Dead . . . If the owner of that shield were dead, it should be with him on the funeral scaffold, so that he might use it on the Other Side. It must be one way or the other, yet it was not. Other strange thoughts flitted through Wolf's mind. Why were there no dogs? A camp of this size would usually have a large number of dogs, yet there were none. Was this a nation who did not have dogs? Surely not. Could there *be* such a nation? The People had used dogs to carry packs since Creation, it was assumed. Dogs were not so important for that purpose now, since the coming of the horse. Their other use, though, was still valid, especially in a season of poor hunting. The People had long had a small, chunky sort of dog, different from the one they had used as a pack animal. Both could be used as food, but the meat type fattened well on scraps from the cooking of food for the families of the People . . .

Where were the dogs of this village? Wolf could only think that the dogs always follow a band when the lodges are struck for a move. But they follow the *people,* not the lodges. The strangers of this band, then, must have left their camp, because there were no dogs. But, to leave their lodges . . . ?

"There are some horses," Beaver Track pointed.

Across the ravine, a scattered group of horses grazed peacefully. No more than ten or twelve . . . Those that might be left behind in an urgent situation, it appeared.

But *what* urgent situation? Not an attack . . . There was no damage evident. Something from which people were dying, yet there had been others to prepare them for burial. Then, suddenly, *they* decided to leave. Had they been afraid? Of what? *Of whatever killed the others,* Wolf realized.

A chill gripped his heart, and he was not certain that he wanted to know. At the same time, he realized that for the safety of the People, they *must* find out.

4
»» »» »»

Very gingerly the three riders made their way down the slope and into the village.

"I am made to think," said Singing Wolf, "that we should touch nothing until we know more."

His voice sounded high and strained, even to himself. He had not encountered a feeling like this before. An unfamiliar spirit hovered here, one that was evil and very dangerous. The horses were skittish, snorting at the smell of death and sidestepping nervously.

Besides that smell, though, Singing Wolf felt that there was another. He had dealt with much sickness as a holy man of the People. The spirit of every illness, his father had taught him, has its own smell. Animals were more sensitive to such things, accounting for the behavior of the horses. He had wondered, sometimes, if man had lost the keenness of smell when he learned to speak. But no, that could not be it. According to the old legends, all animals and all humans once spoke a single language. Maybe the animals had been given the gift of a sensitive nose when they *lost* the power to speak. No matter, now . . .

But his nose was picking up a special scent, a completely unfamil-

iar one. He felt that it was related to the spirit of whatever illness
. . . yes, it was surely a sickness that had caused this destruction. He
reined his horse to a stop and the others did likewise.

"Let us look around from here for a moment," he suggested.

They were among the first of the big lodges. Lodges so much like
their own that Wolf felt he might have understood these people and
their ways. There were differences . . . The shape of the doorway,
the unfamiliar designs painted on the lodge skins. But the basics were
there. The east-facing door, the construction of the smoke flaps, the
placement of the poles. It was all familiar.

"Look!" Beaver Track pointed to the doorway of one of the lodges.

A moccasined foot was exposed to view. That of a man, probably,
from the size. Above that, a bare calf. Wolf moved his horse a step
closer, to see farther into the lodge.

"Be careful," urged his brother, gripping his ax.

Wolf felt that whatever this danger, it could not be successfully
faced with an ax, but he said nothing. He could see more of the man's
leg now. The color was bad, a sickly bluish hue. Unquestionably, this
individual was dead. What sort of people, Wolf wondered, would
leave without caring for their dead? It would be unheard of in any
tribe he had ever known. A dishonor.

The leg, he now saw, was disfigured with several wounds. Small,
blackened circles, much like the holes made by the lead ball from a
musket. But there were several. He could see three or four between
the knee and the ankle. Flies buzzed or crawled around and across
them.

"*Aiee!*" called Beaver. "Another!"

Wolf turned to follow his brother's pointing arm. There, in full
sight before another of the lodges, sat a man, naked except for a
breechclout. Dead, like the other, but seated in a natural pose, this
one leaned against his willow backrest. He, too, had been dead for a
number of days, Wolf guessed.

"He is *spotted!*" blurted Beaver Track.

"Yes . . . like the other," Wolf agreed.

Not wounds, he thought, *but sores. This is the deadly spirit!*

He felt an urge to flee, but there was a need to understand more. It
was apparent that there were other bodies, scattered through the
camp. Some were old, but often there were men and women who had

been in their prime. Children, too. This sickness seemed to spare no one.

Stirring in the back of his mind was something he had heard last season when they had camped at the French trader's. Old Three Fingers, the trader, had been conversing in hand signs with some Kenzas from upriver. They told of such an illness among a distant people to the northeast, the story told to them by a traveling trader. It would strike suddenly, with fever and coughing, followed by many sores like insect bites. Soon these turned to festering spots that covered the victim's entire body. Usually, he died, the Kenzas said.

Yes, Three Fingers had answered, this was a sickness known to his people. *"Poch,"* he called it. Very dangerous . . . *What had he said?* It jumped from the sick to the healthy, leaving its deadly round tracks behind.

"Do any survive?" Singing Wolf had asked.

"Oh, yes," said the trader. "Usually far more than half. But it jumps easily. One does not touch the sick, or anything they have touched."

That statement had impressed Wolf. Several sicknesses of that sort were known to the medicine men and women of the People, so it had stuck in his mind. Even so, it was probably only luck that he had suggested not touching anything as they rode in. Or maybe, guidance. Certainly, he had not expected anything like this. This, he now realized, must be the dreaded *poch* that the French trader had warned of.

One other thing now came to memory. The Kenzas who had told the thirdhand tale had argued, insisting that maybe three out of four had died among the sick, as he had heard it. Most of the listeners had assumed that this was an exaggeration, produced by the retelling of a good story.

Now Wolf was not so certain. This band, the people who had died here . . . He had estimated from the number of burial scaffolds that many lodges were in mourning. Now it seemed to be that there were more dead, a corpse or two abandoned in perhaps half of these dwellings. He did not want to investigate too closely. He was still convinced, however, that some of the people of this band had departed, followed by the dogs and taking most of the horses.

"What has happened here, holy man?" asked Broken Lance, bewildered by the enormity of the scene before him.

"I cannot be sure, my chief," said Wolf slowly. "I am made to think it is this way: I was told of such an illness last season, a very danger-ous new spirit-sickness. It jumps from the sick to the healthy."

Beaver Track looked around them uneasily, and Wolf continued.

"These people had this bad thing, and some died." He pointed to the scaffolds. "Then, those who prepared them for burial died, too. Those still alive hurried to leave, in fear of their lives. I am made to think that those who touch the sick or the dead are struck down, too."

Broken Lance nodded. "Then it is important that none of the Peo-ple touch anything here, no?"

"That is true, Uncle."

"Then let us leave."

The old chief reined his horse around and rode majestically back up the slope toward the wolves at the crest of the ridge.

"Pass the word," he ordered. "No one is to touch anything here. We move on. We will stop early for a council, and Singing Wolf will tell us all of the evil thing that is here."

"My chief," suggested Wolf. "It might be good to tell them some-thing now. Some of the curious, or those who might want to look for something useful . . ."

"That is true," agreed the chief. "Wait!" He called to the scouts. "Tell them we will draw back a little and hold the council now, to explain. But no one goes in!"

To emphasize that, he signaled to one of the Bowstring Society with hand signs. The warrior relayed the message and the Bowstrings moved into position along the ridge.

There was much excitement and many rumors as the People drew back from the slope and toward a level meadow where they could hold the impromptu council. The chief's pipe bearer selected a site for the fire and a few people began to bring sticks and chips. A fire would be necessary as a symbolic gesture to the spirits of the place, a sort of permission to camp. Or, in this case, to stop only long enough to hold the council. The fire was perhaps even more important, thought Wolf, to appease the spirits of the evil thing that lurked just over the ridge.

Broken Lance opened the council, performed the ceremony with the pipe, and passed it to the subchiefs seated in the circle. The pipe passed more quickly than usual, because an urgency hung heavy in the air. Finally Broken Lance spoke.

"My brothers, this is a dangerous thing of which we speak. As I am sure you already know, there is a village over the ridge, there. A camp where everyone is dead."

There was a gasp from the crowd. Some may not have heard the rumors yet, and some who had might not have believed. Now, to have it confirmed by their leader himself . . . *aiee!*

"Singing Wolf will tell you of this," the old chief went on.

Wolf rose, not quite prepared to have the council turned over to him.

"My friends," he began. "There are things I do not understand about this. I heard of it at the trader's last season."

A few nodded their heads. Some others had heard the story of the Kenzas, too, it appeared.

"This is a new sickness, and it kills many. There are dead ones over there, with many spots on their bodies, the wounds that kill. I am made to think . . . Well, this is what the trader, Three Fingers, said, too . . . This is a spirit that jumps easily. Anyone who touches a person sick with these sores will be in danger. Oh, yes . . . these same spirits may stay on anything that the sick one has touched. That is why no one must go into that camp of the dead. I am made to think, my chief," he turned to Broken Lance "that we should travel quickly, well away from this place, before we sleep."

There was a murmur of approval, and Broken Lance nodded.

"Let it be so," he announced.

There was a flurry of activity, as preparations for departure were hurriedly completed. People were already mounting their horses and shouldering their packs when there came a cry of terror. One of the women had stepped behind a fringe of sumac to relieve her bladder before starting to travel. Now she came running back toward the others, terror in her face.

Several warriors sprang to help her, weapons ready for anything that might appear. A couple of the Bowstrings, already mounted, kicked their horses into a lope and converged on the sumac thicket. Then the nearest of the horsemen pulled his mount to a sliding stop, wheeled and retreated.

What can it be? thought Singing Wolf. *A bear, maybe?*

Everyone was retreating now. The thicket parted, and out stepped a child. A little girl, it appeared, of five or six summers. She staggered as she walked, a ragged dress of skins hanging loosely on her emaciated body. She was whimpering as she moved slowly toward the half-formed column, while brave warriors retreated before her.

Now Wolf understood. Every exposed portion of the thin body was marked with circular pustules, yellow and ugly and with a blackening crust in the center of each.

5
»»»

"**S**he is dying anyway," said one old woman. "Kill her to keep her from following us!"

"She could not keep up," insisted another. "Just leave her behind. She cannot last another day."

"But surely we can do something for her," a more compassionate voice joined in.

"The holy man said that those who touch her will have the sickness."

Singing Wolf did not know what to do or say. He almost felt personally responsible for this dilemma. How could he have known that there was a survivor? Or that it would be a small child? And even if he had known, what would he have done differently? Here was a major threat to all of the People. His heart went out to this dying child, but it was as someone had said. Nothing could be done for her. The decisions of the People must be for the good of the People. This dying child was an outsider, a member of some unknown tribe. It was an inescapable fact that even her own people had abandoned her in fear of the sickness that she carried. Probably her parents were dead, and everyone else was afraid.

As the People are now, Wolf reflected. What *should* be done out of pity, when nothing can really be accomplished, and any contact is dangerous?

The girl wandered toward a group of children, whimpering and babbling in some unknown tongue. The children scattered, some squealing in mock terror, others laughing hysterically from the tension of facing the unknown. One of the mothers swooped in to pick up her own child, a boy of three or four.

"Go away, girl," she screamed at the pitiful stranger.

Beaver Track had ridden in a big circle around the encampment, and now returned to talk to Broken Lance. People were remounting their horses, preparing to leave the area, which had become dangerous.

"My chief," Beaver Track reported, "their trail is there . . . They headed north."

"How many?"

"No more than ten or twelve, I am made to think. They took the horses. It was a very poor plan."

"What do you mean, Beaver?"

"I am not sure. They seemed to gather up part of the horses. The tracks say that most of the horses just followed. Their trails wander a lot."

Broken Lance nodded. "Maybe they do not have enough men to drive a herd?"

"Yes, that was my thought."

Singing Wolf thought about this new information. This was a dreadful threat, one that the People might not completely recognize. This sickness had come suddenly, and had all but wiped out an entire band like his own, apparently in a matter of days. Those who had not yet become ill had finally departed in what amounted to panic. They had undoubtedly prevented the dying child from following them. Little prevention was necessary, actually. They had simply departed, and the little girl could not keep up. There may have been someone who warned her to stay back, not to follow. It was a real concern. He was pleased, actually, that the People *were* avoiding the child. His own band could easily meet a fate like that of this camp of the dead.

It might be possible, though, to learn a little more before they departed.

"Go on," he called to Broken Lance. "There is something I must do."

The chief waved in answer. One does not question the duties of the holy man. The column began to form, changing direction slightly to avoid chance contact with the survivors of the sick camp.

Singing Wolf placed a pinch of tobacco as a spirit-offering on the coals of the dying fire. Then he cautiously approached the stricken girl. He kept a reasonable distance between them for safety's sake, but he felt that he must talk to her, if possible. Surely she would know some hand signs.

"*Ah-koh!*" he said aloud in greeting.

The girl, who had curled up on the ground and closed her eyes, now jumped in terror. She looked as if she expected him to strike her.

She must have been threatened, perhaps even beaten. *Ah, to prevent her following,* he thought.

She stared at him with wide dark eyes, sunken in a pallid face marred with the pustules.

"I will not harm you," he told her in hand signs. He took out some strips of dried meat and tossed them to her, still keeping a few paces away. Hungrily, she picked them up and began to chew.

"How are you called?" Wolf signed.

There was no response for a few moments, and then she paused in her ravenous eating to sign briefly.

"I am Gray Mouse."

"Where are your people?"

"Gone . . . dead."

Tears filled her eyes and overflowed down sallow cheeks, but only a drop or two. Wolf had the impression that the child was wrung dry of tears. Possibly it was part of the process of dying from this *poch* sickness.

"Your mother? Father?"

"Dead. Are you going to kill me?"

"No."

"The others said they would."

What others? he thought, confused. *Her own people?*

"If you followed them?" he signed.

The girl nodded.

"When did they go?"

"Two sleeps, maybe. Who are you?"

"I am called Wolf. Those are my people." He pointed to the departing column.

"They left you behind?"

"No, I will go with them. I will leave you some food."

He was wishing now that he had not even tried to talk to the child. She was dying, almost too weak to walk, but now that he had talked to her, even in signs, she was a person. His heart went out to her. Well, it was too bad, but she would be dead in a day or two. The tragedy would be over for her. Not for him, he feared. He would always remember the haunting look in those dark eyes.

"It will be good," he lied. "Your people will come back for you."

In a way, he tried to convince himself, he was not lying. In a way, she would rejoin her parents on the Other Side, and it would not be long. He rose to go, glancing back over his shoulder once. The child had curled up again in the fetal position, and already appeared to be asleep, still sucking on a strip of dried meat. She was probably exhausted from the excitement, he thought. He would never know. Quite possibly she might never move from the spot where she now lay. Guilt lay heavy on his heart, but what could he do? He left a little packet of meat and slipped quietly away to where he had left his horse.

Running Deer had been badly shaken by the events of the day. She rode along, oblivious now to the discomforts of travel. She could not remove from her mind the picture of the dying girl. Old memories of the loss of her own daughter came flooding back. It had nearly torn her heart out at the time. The mourning ceremony had helped, but her mourning had not ended after the prescribed three days. Not until she found herself pregnant with the child who would become Singing Wolf did she begin to rejoin the real world.

Now it had all come back, as she watched the People, her people, step quickly aside to avoid any remote contact with this pitiful child. Life was not fair. Of course, no one had said it would be, but it seemed that her own life had had more than its share of sorrow.

Then she felt again the guilt of feeling self-pity. There were others with so many troubles, and worse. The dying child . . . It had not taken long to realize that the girl's parents must be dead. Among the People, and probably among the child's people, too, relatives would normally take her in. In this case, the relatives, too, might be dead.

Dead, or too terrified at the threat of the horrible sickness to have concern for the child.

And, after all, the little girl was dying. A day or two . . . She could understand. Friends, relatives, other survivors of that village of death could not risk their own lives to care for a dying child. They might have families of their own, and their first duty would be to those. *And I have no one,* she thought glumly. *No husband, no children. They are grown and successful. No one really needs me. I am more a burden than a help to anyone.*

How ironic, then, that she was of no use while the dying child had no one to care for her in her last days. Deer ran this strange situation through her head again, and came to a conclusion: *This is meant to be!*

She very nearly wheeled the gray mare around at that very moment, but realized that there were those who would try to stop her. No, she would bide her time, act as if she had no such plan, and then slip away after dark.

Yes! This was even better than her original plan, to challenge Cold Maker in the Moon of Starvation. She could bring comfort to a dying child. Probably, she would then die with the sickness herself. It struck her as appropriate, somehow, that she would bring comfort to the dying, and then she, too, would cross over to the Other Side. What better place to be when one was ready to cross over than among the dead? She smiled to herself.

It was not long before shadows grew long and the band stopped for the night. Running Deer was careful to place her saddle a little way apart as they settled in. She hoped that the mare would not be too hard to catch. She busied herself with her few belongings, managing to hide a stout length of rawhide thong for a rein. No one must suspect her purpose, or they would stop her. But once she was successful in reaching the abandoned camp, there was nothing anyone could do. She could *not* rejoin the People.

She had been very careful to note landmarks that could be seen at night, so that she could find her way back. There should be a nearly full moon tonight to help her on her way.

Her sons would come back to look for her, of course, but by that time they could do nothing. The People would long tell the tale of Running Deer, the old woman who took pity on a dying child. She did not know how painful such a death as this might be, but surely it

was no worse than freezing. She would greet it with dignity. The
People knew how to die with pride, and she could do this thing.

She lay sleepless, waiting for the camp to quiet down. It seemed a
long time. Finally she rolled out of her robe and stretched. This must
look as if she were only going to empty her bladder, in case anyone
noticed her. She might need the robe . . . At first she cast it aside,
but then came back, hugging her shoulders as if she were cold, in
case someone noticed her. She picked it up and drew it around herself, walking toward the brushy area which the women were using to
answer the call of a full bladder. No one seemed aware of her.

Once out of sight, Deer waded through the stream and paused to
locate the young man who would be watching the horse herd. He
must be avoided. *Ah, there, by the tree!* She edged around the other
way, threading her way among the horses. It was dark . . . But now
she saw the gray mare, and moved in that direction.

Three tries she made. Each time the animal waited until Deer
touched her neck, and then spooked away. Deer felt her anger rise.
Well, enough! The longer she remained here among the horses, the
greater the chance that she would be discovered.

"Stay, then," she muttered to the gray. "There are many better
than you!"

She slipped her thong around the neck of a bay that stood quietly
and allowed her to do so. The horse did not object when she led it out
of the herd and to the brushy area where she had left her saddle.

It required some effort to swing up. It was a long time since she
had mounted without one of her sons hurrying to help her. There was
a satisfaction in it.

Very quietly she walked the horse away from the camp. When she
thought it safe, she urged the bay into a trot. It was a rough gait, not
nearly so comfortable as that of her gray mare, but so be it. It was not
for long.

She sighted across the hills to verify her landmarks, and headed
toward the village of the dead.

6
»»»

"**H**ave you seen our mother this morning?" asked Singing Wolf.

Beaver Track glanced up from his task, tying packs to the *travois*. "No . . . Why, Wolf?"

"I do not know. No one has seen her."

"Were her robes slept in?"

"Her robes are not here."

"Was she not with your family, Wolf?"

"Near us, yes. You know how she draws aside to be alone sometimes. We thought she might have joined you."

"No!"

Both were alarmed now. They widened the circle of inquiry. Someone thought he had seen her go to empty her bladder, but no one was certain.

"Her horse!" exclaimed Beaver Track. "Maybe she rose early to catch her horse."

The two men hurried out to the herd, where people were catching their animals and preparing for travel.

"There is her gray mare," Wolf noted.

Their attention was diverted by an argument between one of the young men who had guarded the horse herd and an older warrior.

"I do not know, Uncle," the young herdsman said respectfully. "I saw nothing."

Wolf recognized the older man as Quick Otter, a respected sub-chief.

"What is it, Uncle?" he asked.

"My bay pack horse, Wolf. It is not here."

"Maybe he strayed away."

"No. My black does that sometimes, but not this one." Otter turned back to the nervous youth. "Nothing at all? You saw nothing?"

"No, Uncle. They were a little restless about half through the night. I looked, but found nothing, and then all was quiet."

Beaver Track had left the group to circle the area, and now came trotting back, an anxious expression on his face in the early light of day.

"Someone led a horse from the herd and across the stream there," he announced.

"Of course," snapped old Otter. "Many have, this morning."

"No, Uncle, *away* from the camp. They stopped, to saddle maybe, in the brush there. Does your bay paddle a little on the left front foot?"

"Yes! He does!"

"This was the horse, then. I found the tracks on the sand bar where they crossed."

"But this makes no sense!" protested the herdsman. "If one steals a horse, he steals the best buffalo runner, not an old pack horse. Besides, we have no enemies here."

"Not that we know of," Singing Wolf agreed. "But he is right, Uncle. Why? Would anyone want to play a joke on you?"

"No. It is a bad joke, anyway. The bay was not worth much, but he was always easy to catch. Even a child could catch him."

The sons of Running Deer looked at each other, a light dawning.

"Or an old woman," said Wolf softly.

"What?" demanded Quick Otter.

"Nothing, Uncle. We will try to find your horse."

Wolf and Beaver Track drew aside.

"Could the tracks have been hers?" asked Wolf.

"Maybe. They were small. I was thinking of a young person . . . a joke."

"But where would she go, and *why?*"

It took only a little while for Beaver Track to determine that the rider on the stolen bay had headed straight on their back trail.

"Maybe she forgot something," he suggested.

"Maybe," his brother agreed. "But I am afraid there is something more here, Beaver. Our mother has been acting strangely, has she not? I am afraid that she has some strange idea about that camp of the dead."

"But what . . . ?"

Wolf was already turning back toward their own camp.

"I do not know. Let us get our families ready for the trail, as quickly as we can. Then we will go back, you and I."

Running Deer had reached the area she sought a while before the gray-yellow of the false dawn began to make itself seen in the eastern sky. She stopped the horse and slid to the ground. It had been an uncomfortable trip at best, and *slow.* The frustrating slow walk of the old pack horse had driven her nearly to distraction, and any faster gait jarred her bones unmercifully. She had not realized how grateful she should have been that her husband had always insisted on the best of horses for the family. Even her gray mare . . . *aiee,* what a differ- ence.

She stripped the saddle from the bay, and untied the bridle thong from its lower jaw to release it. The horse ambled away, grazing contentedly. *He paddles on the left front,* she noticed. Maybe that would partly account for his rough gaits. Beaver Track would have known. He was the horseman of the family. No matter, now . . .

Deer sat down, waiting for daylight. She did not want to go wan- dering around in the dark looking for the child. A night bird called from the trees downstream, where the burial scaffolds were. An eerie sound . . . There was a time . . . When she was a child this whole scene would have been filled with terror. Now it almost pleased her to face it. From another direction came the hollow cry of *Kookoos- koos,* the great hunting owl. His was a powerful spirit of the night. She had always felt a closeness to *Kookooskoos,* and as he called the hollow rendition of his own name, it was a comfort. Then a soft, noiseless spot of darkness floated past her against the paling sky, and was gone.

"Thank you, *Kookooskoos,*" she murmured. "Good hunting!"

As it grew lighter, Deer could begin to recognize landmarks from the day before. Yes, over there . . . that was where she had last seen the dying child. The girl might even be dead now. If so, she would abandon her plan, catch the horse, and follow the People, she supposed.

But there . . . yes! There lay the child, near where she had last been. The girl was sitting up, looking around in confusion, and crying softly. Running Deer hurried toward her, and the child started to run away.

"Wait!" called Deer.

The girl turned to look, and paused, still anxious. Deer quickly made the hand sign for peace, which says literally "Look! I am unarmed!"

The child seemed to relax a little, and Deer approached slowly.

"How are you called?" she signed. "Gray Mouse, is it not?"

The little girl nodded, perplexed.

"How are *you* called?" she signed.

"I am Running Deer."

"Will you hurt me?"

"No, no, child. I want to help you."

"It cannot be. They told me. They went away!"

The girl pointed in the direction where the wolves of the People had discovered such a trail.

"I will not go away, little one. I came to stay with you."

There was doubt in the pitiful little face. Gray Mouse made the sign for a question. It can be used for many purposes: who, where, when . . . But in this case it was almost surely *"why?"*

Running Deer held out her hand encouragingly.

"I want to be with you. You will be my daughter."

"You are my grandmother?"

Deer thought for a moment, and then smiled.

"Yes, child, if that is what you wish."

With a sudden rush, the little girl flew into her arms. For a moment Deer felt a revulsion at the scabbing sores. They were even worse when seen at close range. She closed her eyes, and that helped. Now the child was a person again, a small person who needed someone very badly. Running Deer enfolded the sobbing little form in her arms and rocked gently. Tears flowed down her own cheeks. She drew her warm buffalo robe around them both, warming the shivering little body.

There flitted through the back of her mind an undeniable fact: there was no turning back now. Close on the heels of that came another, in the form of the words of the Death Song.

> The grass and the sky go on forever,
> But today is a good day to die.

At least, to begin to die, she thought.

The two men approached the area which was already being called the Camp of the Dead before mid-morning.

"Look!" exclaimed Beaver Track.

A bay horse grazed peacefully in the meadow where the People had stopped to wait while they had scouted the camp.

"It may not be the same bay," suggested Wolf, but in his heart, he knew.

"Why would she come back here?" Beaver Track wondered aloud.

Singing Wolf was afraid that he knew that, too. The child . . . the hearts of many had gone out to the pitiful figure. It had been a shame to abandon the girl, but the safety of the People had demanded it. Anyone who touched the child would undoubtedly risk death, but worse, the bad spirit would be carried to the rest of the band. Then everyone might die. Wolf wondered whether that was how it had been with the people who lay dead in the ravine just over the ridge.

But a more pressing problem lay with his mother. If, as he suspected, she had come back to look after the needs of this dying child, Running Deer must not be allowed to rejoin the People. She, too, would die here, among the other victims of the dreaded *poch.*

"Smoke!" muttered Beaver Track, turning his horse aside.

They rounded the shoulder of the hill, to see a fire and a woman kneeling beside it.

"Mother!" called Beaver Track, kicking his horse forward.

"Be quiet!" she scolded. "The child has just gone to sleep!"

"But . . . I . . ."

"Do not come any closer!" Deer warned.

Singing Wolf glanced around the area. It was well chosen. Some shade, from a cottonwood partway up the slope. Level ground . . . Not too far from water . . . Upstream from the abandoned village . . .

He got the distinct impression that this was not a temporary camp. His mother's entire attitude said so. The statement suggested by the presence of her campfire was unmistakable, a message to the spirits of the place: *Here I intend to camp.* It was a challenge, a statement of defiance to the spirits that carried the *poch.*

"Mother! What are you doing?" blurted Beaver Track.

"I came back to care for my child here."

She pointed at the sleeping girl.

They noticed that she was gently fanning the fevered little face with a hawk-wing fan, brushing away the flies.

"But Mother . . ."

Running Deer interrupted.

"My sons," she declared firmly, "there is nothing to say here. It is my choice, and you can do nothing about it. I have chosen . . . I have sung the Death Song, and I will fight. I have the right to do this, to help this child in her last days, and mine."

Her sons were speechless, and there was an awkward moment of silence.

"Give my lodge to someone. There will be a gift dance this fall, no?"

"Well, yes . . ."

"Then so be it! Go now. There is danger here."

"But not all die with this *poch,* Mother," Singing Wolf argued.

She shrugged. "Then so be that, too. If it is to happen that way, I will rejoin the People."

"Winter camp will be on the river of . . ." Beaver Track started to tell her, but she interrupted angrily.

"I do not care where winter camp is to be, Beaver! Now go, you will bother my child's rest!"

The two turned their horses and walked slowly away. There was nothing more to do, nothing to be said.

"She is crazy!" muttered Beaver Track, glancing back over his shoulder and wiping a tear away.

"Maybe," answered his brother, his voice unsteady, "but it is hers. She has had little that *was* hers for many moons, Beaver."

. . . . .

Running Deer watched them go, with tears streaming down her face. She would have loved to hold them in her arms one last time, but it would not have been possible. They would have stopped her in her plan if they had known. And they would have suspected something if she had acted differently in any way.

"Goodbye, my sons," she whispered. "May all go well with you and yours."

The hearts of all three were very heavy.

7

>> >> >>

"**W**hat can we do?" asked Beaver Track as they rode away.

"Nothing," his brother muttered. "She planned well, so that we could not try to stop her. But it is as she says. It is hers to decide. Here, let us catch the horse and take it back to old Otter."

He dismounted and fastened a lead thong to the horse's jaw. It followed willingly.

"But . . ."

"Look, Beaver," Singing Wolf interrupted, "you remember . . . no, maybe you were too young. The People had a bad winter. The Fall Hunt had been poor."

Beaver Track nodded. "I was small, but I remember the telling of it."

"Yes. Well, that winter in the Moon of Snows, there was an old man, a warrior of many winters. He walked out to fight Cold Maker, singing the Death Song."

"*Aiee!* He was crazy?"

"No, no. There was much talk about it. It was that he could see that food would be scarce, and some would starve. So, he wanted to save his grandchildren. He *fought* Cold Maker that way, and *won.* His family survived, and Cold Maker was cheated."

"But that has nothing to do with this, Wolf."

"Yes, it has. You know our mother. She is gentle and caring. She feels that the dying child needs care, so she decided to do it."

"But she risks her own life."

"Yes. She does it willingly. I am made to think that she does this as a challenge to the spirits that cause the sickness."

"But Wolf, that is a challenge she cannot win."

Singing Wolf swallowed hard around the lump in his throat. "Maybe not. Yet *she* might think so. You saw . . . She has already brought comfort to the child. Maybe she thinks *that* a victory. You have seen her sadness these last few moons. She has seemed tired. *Aiee!* It is a while since I have seen such fire in her!"

"It is like the old stories of people who asked to be left behind when the band moved on, maybe," mused Beaver Track. "Someone was tired, and asked to be left alone . . ."

"Maybe so . . . That has not happened in our lifetime. It was before the People had horses, I think. The hunt was hard, and food scarce. Many starved."

"But it is not that way now."

"That is true. But maybe it is the same. Someone gives himself to help the children. Anyway, our mother planned it so that we could not stop her."

Riding at a slow walk as they discussed the matter, they were now some distance from the dead village. They rounded the shoulder of a low hill to confront a small band of buffalo. The creatures were perhaps a hundred paces away, two old cows, their summer calves, and one yearling.

"There," said Singing Wolf quietly, "is something we *can* do."

The breeze was favorable, or the buffalo would have scented them already. The animals' vision, however, was poor, accounting for their lack of alarm.

Singing Wolf dismounted and drew his musket from its decorated buckskin case. *A case she made for me,* he thought. He checked the priming, closed the frizzen, and readied the flint. The buffalo appeared restless, and he moved into a better position quickly and smoothly. A stray puff of wind, they would be gone. The yearling would be his quarry, fat and tender.

Sighting over the long barrel of the weapon, he pulled back the jaw holding the flint, hoping that the loud click would not be heard by the animals. When the picture of the buffalo appeared right, the barrel pointed low and behind the front leg, he began to squeeze the trigger. The flint fell, knocking the frizzen aside with a shower of sparks and igniting the priming powder in the pan. A flash of fire and smoke obscured his vision, and a fraction of a heartbeat later the main charge boomed.

Wolf already knew, as he pulled the trigger that his shot was true. A shooter can tell, sometimes, as he can with the bow. The cottony smoke began to clear, and the yearling lay kicking in the grass. The others had fled.

"It is good!" exclaimed Beaver Track, behind him.

They hurried over to begin the task of butchering.

"We cannot handle all of the meat," observed Wolf. "Let us take our mother a haunch, then return here to pack a horse with more for our families."

First, though, he turned the head to a lifelike position, propped it there, and stepped back to address it.

"We are sorry to kill you, my brother, but on your flesh our lives depend, as the lives of yours depend on the grass. May your people prosper."

The apology finished, they began the work. The day was becoming hot, and flies gathered quickly.

"This is not going well," mumbled Beaver Track. "We have no pack saddle. How can we travel with meat?"

Singing Wolf was beginning to feel the same way. Meat, not cared for properly, would begin to spoil quickly on a day like this. Usually the women supervised the butchering and processing, while the men helped with the heavier parts. Just now, the two found themselves clumsy at the unfamiliar work.

"Let us take our mother some of the better parts. We can wrap the meat in part of the hide," suggested Beaver Track.

That plan was quickly accomplished. They removed a large, irregular piece of the skin and spread it on the grass, flesh side up. On this, they began to place choice cuts . . . the tongue, loin, part of the liver, and strips from the haunch that would cure easily by drying.

"We cannot handle much more," said Beaver Track finally. He glanced at the sun.

Neither mentioned it, but the day was passing. They would not overtake the band until nightfall. They tied the clumsy bundle to the saddle of Wolf's horse, and he rode the bay bareback, retracing their path to the camp of their mother.

"I did not need anything!" she flared angrily. "You should be taking care of your own families! Go now!"

She had heard the distant shot, and was concerned for a little while. Yet, since there was only one, she had reasoned correctly what had occurred. She was not surprised when her sons returned with the gift of meat. Her face softened.

"Still," she said, "it was a good thought. No, do not come any closer. I will pick it up after you leave. Just drop it there."

The two untied the bundle and lifted it to the ground. Wolf adjusted the saddle, mounted, and picked up the rein of the bay.

"*Aiee*, Mother," he said. "You might have stolen a better horse!"

Running Deer smiled inwardly. She well understood that remark. The gaits of the bay were quite uncomfortable, as she well knew. She appreciated her son's wry humor. Maybe, even, it was an attempt to tell her that he understood. But she did not want to show weakness. She swallowed hard and tried to sound stern as she spoke.

"It was a good thought, to bring the meat," she repeated, "though we did not need it. Maybe you were raised well, after all. Now go. You have far to travel."

The two men did not speak until they reached the buffalo kill. They stopped and dismounted. Buzzards were gathering overhead, circling warily high above before descending. On a knoll a little distance away, a coyote sat, watching.

"Beaver," said Singing Wolf, "I cannot ride that pack horse all the way to the night camp. Maybe we can each carry a bundle of meat, tied to our saddles."

His brother nodded. "Maybe. Would it keep, on a day this hot?"

"Maybe not." Spoiled meat could be dangerous.

"Wolf, I am made to think we have done all we can. Our wives will be worried about us. Let us hurry on."

Singing Wolf thought about it for a little while, then turned to look at the distant coyote.

"Grandfather," he mused, "the rest belongs to you. Share with your winged brothers up there!"

Wolf referred to an old Creation story. Coyote had agreed to steal fire from Sun Boy's torch as it slipped over Earth's rim to the other side. As he ran with the burning brand in his mouth, the flames fanned backward with the wind of his passing, scorching his flanks and marking the race of all his descendants. He gave the fire to Man, and by their previous agreement, is to receive the leavings from every kill.

The brothers remounted and hurried on. The bay pack horse led well, but even so, shadows were springing up from low spots in the rolling prairie, to creep across the earth, growing as they went.

The trail was plain, even after darkness was nearly complete. Faint starlight was sufficient to reveal the broad pathway made by hundreds of hooves and hundreds of lodge poles whose butt ends had scored long scratches in the prairie sod.

The Seven Hunters had hardly begun to circle around the Real-star, however, before they saw the twinkling fires of the night camp. No one seemed to have sought the sleeping robes yet. A curious crowd came out to meet them, and it was apparent that there were many rumors. Singing Wolf saw Quick Otter among the others.

"Here, Uncle," he said, handing the rein to the old warrior. "Your pack horse. Our mother had borrowed it."

"Where is your mother, Wolf?" Otter asked. "Is there trouble?"

The young holy man drew a deep breath. It might as well be told now.

"Our mother," he began, clearly and loudly enough for all to hear, "will not be rejoining us. She wished to stay with the child at the Camp of the Dead."

There was an excited murmur.

"But will she not die, too?"

"Maybe." He could say no more, and they turned away to care for the horses.

It required only a little while to strip saddles and bridles and release the tired animals. They shuffled off toward the herd, and the men turned toward their families. From the camp came the wail of the Mourning Song. It sounded to Wolf like the voice of his wife, Rain. This was not going to be easy. Should one be mourned who is not yet dead? But then, how would they know *when* to mourn, otherwise?

A half day's travel away, Running Deer settled down for her first night with the dead. She did appreciate the fresh meat, and now regretted having spoken so harshly to her sons. But there had been no other way. She had to make them leave her, did she not? They would have loitered around, endangering themselves, and in the end it would have done no good. No, better this way.

Gray Mouse was awake now, staring at her in wonder from large dark eyes. The child actually looked somewhat better. She had taken a few bites of raw liver, a known effective treatment for anyone with questionable health and stamina. Then a little broiled meat . . . Deer wondered what the child had been eating, and for how long. In hand signs, she tried to inquire.

"Dried meat. There is plenty," the child signed, pointing.

"At your lodge?"

The girl nodded. "At any lodge. There was no one to eat it."

The old woman thought about that for a moment. Tomorrow, she would explore the abandoned camp. There might be many things that would be useful to the two of them.

As long as there were two of them, anyway. That might not be long. She wondered how long before she would start to see the first signs of the disease in herself. And what would they be? No matter, she would know soon enough . . .

"How long have you been alone?" Running Deer signed.

The little girl shrugged, and her eyes filled with tears.

"Three, four sleeps, maybe."

The heart of Running Deer overflowed with pity for this child. Several long nights in the darkness, with the dead bodies everywhere . . . her own parents . . . *aiee*, how had the girl survived at all? Even Deer, an old woman, was uneasy in the area where so many spirits had recently crossed over. She shivered a little, tossed a few sticks on the fire, and then turned to spread her arms.

"Come, little Mouse," she paused to sign. "You are not alone now."

Somehow, she noticed, as she enfolded the thin body in her arms, *I am not alone, either.*

Close on the heels of this warm feeling, though, came another.

I will lose her soon, now when I have just found her.

Running Deer was afraid that another such loss would be more than she could bear. But then, she would follow soon, anyway. No matter . . .

8
»»»

The following morning was the first opportunity to really investigate the Camp of the Dead. Even knowing the situation, Running Deer was not prepared for the horrors that she encountered. Little Gray Mouse clung tightly to her hand. She had wished to leave the child outside the village while she explored, but Gray Mouse would not have it so.

"You will leave me!" the little girl protested in hand signs, tears streaming.

"No, no, child! Well . . . come along," she beckoned. *Though I do not like what we will see,* Deer added, to herself.

The People had been aware of dead bodies in the camp, but had not investigated in much detail because of fear of the spirits that might cause the dreaded *poch.*

"Do not touch anything," Running Deer signed. Instantly, she recognized how ridiculous that advice was. The girl had already been struck down by the *poch.* How could she be further harmed?

Slowly, they walked through the camp. The air was still, and the fetid odor of death hung over everything. Bodies were beginning to bloat.

We must leave this area, thought Running Deer. *It is not good for a child* . . . Or for herself either, she realized. She tried to choke back her nausea as a slight stirring of air brought a heavier scent of rotting human flesh.

She must remember her purpose here . . . finish her salvage and get out. Weapons . . . she took a bow in its case from the pole before the lodge of a warrior who would not need it again. Arrows, from the same weapon stand.

Walking among the lodges, Deer looked into the doorways. Most were empty, but some contained corpses in various stages of decay. *An ax would be useful,* she thought. She saw one, a shiny metal throwing ax, in the belt of a young warrior who lay on his willow backrest . . . *He will need it on the Other Side,* she told herself. That was better than admitting that she could not bear to take it from the dead warrior's belt. She would look for another . . .

It was not long before she found one not in the possession of the dead. That was added to her plunder, along with a good steel knife and a small skinning knife that was better than her own. There was some guilt in taking the possessions of the dead, but after all, they could not use them here. She finally solved her dilemma with a short prayer to the spirits of the former owners.

"I will bring them to you when I cross over," she promised. She wondered if she had become a little crazy.

What else now? Food! Gray Mouse had told her that there was plenty.

"Where is the food?" she signed.

"There . . . and there . . ." The girl quickly pointed to several lodges. "That lodge is mine," she added.

Running Deer approached the lodge, and stooped to peer inside. She pulled back the hanging doorskin . . . a little different in shape than those of the People . . . Two bodies, a young man and woman, on beds of robes opposite the door. And the powerful, ever-present smell of death and decay.

"There is nothing here," she signed. "Your mother and father have crossed over. Let us go."

Gently, she allowed the doorskin to fall back in place. Then she drew it aside again and reached inside. She had seen a child's doll, just to the right of the doorway. She drew it out . . . It was made of sticks, dressed in soft-tanned buckskin. Facial features were painted on the round head, made of the same material. A smiling face . . .

A faint odor of death clung faintly to the doll, but sunshine and fresh air would help that. She glanced at the girl, who was looking at the ground near her feet and sobbing quietly. Running Deer touched the small shoulder to attract the child's attention, and held out the doll.

"Is this yours?" she signed.

A new rush of tears burst forth. Gray Mouse gathered the doll to her in a two-arm embrace that enfolded also the knees of the older woman. Running Deer patted the girl's head.

"Now, now," she crooned in her own tongue.

The girl could not understand the words, but the language of grief and of sympathy is universal, is it not?

"Come, child," she said. "We must leave this place."

Running Deer investigated several of the better-kept lodges for food, choosing those which held no corpses. In a short while she had assembled as much dried meat as she thought she could carry. A small amount of pemmican . . . She would have liked to carry more pemmican, especially from one large dwelling that seemed especially well managed. The wife or wives of that lodge had been skilled in food preparation. The pemmican, stored in casings of buffalo intestine, seemed of high quality. Not only pounded dried meat, but an assortment of berries had been kneaded into the mixture with melted tallow. The maker of that supply had been a woman who understood fine foods.

Running Deer sighed with regret. The weather was hot, and would be hotter. The pemmican would not keep well, because the tallow would become rancid. Although it would be a treat, it would not keep like the crisp strips of dried meat . . . She must plan for the future. *As if there will be a future,* she thought wryly.

She compromised at last, taking a few links of pemmican and all the dried meat they could carry. She bundled it into a bright-striped blanket from the same lodge, the clean one, adding a sack of dried corn.

She remembered Singing Wolf's warnings, that the evil spirits of the *poch* cling to objects, but that was certainly a good blanket, practically new. Maybe she could cleanse it. A scrubbing in the stream with yucca suds, exposure to healing rays from Sun Boy's torch.

Just now, she must escape from this place. Physically and emotion-
ally, it was beginning to weigh heavily on her. More than she could
bear for much longer. Even now, each time she took a deep breath,
she could tell that the death-smell had saturated her own lungs. It
would take some time . . . If she *had* time . . .

"Come," she signed to Gray Mouse. "We go now."

Back at their little camp, there was much to be done. Too much,
really. Gray Mouse, exhausted in her already weakened condition,
had fallen asleep almost instantly. *I should not have pushed her so
hard,* thought Deer. *She must be very weak.*

For now, while the child slept, Running Deer built up her fire and
cooked some of the fresh meat that her sons had brought. That was
thoughtful, though in reality, it made more work for her. *They did not
realize that,* she assured herself. She cut thin strips of the meat, hanging each on a rack of willow sticks that she had constructed just
downwind from the fire. The smoke would discourage the flies that
were always a nuisance when drying meat.

She smiled, amused at herself. Here she was, working hard to
prepare the fresh meat for future use . . . *Why?* There was more
than enough already in the supplies that she had salvaged from the
lodges below. It was likely that the future was very short anyway,
both for herself and for the sleeping girl there. The child looked so
tiny, so helpless.

Deer's attention focused on a large circular sore directly in the
center of the girl's forehead. It was yellowish and wet-looking, as
wide as a man's finger, and dark in the center. It seemed darker . . .
no, the dark portion was *larger,* than on the previous day. A wave of
alarm swept over her. It was apparent that the sores on the dead
bodies in the camp were completely black and scabbed. She realized
now that this must be how it happens. The sores become dark and
dry and the sufferer dies. Yes, there on the shoulder . . . a smaller
circle, but it, too, had a dark center today. Young Gray Mouse was a
day closer to death than she had been yesterday.

But so am I! Running Deer thought. *So is everyone!* She smiled
grimly.

While the child slept, she carried the bright-striped blanket to the
stream and scrubbed it, then stepped out of her dress and slipped
into the cool water. She cleansed her body completely, washed her
hair . . . She wished that it was possible to wash out her lungs. A

deep breath still caused her to taste the scent of decay. She experimented with several very deep breaths in succession, hoping that this would force out the remnants of stale air. She could not tell whether it made any difference.

The bath did make her feel better, though. She was still luxuriating in its cool comfort when the girl stirred and woke. Deer hurried out of the water and picking up her dress, and the blanket, quickly covered the few steps to the camp.

"Where were you?" Gray Mouse signed.

"In the water. Soon you can do that, too."

She felt that she lied. She did not know what the effect of water might be on the sores of the *poch*, but did not think it would be good. It seemed unlikely that this child would ever be able to swim again.

Running Deer spread the striped blanket over a bush to dry in the sun, and turned to the fire. The broiling meat was nearly done . . . She rotated it, and then looked at the drying rack. That, too, was progressing nicely. A little more wood on the fire . . .

"We can eat soon," she signed.

"It is good."

They ate, and the exhausted little girl fell asleep again. Running Deer felt a pang of guilt at having kept the child on her feet so long while they explored the village. *But what could I have done? The child would not stay alone . . .*

Running Deer had donned her dress again, after her skin dried in the sun. Now she sat, watching the sleeping girl. What was to be done? Seldom in her life had there been a time like this, with no pressing tasks. Even after her husband's death, there were things in need of doing. Now . . . it struck her that she did not know what was needed. *How long* would they need food, shelter? There was no way to know.

Out of sheer habit, she inspected the ragged half of buffalo skin brought by her sons. It might be useful, and nothing should be wasted. She spread the skin on the ground and began to dress the flesh side, scraping all the scraps of fat and tissue away.

Running Deer had nearly completed her task with the buffalo skin when the girl awoke again. *A long sleep, good for the sick,* thought Deer. She left the skin, and approached the child.

"How is it with you?" she signed. "Would you eat again?"

The girl nodded eagerly. *Odd,* Running Deer thought. *She looks stronger, almost, after her sleep.*

They opened one of the tubes of pemmican, which did prove to be of high quality. Its richness prevented them from eating very much, but it was filling and good.

Evening was approaching, and Running Deer began to prepare for the night. More firewood . . . *It might be good,* she thought, *to have a better shelter. A frame of poles, maybe, a part of one of the abandoned lodge skins* . . . Well, she could consider that tomorrow.

It was nearly fully dark when little Gray Mouse approached her and crept into her lap.

"Are you cold, little Mouse?"

"No. Grandmother, tell me a story?"

A story? In hand signs? Deer chuckled.

"Maybe," she signed. "We will try. I will use words, too."

"In long-ago times," she began, "all people and all creatures spoke the same language."

The girl nodded eagerly. "I know of this!" she signed. "Your people know this, too?"

Running Deer gave her a quick touch in approval.

"Of course. Now, do you know why Bobcat has such a short tail?"

The little girl smiled. "Yes, but tell me again, Grandmother."

And again, this was good.

It was a day or two later. Darkness had fallen, and they were settling down for the night when there was a noise in the darkness just beyond the circle of firelight. Running Deer quietly reached for her ax, and prepared to rise. Probably nothing . . . a stray skunk or possum, but it was good to be ready. The creature seemed larger than that, though. It was making a lot of noise, rustling around in the brush and making an odd snuffling sound.

Then into the circle came the object of their attention. A half-grown dog. It would be a large animal when it matured. Running Deer wondered why they had not seen it before. Well, they had not searched the village completely. The puppy might have been in one of the lodges. At this age it could be expected to wander around rather illogically and to do stupid things. *Much like young humans,* she thought. Maybe it had been out wandering the prairie. At any rate, it had been left behind.

The friendly yellow pup walked directly to Gray Mouse, wagging its tail and trying to lick her face. The girl giggled weakly and patted its head.

"Do you know this dog?" asked Running Deer in hand signs.

"No. But he is good. Can he stay, Grandmother?"

Deer thought for a moment. *Why not? The child is pleased by it. It will probably not be for long anyway.*

She smiled and nodded. The girl smiled.

"It is good! I will call him Yellow Dog."

Deer fed the animal a few bites of meat so that it would stay. If it made the child happy in these last days . . .

"You have to hunt for yourself, dog," she told it. "I will not give you all your food."

When they fell asleep, Yellow Dog was curled near the sleeping robe of young Gray Mouse.

9
>> >> >>

This child is stronger, thought Running Deer. *She should be growing weaker, but she is stronger.*

It had been four . . . no, five days now, since their lives had been thrown together. There were times when Running Deer thought that her sons were right, that she had gone completely crazy. It was still a problem to communicate with young Gray Mouse, but usually there was not much need to do so anyway. The simple needs of the day . . . food, water, sleep . . . Deer had dug out a cooking pit, and lined it with the scrap of buffalo skin. That, with a few cooking stones, had allowed her to make nutritious soups from the pemmican. The little girl had seemed to enjoy this.

Of all the needs and wants of a child of five summers, though, perhaps the most important is that of affection. The two spent much time close together, or with the girl sleeping in the arms of Running Deer. That was how Deer noticed the change, slow as it was.

There is not so much fever, she had noticed on the morning of their third day together. Later that day, she decided that she had been mistaken. The skin of little Mouse felt hot and dry. When it was that way, the girl was very quiet and listless, and showed little interest in anything. And, Deer noticed, the girl always seemed at her best in the morning, after a night's sleep. So, the answer seemed to be more rest. When the child became listless, Deer would hold and rock her, and when sleep came, lay her gently on a soft robe. Then she would fan the little face, stirring the air to keep the flies from annoying or disturbing the needed rest.

Now . . . *Yes, she is stronger,* thought Deer. She studied the child carefully for the next day or two, and realized that Gray Mouse had become much more active. Her need for rest was still present, but the periods of sleep were shorter and less frequent. The childish play became more active, more normal.

A favorite place to play was on the gravel bar where they dipped water from the stream. White, smoothly polished stones lay piled there by the current of the stream when it had been swollen in some flood time . . . maybe long ago, maybe last spring. The stones ranged from the size of a goose's egg down to no larger than one which could be concealed in the palm of a child's hand. Not all were round. Some were flattened or gnarled in strange shapes.

"Look! This one is a dog!" the girl would sign, bringing a special stone for Running Deer to examine. "And here is one like a bird."

Deer had used some of the better, rounder stones, from well above the water line, for cooking stones. Heated in the fire, they could be transferred to her little cooking pit with willow tongs until the water was boiling and the meat cooking. As the stones cooled, they were returned to the fire to be replaced by reheated stones. Most of the People had cooked in this way when Running Deer was young. She was expert at it. She could have used one of the several cooking pots that she had seen in the camp of the dead ones, but felt that it would not be right, somehow. It felt better to go back to the old ways. It was simpler, cleaner and more pure, maybe. Anyway, it *felt* better. She was not certain how the spirit of the *poch* sores made its leap to another victim, but maybe the old women were right. Maybe it was the result of all the modern changes that had come about in her lifetime.

Aiee, I am thinking like an old woman, she admitted to herself. Then she chuckled aloud. *I am an old woman! Maybe that is why.*

She lifted a heated stone and dropped it into the stew. There was a hiss and a puff of steam, and the liquid continued to simmer. The smell was good . . .

A sudden cry came from the gravel bar where Gray Mouse was playing. The child had fallen, and now jumped to her feet to run to her "grandmother" for comfort, wailing from the hurt. Had the boisterous dog knocked her down? Maybe not . . . It always seemed concerned for the girl's welfare. It was apparent that she was not badly injured, but she was holding a hand over her other arm.

Running Deer opened her arms to give consolation and comfort. That was a function that she had missed when her own children had grown and no longer needed such hugs. The little girl flew into her ready arms, and Deer suddenly realized that the child's arm was bloody. The bleeding seemed rather profuse . . . what . . . ? She examined the injury and relaxed somewhat. It was only that the fall on the rocky shore had dislodged one of the round scabs that dotted the girl's body. It would soon stop bleeding, but . . .

Wait! she thought. She looked more closely. She had noticed that the black centers of the pustules had grown, day by day, until the entire sore became dry and black and scabbed. She had thought that an ominous sign. Many of the dead in the abandoned camp had sores with that appearance. Yet, as those of Gray Mouse dried, she had grown stronger. Now, looking at this fresh injury . . . the drainage was not the yellow of the vile fluid that had been there before. This was *blood.* Bright, healthy-looking blood, not like that from the sores of the *poch!*

She hugged the child to her, rocking gently and murmuring the soft singsong words of comfort. Tears came easily, as one thought kept repeating over and over in her head: *She is going to live!*

In the happiness of newly recovered life, there were a glorious few days. Gray Mouse, of course, did not understand the significance of what had happened. She only knew that she felt better, and that the grandmother who had come from nowhere to help her was now happier.

They played the games of childhood, by which one learns to count, to reason, and to become a responsible adult. They enjoyed stories together. Gray Mouse was rapidly learning the language of the People, which made the stories easier and more interesting.

For Running Deer, it was a time of ecstasy, the return of the daughter she had lost. It was easy to forget all the problems that had confronted her, all the sadness and tragedy. This was here and now, and nothing else seemed to matter. The weather was warm, they had food in plenty and water to drink, and shelter. She had salvaged part of a lodge skin to cover a sort of lean-to that she built against the hillside. She did not have the physical strength to erect one of the big lodges. There was no need for one, anyway. At least, not for now.

Deer woke one morning, her throat just a bit sore and her eyes watering. *Aiee, the season!* The blooming of some of the late summer flowers had always bothered her. She rolled out of her robe, somewhat stiffly. More stiffly than usual . . . She glanced at the sky. A storm? That always made her bones ache. But the sky seemed open and clear . . . Just a cold, maybe.

She started to build up the fire, but found that she was quite dizzy. She sat down . . . *Maybe I rose too fast,* she thought.

The little girl crawled sleepily from her sleeping robe and stumbled over to sit in Grandmother's lap. Running Deer did not particularly feel like holding a child right now. She was nauseated and weak and could not seem to think well. Gray Mouse took her hand.

"*Aiee,* Grandmother, you are hot!"

Only now did Running Deer begin to understand. She was ill. In the happiness of the past few days she had pushed it into the farthest reaches of her mind. Now it crept into her thoughts again, and a dreadful fear gripped her heart. She had not known, but she did now, how it would begin. *This is the evil thing. This is how it feels.*

The *poch* . . .

Something like terror gripped her. There was a passing temptation to run, and try to get away, yet she knew that was useless.

Then anger . . . *Why me?* she wanted to shout. The answer to that came quickly to her: *Because I chose it!* That angered her even more. *This was not part of the bargain!* her mind protested. *The child was dying. I only wanted to comfort her in her last days. Then I would be ready to cross over, too.*

This was not right. She had only made things worse. The child had survived, but for what? Only to die alone, later, when her protector was gone. Running Deer tried to console herself with thoughts of their few days of happiness together, but it was no use. Without her help . . . The child's senses were already dulled. Death would have come, gently and without notice, in a day or two. And she, Running Deer, had tried to intervene in what was meant to be. It had seemed successful, at first, but now she knew. It had been only a trade, her life for that of the girl.

The bitter part, the cruel result of the entire affair, was that it was not even a fair trade. Without her help, the child would now die alone on the prairie. It would take a little more time, that was all. Deer had thought herself so clever in this attempt to challenge the way of things, but not clever enough.

You cheated me, she thought defiantly, directing her anger toward the dreaded spirit of the *poch. This was not the bargain!*

"You are hot, Grandmother!" Gray Mouse was saying. "Here, I will cool your face!"

The little one was bathing her cheeks with fresh cool water, and it felt good . . . But now, there were more important things . . . She had only a few days to live, she did not know how many. In that short time, she must teach the child everything she could about survival. Even so, it would be a hopeless task. How could a girl of five summers survive? There would be food for a little while, and then . . . Deer could not guess which might come first. Starvation, or Cold Maker's chill hand. Tears came freely.

"Do not cry, Grandmother," signed Gray Mouse. "I will take care of you."

That was perhaps worst of all.

10
>> >> >>

"**I**t is a miracle that was granted to me," No Tail Squirrel was explaining. "It is good, no?"

The People were several sleeps away from the Camp of the Dead, still traveling toward the selected summer camp site. There was always a certain confusion during the days of travel. Travel left no time for socializing or the leisurely casual smokes and conversation. Only for a short time as daylight changed to twilight was there any time for such things. Even then, most of the People were too tired.

This evening, though, they had halted early. A good day's travel . . . They had reached the intended camp site somewhat earlier than expected. The young men were taking advantage of the extra daylight for some gambling, boasting, horse trading, and casual visiting.

"No, I do not want to trade him," No Tail Squirrel said indignantly just as Singing Wolf walked past. "I want to use him."

Wolf paused. A group of young men about to aspire to one of the warrior societies were gathered around a magnificent horse. He did not think he had ever seen the animal before, and he paused to admire it. A strong, broad-chested stallion, heavily muscled through the hip and stifle . . . A buffalo runner, maybe. The foreparts were dark, black to bluish roan, and the hips were white as snow with scattered black spots. Some of these were grouped like hand prints, the powerful ritual markings placed on a horse's shoulder or rump to insure a successful hunt or battle.

"You have painted him?" asked Singing Wolf. It was customary to do so only as the party prepared to leave.

The young men laughed. "We asked him that too, Uncle," one said respectfully. "Squirrel says no."

Wolf stepped to the horse's side, touching the black spots. It was true. This was not paint. He could feel the texture of the hair . . . A trifle thicker and softer, maybe, in the dark spots.

"When did you get him, Squirrel?" asked the holy man.

"It is as I was telling them, Uncle. It is a miracle. He came to me as I was riding behind the column. As wolf, you know. I was tired of the dust and sweat . . . maybe I closed my eyes for a heartbeat or two. But then I heard the horse call out. And there he stood before me. It is a good sign, no?" he asked eagerly.

"Of course. He is well trained?"

It was obvious that this was no wild horse. It stood calmly, allowing itself to be handled.

"Yes, Uncle. I think so. I have ridden him a little, and his gaits are good. *Aiee,* he can run. I think he runs to the right."

"And you use the bow?" Singing Wolf inquired.

"Of course. If I did not, it would be worthwhile to change, no?"

There was a ripple of laughter. Usually, one would learn the use of bow and lance, and decide on the basis of preference. Then, choose a horse that would fit the hunter's style . . . one that pursues a running buffalo from the right for a bowman, a left approach for use with the lance. Yet, as No Tail Squirrel said, for a horse as good as this, one would be tempted to change. But looks and gaits are not everything.

"Well, see how he works at the hunt," Singing Wolf advised as he moved on.

It was nice to have a pleasant diversion, and his heart was good for the young man. His heart had been unbearably heavy for some time . . . through the prescribed three days of mourning for his mother, but still to this day. He could hardly force himself to go about daily tasks, knowing what Running Deer might be experiencing. It was hard, to know that although mourning was over, she was probably still alive. It was only her stubborn demand that prevented him even now from returning to see about her welfare. That and common sense. If he did go back, there was nothing he could do, whether she was alive or dead.

Maybe this puzzle of No Tail Squirrel and his wonderful horse was good. It would distract him. There were some strange things about the event. He was certain that Squirrel was telling the truth. There was no reason *not* to do so. But someone had trained and used such a horse. It had not simply materialized. At least, he did not think so. True, there are always strange events where the spirits are involved, but this? No, in all his experience as a holy man, and even the experience of his father, nothing like this. There was something here that did not ring true, but he could not quite identify what it was.

Several other things, insignificant things of routine nature, distracted him for a few days before his mind turned again to Squirrel's mystery horse. One of the children had blundered into a lodge of bumblebees and suffered many stings. A lame pack horse . . . that had required repacking and the use of a different animal. It was that event that finally called his attention to horses again. What about the horse that Squirrel had found? He had heard nothing more of it.

Singing Wolf went out to where the horses of the People were herded to graze for the night. It was nearly dark. The animals were greedily cropping the lush grass of the meadow. They must spend half their time eating to build strength for the other half, such as travel.

He saw the stallion of No Tail Squirrel. It was unmistakable, even in the fading light.

One of the young herders approached him.

"*Ah-koh*, Uncle. How is it with you?"

"It is good."

"Did you want one of your horses?"

"No. I was looking for No Tail Squirrel. He is not herding?"

"No, Uncle. Squirrel does not herd much any more. He rides as wolf now."

"Of course. I should have known. Well, you too will ride as wolf someday, no?"

"Yes. Soon, I hope."

"May it be so! Does Squirrel ride the big horse?" Wolf gestured toward the stallion.

"Sometimes. Not today, I think. His brother, there, says he is sick."
The herder gestured toward the other young man on night-herd duty.

"Ah! His brother?"

"Yes, Uncle. Over there by that tree."

"Good. I will talk to him."

He made his way around the herd, trying to remember . . . what was the name of Squirrel's younger brother . . . ? No matter.

"*Ah-koh,*" he called, and the youth rose from the rocky outcrop where he had been seated.

"Yes, Uncle?"

Wolf walked over to sit beside him.

"Your brother is No Tail Squirrel, who found the horse?" he asked.

"Yes. Is it not a wonderful thing for him? You saw the horse, no?"

"Yes. A fine animal."

"Good fortune for my brother! *Aiee,* what a horse! And a good saddle and blanket, too."

Instantly, a chill gripped the heart of Singing Wolf. His stomach tightened.

"There was a saddle?" he asked casually. "I had not heard."

"Oh, yes, Uncle. A good saddle, a forked wooden tree. Not a pack saddle. An almost new blanket, too. A bright-striped blanket, from the traders."

Wolf's heart sank. This was the missing part . . .

"When did he find this horse?"

"Ah, I do not remember, Uncle. Several days ago. No, more than that, maybe. I know . . . two or three sleeps after we saw the Camp of the Dead."

"Someone said your brother is sick?"

"Yes, too bad. He took sick yesterday, but he will soon be better."

"Yes, I hope so. Maybe I will go and see him."

"It is good. Squirrel would like that."

The young man lay near the campfire of his parents, his face flushed and sweating. His mother was bathing his face, neck, and chest, and there was concern in her eyes. She rose and the two stepped aside.

"He is very sick," she said, her voice trembling. "He rode the *travois* today."

It was apparent that the young man must be very sick if he would ride a pole-drag, usually reserved for tiny children, the elderly, or the incapacitated. It would have been beneath his dignity if he had the strength to protest.

"Yes, I see, Mother," Wolf said.

"He has not been the same since the coming of that horse," she lamented. "It seemed to take over his life. He is almost crazy over it. I wish he had never found it!"

"I, too, Mother," he said sadly. How strange, that the woman should have identified the threat, but did not understand it.

"It was said that the horse had a blanket?" he asked.

"Yes. He is proud of that, too," the woman said with disgust. "It is new, but stained and dirty. But he insists on sleeping in it. *Aiee,* look at him there."

Wolf looked, and his heart was heavy. He must find Broken Lance and discuss this. This threat was very real, not only to the family of No Tail Squirrel, but to this entire band of the People.

He wished that he had the wisdom and advice of his father. There were harsh decisions to be made.

11
»» »» »»

The council was quiet tonight. Participants spoke in hushed tones, due partly to the heavy dread that hung over the People. Singing Wolf, the holy man, had been right. The *poch* had descended on the band. There had been arguments and denial at first. Everyone, even the family of No Tail Squirrel, denied any contact with the Camp of the Dead. Everyone was telling the truth, Singing Wolf agreed, but the curse *had* followed them. How? In the blanket of the horse found by Squirrel, Wolf was convinced.

Again, denial. Who had ever heard of such a thing? Wolf related it, as he had been told by the French trader. The *poch* could ride on blankets or robes. Still there was disbelief until No Tail Squirrel died in agony, with great round sores on every part of his body. By this time, his mother and his brother were sick, too.

Panic flew swiftly through the camp. Two or three families quickly packed and departed. That was not a bad plan, Singing Wolf thought. For the People of the Southern band to scatter would lessen the danger of spread of the evil *poch*-spirits. Yet it was also dangerous. They were not totally without enemies. Suppose, for instance, that Shaved Heads to the east or the Horn People to the north of the

People's range discovered what was happening. Both were nations with whom they had warred in the past. The news of scattered families of the People, virtually defenseless on the wide prairie, might bring war parties down into the Sacred Hills like wolves to the bleating of a lost calf.

But something *must* be done. Wolf was not certain what. And, this time, Broken Lance came straight to the point of the council, and no one seemed to care. As a strong leader, the old band chieftain knew when to call for discussion and when to say how it will be. In this case, he did the latter, and no one objected, because no one had a better idea, and they were all afraid.

"Something that I can fight, I do not fear," said one old warrior. "But this . . . *aiee!*"

"So be it," Broken Lance announced. "Any lodge that shows the sickness will stay behind. *All* those living in that lodge, sick or well. The rest will keep on moving until the *poch* is left behind."

"Then where is summer camp to be?" someone asked.

"We do not know. Wherever we are when the spirits leave us alone, maybe," said the chief. "But . . . let us winter on the Sycamore as we had thought to do. Is that not good, holy man?"

"It is good, my chief."

Wolf did not really know. Surely this horror would be over by then. If not, the survivors could still gather and decide what to do about the coming winter.

"What is to prevent those left behind from following us?" asked someone.

"Honor," replied Broken Lance. "If that fails, the Bowstrings will stop them."

It was possibly the harshest rule in the history of the People, yet few objected. But of course, in a matter of honor, there was little possibility that enforcement would be needed by the Bowstrings anyway.

"What of the horse? Is it not the cause of our trouble?"

They were still camped where death had overtaken No Tail Squirrel, while his family performed the burial arrangements. They had already decided to stay behind to care for their younger son, who had now sickened. The mother had used Squirrel's blanket to wrap his body, so Wolf had not made further suggestion on that.

But the horse . . . ? It was not unknown to sacrifice a horse for the dead hunter to ride on the Other Side. Some tribes, Wolf knew, even tied the animal to the burial scaffold and let it starve to death, but the love and respect that the People had always held for the horse usually prevented that. ("Are we not called the Elk-dog People by others?")

Some felt that the horse should be killed, but the argument was feeble. Singing Wolf was glad. He was still sure that it was not the horse, but its *blanket*, on which the *poch* had been carried, but it could not be proved. The blanket was now out of consideration, so he said nothing more of his theory. But after all, the *poch* was French, and so was the blanket, no? It made sense.

It was decided that the safest thing to do was leave the horse behind, and to drive it away if it tried to follow.

"*Aiee*, what a loss," observed Beaver Track as he took one last look over his shoulder at the proud stallion. "I would breed all my mares to him."

Singing Wolf felt much the same.

"You did breed all that you could, Beaver, did you not?" he chided as they moved out.

Behind them, the mourning family of No Tail Squirrel looked pitifully defenseless. They grew smaller in the distance, standing beside the burial scaffold of their son, until the column crossed over a low rise and they were not seen at all.

There were a few days when it seemed that the world had returned to normal. A good day's travel, a halt for the night, move on. The prestige of Singing Wolf rose, because the holy man's advice had enabled the band to avoid the deadly sickness. The loss of one lodge and its three warriors was regrettable, but did not seriously affect the defensive strength of the band. There was a spirit of optimism, and there was talk of considering a place for summer camp.

Then the *poch* rose again, striking down a young man who had been a friend of No Tail Squirrel. The connection was obvious. There was much concern, but little panic as the band left another family behind and hurried on. They changed directions this time, at the suggestion of one of the older men of the band. It might confuse the bad spirits that pursued them.

The course was now more southerly than their previous southwest direction. In another two days they changed again. This began a zigzag pattern that was not really a recognizable pattern at all, to further baffle the spirits. Wolf was not certain that it was a valid theory, but it could do no harm.

Another family announced that, although there was no sickness in their lodge, they were leaving the band.

"We are tired of running," said the woman. "We will stay here, and join the band for winter camp. Sycamore River, no?"

"Maybe," answered Broken Lance. "Where will you go now?"

"We stay here. There is water, grass . . . the place is pleasant, no?"

"That is true. May it go well with you."

"And with you, Uncle!"

The others moved on. The band had begun to look alarmingly small to Singing Wolf as he looked back along the column.

Many sleeps away, a small girl dozed fitfully by a dying fire.

Her little world had been a happy one. Plenty to eat, loving parents, other people that she knew and trusted. There had been other children, with whom she played. They had learned many things . . . The Children's Dance . . . that had been sheer enjoyment and excitement. The rhythmic thump of the drums, the hopping steps, the praise and pride that had been hers.

And the stories . . . she loved the stories of long-ago times. How Bobcat lost his tail, why Rabbit has only a little fat . . .

She could not remember when or how things had begun to change. There had come a time when the dance drums were silent and there were no more stories. There was singing, a sad chanting that made grownups cry. Some of the people that she knew lay still and cold. They were wrapped in robes or blankets and placed on platforms of poles like lodge poles, with much more crying and singing, and they did not come down. They were seen no more. That she found disturbing, and even more so when it happened to some of her playmates. There was the day when Songbird could not come out to play, and then was not even there any more. Why would her friend leave her that way, without saying anything? Mouse's mother said that the girl had "crossed over."

At least her parents were one solid strength on which she could depend. She sat on her mother's lap at a council one evening, frightened by the serious tone of the talk. She had hoped when they gathered that this was to be a story fire, but it was quite different. Old men discussed in worried tones what should be done. Gray Mouse did not understand why there should be such worry. The talk was boring, and she fell asleep in the pure protection of her mother's arms.

Then her mother had fallen ill, and great ugly sores grew on her face. People tried to keep her away from her mother, which made the girl frightened and angry. When she was told that her mother had crossed over, it was devastating.

"She left without me!" Mouse wailed.

By that time she was sick herself. So many were crossing over that there were not enough left to wrap them and sing the sad songs. There were not enough to look after each other among the living, either. Mouse found herself wandering among the lodges. She had been told by those who had been caring for her to go away. Confused and weak, she sought her own lodge. Maybe her father was there . . . she would be safe with him.

Father was there, but he, too, was still and cold, beside the bed where her mother lay. Frightened and crying, Gray Mouse crept close to her mother and sobbed until she fell asleep.

When she awoke, there were shouts and confusion. People were saddling horses and packing belongings, obviously preparing to travel. She was puzzled as to why most of the lodges were still standing. She approached a woman in the lodge next to her parents, a woman she knew. Surely Left-hand Woman would help her. But the woman looked at her and recoiled in terror.

"Go away, girl!" the woman shouted. "We are leaving."

"But I . . ."

"Stay back! We will kill you if you follow us."

Gray Mouse did not understand at all. She was frightened and still angry. Why would everyone leave her, when she needed them . . . ?

She woke, terrified. She had dreamed it again. Almost every night, it happened. Quickly, she looked to see that the grandmother was still there. Yes, soft snores came from the robes beside her.

And Yellow Dog . . . he raised his head and wagged his tail. At least these two would never leave her. They had not yet, anyway. A shadow of doubt crossed her mind. The grandmother was sick, and looked much like those she had known who had crossed over. Would she, too?

12
»»»

There were many things that Gray Mouse did not understand. One was the grandmother. She did not even know who this woman might be, who had come out of nowhere. It had been good . . . This was the first human who had treated the girl with kindness in a long time, it seemed to her.

But, kind though she might be, there were puzzling things about the grandmother. Her strange language . . . Her garments, slightly different than the ones familiar to Mouse. The manner in which her hair was plaited . . .

These things were not really distressing, because it was apparent that the woman was kind. The lap, the comforting arms, were those of a woman who understood the needs of a lonely child, abandoned and frightened. Gray Mouse had perceived immediately that here was a mothering-person. A person older than her own mother, though, so it must be a grandmother. Mouse had inquired, through hand signs, and it was verified.

That was when the girl felt her very worst. There were a few days that she did not even remember very well. The mind blocks out and forgets much of the unpleasant and the painful to spare us part of the bad memories.

Grandmother talked to her a lot. At first Gray Mouse knew none of the words at all, and was too sick to care. Then, with repetition, she began to recognize words and phrases. *Water, food. Go to sleep. Dog, lodge, corn, meat . . . fire.*

The woman had built a sort of lodge to shelter them. Poles and sticks and a big sheet of hide that she had cut from the lodge skin of Stumbling Elk in the camp below. Elk had no need for it, Grandmother told her. That was true. He was on one of the scaffolds downriver now.

Among the very confusing things were the stories. Mouse had seen stories in hand signs before, when a traveling trader had camped with them, so that part was nothing new. The stories themselves, however. She, Gray Mouse, had requested stories. Stories told by her mother or her father had always been part of happy times, and had made her feel better. She had wished for things to be happier. The new grandmother had agreed, and had held her in comforting arms, had sung and rocked her, and had told stories in words and hand signs.

Now came the confusing part. The stories were different. Bobcat . . . *Do you know how he lost his tail?* the grandmother had asked. Yes, Mouse knew and loved that story. Bobcat had had a long tail at Creation. He had lost it when he stood motionless, watching Rabbit, with the long tail hanging down in a pool of water. A sudden shift in the weather had frozen the pool, and when Bobcat pulled away, his tail, frozen in the ice, broke off short. This is why even now, the bobcat's tail is short and he does not like water.

It was with great surprise, then, that Gray Mouse heard a quite different story. The new grandmother had said that Bobcat had slipped into a hollow tree to hide from a hunter. But his long tail *(that was the same)* . . . his tail stuck out through a knothole, and the hunter had chopped it off to decorate his bow case.

This was quite puzzling. *Which story is right?* thought the girl. She was sure that her own version, that of her parents, must be the correct one. She was almost indignant that anyone who did not even know how it *really* happened would try to tell the stories. But she had been too sick to care, really. The important part had been that she had been held, rocked, and comforted. So she decided to say nothing.

Now confusion and worry had fallen on her again. The new grandmother was sick. There was a feeling of panic . . . *What if she leaves me, too?*

Gray Mouse had decided to be as helpful as she could, so that maybe the grandmother would not leave as everyone else had done. The reassurance that she had tried to give, that "I will take care of you," had been a desperate attempt to hold the sick woman, to induce her to stay.

For the next few days, Gray Mouse tried to do all she could. She brought food and water, though sometimes the grandmother was too weak and feverish to eat. At those times Gray Mouse would bathe the hot face and hands, and would sing to the sick woman. That had been a comfort to the girl when she was the sick one, so maybe it would help. Even so, the grandmother spent much time in crying.

Gray Mouse herself ate, slept, and played with Yellow Dog sometimes when Grandmother slept. Day followed day . . .

For Running Deer, it was a terrible time. She was feverish, weak, and probably dying. Over and over, she relived her life, and every event that she wished she had handled differently. It was a sort of desperate sadness, a regret for a life that had gone nowhere, and was now to end in even further tragedy. She told herself that at least she should try to teach the little girl some things that might help her to survive a little longer. But she could not seem to summon enough energy to do so.

She was repelled by the sores that erupted on her body, as well as by the pain and itching that never seemed to subside. Finally, she was burning with fever, hallucinating, talking with people who were not there.

Much later, she realized that she had been confusing her own child, dead these many seasons, with the pitiful child who had been abandoned. One became the other as she drifted in and out of consciousness, and they became inseparable.

"Thank you, Little Bird," she said, as she sipped cool water from the gourd that the child had brought.

"What, Grandmother? What did you say?" the girl asked in hand signs.

Why does she sign, instead of talking? Running Deer wondered. "Bird, what is it?" she snapped irritably. "Talk, do not sign! I am too tired to play games!"

Bewildered, Gray Mouse retreated. She had not been able to understand a word of the outburst. What had she done to anger the grandmother? She crept away, tears welling up.

Out of sight, she buried her face in the thick fur of Yellow Dog's neck and cried softly to herself.

Several more days passed. They were unpleasant days for both of them, the frightened, confused child and the sick, demented old woman.

Afterward, Running Deer remembered very little of it. At the time, her illness was so severe that she saw things and people who were not there. They were so real that she talked to them, and sometimes they answered. Well, the dog never answered. At least she thought not. It did lick her hand sometimes, and her face.

And there was the child. *Her* lost child, Little Bird. Bird was there much of the time. She brought water, and food which Running Deer was unable to eat. And she talked, that one. Yet that was even more frustrating. When Little Bird spoke aloud, she spoke in words that were completely without meaning. Running Deer was puzzled at this. In her more lucid moments when her tormented mind tried to reason, it seemed to her that it must be the language of the dead. Little Bird had crossed over long ago, and must be here to welcome her mother to the Other Side. And, since this tongue that the girl was speaking was unknown to Deer, it must be that which is spoken there, by those who had crossed over.

Strange . . . she had never thought of it . . . What language *is* spoken on the Other Side? Will it be all one, used by all humans and animals, as it once was long ago?

It angered Deer, though. Little Bird, though she appeared to be trying to comfort her mother, persisted in speaking that tongue.

"Have I not taught you better?" Deer flared at her once. "Why do you speak in words that I cannot understand?"

The girl shrank away, frightened at the tirade, and Running Deer was almost sorry for her outburst. Almost, but not quite. She drifted away in confusion again, and roused to find the girl using hand signs. *Has she forgotten her own tongue?* Deer thought irritably.

One thing really bothered her about the hand signs, too. Granted, the signs vary a little from one tribe to another, but they, above all, must be understood by all. Would hand signs, then, be different on the Other Side? There would seem to be no purpose if they were all different. And it would seem that there should be no need for hand signs there, if everyone spoke the same tongue . . . *Aiee!* It was too much for her fevered brain.

The hand signs, though, used by Little Bird . . . *What was I thinking? Oh, yes* . . . Why did her daughter persist in using the sign for *grandmother?* Several times Deer tried to correct the child. *Mother, not Grandmother!* she signed. But the child's eyes would fill with tears, and she would shake her head, and Running Deer was too weak to argue. It was no matter anyway. Soon she would cross over. *Or finish crossing* . . . She thought she was probably partway over already. Was her daughter not here? When she finished crossing, she would understand the language of those who had already crossed. Then she could *demand* an explanation for this insulting treatment.

She wondered if she would understand the new language instantly, or would she be required to learn it? Surely, she would not be submitted to that indignity. *But who knows?*

She slept again, and wild and frightening dreams raced through her head. Nothing was clear . . . there were fragmented pictures of abandoned lodges and empty landscape and then she would come upon piles of rotting corpses and flies everywhere, and the smell of death . . .

Running Deer woke, and it was early morning, not yet full daylight. She looked around, trying to remember. Yes, her little camp . . . this lean-to . . . but why . . . *oh, yes, the girl. And I was sick, so sick!*

Almost at the same instant she realized that her fever was gone. She started to rise, and fell back. *Aiee!* She could hardly hold up her head. *Ah! I have crossed over,* she thought, and immediately knew that it was not true. On the Other Side, there would not be the pain and stiffness that she felt in every part of her body. *Would there?* She thought not. But the girl . . . *What girl?*

She realized that she was having trouble sorting out what had been real and what was part of her fever-dream. She had seen the Other Side . . . or had she? *Wait, now . . . My daughter . . . Yes, Bird was there! She brought water!*

There was a movement beyond the fire, and a large yellow dog raised his head. *Yes, the dog!* But had it been here, or on the Other

Side? The dog wagged his tail, and in the poor light Deer saw that curled next to him was Little Bird, who was slowly awakening.

But what is she doing here? I have come back, but she had to stay, surely!

Then the truth struck her. *This is not Bird! It never was* . . . Yes, the dying child . . . not dying now . . . the *poch* . . .

She cared for me, Deer realized. *All the time I was so sick. I did not know. I thought it was Little Bird!*

As her memory came rushing back, she realized that she had spoken harshly. She had argued and sometimes yelled at the child in her fevered delirium. *Aiee, the poor thing* . . .

Running Deer managed to sit up, and the little girl, rubbing her eyes sleepily, came toward her. Deer spread her arms and then spoke, with both words and signs.

"Come to me, little one!"

Gray Mouse smiled and rushed into the embrace, tears of joy now flowing.

"You have come back to me," she signed. "It is good."

And now both were laughing and crying, all at the same time.

13
» » »

It was a long time before Running Deer completely regained her strength. There were times when she thought that she would never completely recover. She would waken in the morning and look at the dawning day and marvel at everything that had happened since the Sun Dance.

And I am still alive! she would say to herself. *And so is the child!*

She took no credit for it, though perhaps she should have. Sometimes there is nothing left but sheer will and determination. These qualities she had never lacked, although her family would probably have called them stubbornness.

But now the crisis was past. The black scabbed places on her face and body were drying rapidly. Already some of the smaller scabs had dried and fallen away. The others were itching, and it required much attention not to rub or scratch them, especially as she slept.

The lesions on the skin of Gray Mouse had already finished their cycle and the scabs were gone. Left behind were the scars, bright pink against the pale golden brown of the girl's delicate skin. Running Deer supposed that the bright scars would fade, in time, to the color of the normal skin. At least, it would be so with any other scar.

It was too bad, the scars on the pretty young face. Yet as she studied the girl's appearance, Deer decided that it would not be too bad. One large *poch* in the center of the forehead, just above the eyebrows. A smaller one in front of the left ear, and two or three around the neck and shoulders. Some of those, even, would not be visible under normal circumstances.

Young Gray Mouse was completely unaware of her own appearance. She did seem to enjoy having the older woman comb and plait her hair after they would bathe at the stream and cleanse their hair with yucca suds. Occasionally the girl would seem troubled that the plait was "not good." It took a little while for Running Deer to realize that her meaning was "not right, not correct."

Of course . . . The way one's hair is worn is important. It denotes *belonging*. Running Deer had taken little note of how Mouse's people might have dressed their hair. The contact had been much too intense. With a start, Deer realized that she had never seen any of the girl's nation *alive*, except for Mouse herself.

Anyway, she told herself fiercely, *she is mine now, one of the People. She will do her hair as a woman of the People.*

That led to other thoughts of the People, and what was to be done now. It was still something of a surprise that they had *survived*, both of them. She had made no plans that included that possibility. Now what? It was apparent that they must rejoin the People, but summer was passing quickly. It must now be the Red Moon, with its withering heat. Not a bad season, though . . . There had been occasional showers which washed the prairie clean and cooled the air. Nights were always cool.

Running Deer studied the scattered flowers among the tall grasses. Yes, the right flower-heads of the yellow sun-seekers were blooming, and there were purple spikes of feathery appearance. Very nearly the Moon of Hunting. Or of Gathering, she had heard some of the Grower people call it. Yes, now she realized that the real-grass was already pushing up its bluish seed stalks. In a matter of days, they would be as tall as a man, with the three-toed seed head, like the foot of a turkey. Their allies the Head Splitters used that name for it . . . "turkey-foot grass."

Deer had always loved this time of the year. The several other grasses, each with its own character . . . The sights and sounds and smells of the coming autumn . . . The excitement of migrating geese in long lines across the sky . . . Migrating buffalo . . . She wondered if the fall hunt would be good for the People.

She was thinking of these things for good reason. Would it be possible for the two of them to rejoin the band in winter camp? And where was it to be? She should have listened to her son Beaver. He had tried to tell her, but she had been angry, and cut him short.

It would be very hard to travel now. The beauty of the tallgrass prairie and its man-high grasses was overshadowed by its problems just now. At this season, it was very difficult to travel, especially on foot. With the real-grass and feather-grass taller than one's head, it was quite easy to become disoriented and lost. Especially on foot. She wished for a moment that she had asked her sons to leave her a couple of horses. But that would have been ridiculous. She had expected to die here, and to have no need for travel.

But what now? It had come down to this: should she plan to winter here, or try to move to a more favorable site? Eventually she decided on the latter. It would be almost a moon before the tall seed heads of the grasses reached their heaviest and became the greatest of problems. There was a little time to travel.

Besides, the alternative was not a pleasant prospect. She did not relish the thought of long dark nights only a couple of bow shots upstream from a dead village of corpses. Probably they were already being devoured by scavengers. She shuddered.

Part of the shudder was brought on by the realization that she must go back to the lodges of the dead one more time, at least. The supplies that she had salvaged were running low. Distasteful as it might be, Deer felt that another visit to the camp would be by far the easiest way. She could probably find more food in the deserted lodges. The only alternative that she could think of was to try to kill some large animal . . . deer, elk, or preferably buffalo. She could possibly do that, because she had the bow and arrows. Then, however, it would be necessary to prepare the meat. The butchering, slicing, drying, and packing of the food would require some time . . . Time that they really did not have.

No, if they were to move, it should be quickly. A day to prepare, and then they should be on the trail . . .

Running Deer had hoped that she could persuade the girl not to accompany her to the camp. That was not to be. Little Mouse was so terrified at the possibility of being abandoned again that finally Deer relented.

"It will not be pleasant," she warned.

The child nodded, holding tightly to her hand, and with tears still flowing.

Running Deer was shocked to see the changes in the village as they approached. It had truly taken on the look of a dead, abandoned place. She realized that it had been nearly a moon, but *aiee!*

A deserted house, bereft of the supportive spirits of those who lived there, begins to deteriorate quickly. It can be seen anywhere. Windows stare like empty eye sockets, shutters and doors sag, sad and lonely, because the life force that was once there has now departed. How much more apparent in a lodge of poles and skins, which are a few steps closer to the life force that produced them, and has produced all things . . .

Tattered skins hung limply on sagging poles. Painted designs were fading from sun, rain, and wind. Grasses grew tall in front of lodge doors. A small animal, surprised in its solitude, scurried away and *into* a lodge to hide . . . what a strange sensation!

Gray Mouse was clinging to her, silent and afraid. Even the dog seemed to sense something oppressive here, slinking along at their heels.

"Enough!" spoke Running Deer, hoping that her voice would not sound as strained as she felt it was. "Let us look for our food and be gone from here."

She said this without signs, partly because Mouse was beginning to understand more, and partly because she could not sign well with Mouse holding tightly to her hand. The real reason she spoke, anyway, was to bolster her own confidence.

Many of the supplies that they found were spoiled, bundles torn open by raccoons or other small animals, and the contents partly eaten and scattered. A couple of the lodges were damaged considerably, perhaps by a bear.

They were able to assemble a bundle of dried strips of meat. Not enough for the winter, Deer thought, but enough to travel on. She also salvaged a pouch of tobacco. She had never smoked it very much, but it might be a comfort. She had enjoyed the social smokes at their big lodge when her husband was alive. She could almost smell it now, the pungent bluish cloud gathering above the heads of the guests and drifting out between the smoke flaps.

Of course Walks in the Sun had used tobacco ceremonially, too. It was always good to offer a pinch of tobacco to whatever spirits might reside in an area. And now they would be traveling . . . yes, tobacco would be useful to appease the spirits where they would camp, and where they would spend the winter. She should have thought of it before.

She considered taking along a pipe. There were several that were of no use to their previous owners. Not in this world, anyway. Yet a pipe is a personal thing, a thing of the spirit. Tobacco, for the use that Deer had in mind, could be offered in a fire. Just a pinch, tossed in the evening campfire as it grew to a lively start. Yes, she would do it that way. Walks in the Sun had told her once that a ritual itself is not as important as the spirit in which it is done. "If the heart is good, the Grandfathers know," he had said. Running Deer hoped that her heart would be considered good.

"Come, we must go!" she said suddenly.

It was good to leave the place. Long after the lodges had rotted to dust and the bones of the inhabitants were scattered and reduced to nothing, the People would remember this place as the Camp of the Dead.

Yellow Dog trotted ahead. He, too, had been impressed by the dark and heavy mood that hung there.

Back at their own camp, Running Deer built up their fire, and just to be sure, tossed in a generous pinch of tobacco.

Now she must begin to organize their move. She had thought that they had very little, but now as she surveyed her camp, there was quite a lot to transport. Their robes and blankets, the food, the skin lodge cover that formed the lean-to. Yes, they must take it. They might also need *more* shelter for the winter, but one thing at a time.

She had it in mind to head south. She had abandoned any thought of trying to find the People. There was no time to waste in wandering around. But a march of a few days—she did not know how many— would bring them to the area where the tallgrass prairie met the oaks of the red-dirt country. That would be a good place for them to winter. The oaks, holding their dried leaves all winter, would be a good natural windbreak. It was necessary only to camp on the south side of a thicket to hide from the main force of Cold Maker's icy breath.

Besides, the scrub oak thickets harbored deer, turkeys, and squirrels. Yes, they could manage, if they could get there. But so many bundles and packs . . .

Her eyes fell on Yellow Dog. *Of course!* Did not the People use dogs to pull a pole-drag before the horse came? She laughed aloud.

"What is it, Grandmother?" asked Mouse.

"Come, child," called Running Deer. "We will teach Yellow Dog to pull a pole-drag!"

14
>> >> >>

They found the travel not really too unpleasant. There were meandering game trails, which through the centuries had delineated the easiest paths. For the same reason, the tread of a million hooves, the tall grasses were not so vigorous in growth there.

In areas where they had a choice, Running Deer chose the trails that followed the streams. There was better concealment in case they needed it, more fuel for their nightly fires, and of course, water. Always, they worked their way south.

The dog, young and undisciplined, seemed more trouble than he was worth for a few days. His main purpose in life seemed to be to avoid the harness that Running Deer had fashioned to allow the use of a small pole-drag. Yellow Dog was inhibited considerably in his explorations by such a contraption. Eventually he seemed to become resigned to it. Even so, he did break away in pursuit of a rabbit once, destroying the harness and scattering poles and supplies along the stream. There were times when Running Deer was tempted to use her hatchet on the contrary creature's skull. She refrained for several reasons, not the least of which was Mouse's affection for the strong-willed pup. And it *was* a help, not to have to carry all of the heavier bundles. Besides, if the time came when they really *needed* to kill and eat the dog, it would be in the winter, the Moons of Snows and Starvation. Gradually, the headstrong pup became accustomed to pulling a burden, and was actually useful.

The weather held, with warm days and cool nights. They were seeing a gradual change in the land. The stone that forms the shelves and rocky slopes of the Sacred Hills is white limestone, laced with veins of the top-quality blue-gray flint so prized by the People. To the south, the rolling hills appear quite similar to the inexperienced eye. But their base is different, a yellow to brown sandstone. Here conditions are favorable for the growth of a variety of different plants and trees. There are groves of oaks of several kinds, hickory, and pecan, in addition to the massive walnuts farther north.

Running Deer's goal just now was to reach the first of the scattered strips of scrub oak thickets. This was an area favored by the People for wintering, because of the shelter available.

There was a possibility, even, that they might encounter her own Southern band. Deer was not certain how she felt about that. It was too soon to tell. The circumstances under which they had parted made it difficult. Her decision had been final, or so she had thought. She had been angry with her family, with the People, and would die alone, never having to face them again. She had relished the thought of their mourning her. They would be sorry, to think of her dying alone, racked with pain and fever . . .

But it had not happened. With the sometimes puzzling, even perverse ways of the spirit, Deer was still alive. She had planned so carefully, had concealed her departure from the People, planned every detail of how she would comfort the poor dying child of the strangers, and then cross over herself. Her plans had included every possibility *except* this one. Running Deer, in the emotion of planning for her own death, had neglected to think that she might *live*.

There were times now, when she was tired and discouraged, that it seemed to her her entire life was a failure. She tried to console herself with thoughts of her happy marriage, of her successful sons. Yet there always came flooding back the despair over the loss of her beautiful daughter, and later, her husband. It was easy to slip into the dark moods of depression when she thought of such things, and to think that her life had been meaningless. She had accomplished nothing, really, nothing important in her entire lifetime. Any other woman could have been as good a wife for Walks in the Sun, could have managed their lodge as well. Maybe better.

And now, in the twilight of her life, Deer had been given the opportunity to die with dignity, trying to help someone. It had seemed a good thing, but now, even that had turned sour. She had failed in that, too. She had lived. It was not intended to happen that way, and she was unsure of herself. How was she supposed to handle *this?*

Yet even while she thought such black thoughts, Deer was taking the appropriate actions. Her entire life had been one which revolved around doing what must be done, what was *needed.* So, without really thinking about it, she continued to prepare for their food and shelter from day to day, and to plan for the cold moons ahead.

There were, of course, some major decisions. It might have been possible to winter with one of the Grower villages that were dotted along the rivers and streams. The People, hunters by tradition, had traded with the Growers for many generations, exchanging meat and skins for corn, beans, and pumpkins. It was their way. Surely, it would have been possible to ask for shelter in one of the permanent towns. They had passed several as they traveled southward. That had not been a difficult decision, though. First, her pride would not allow Deer to ask for help.

Then, the other thing, more indefinite . . . a dread of closed places. To a nomadic child of the prairie, the thought of the semi-buried lodges of the Growers was repugnant. Deer remembered as a child once when they had camped beside a Grower town to trade. The children had begun to play together . . . there are no cultural or language barriers among the very young . . . Deer had accompanied one of these new friends to her lodge. There was a slope down into a hole in the ground, and inside, the heavy, closed-in smell of human bodies. It reminded her of the smell of a mouse's nest, or of a cave that was said to be a bear's den, near the People's winter camp one season. Young Deer had turned and fled from the earth lodge. How much better to live in a skin lodge, which could be rolled up in summer to catch any refreshing breeze, or pegged down and stuffed with dry grasses in winter . . . No matter. She did not think that she could survive a winter in a hole in the ground. That possibility was quickly rejected.

Her plans were rather vague beyond that, however. She could have inquired as to where the Southern band of the People were wintering. Growers gleaned gossip and information such as this from everyone who passed. But Deer was not certain that she was ready to rejoin the People. Pride . . . *Aiee,* sometimes it makes us work harder. Deer was not certain . . . Maybe she merely wanted to prove herself . . . Maybe she merely hesitated to let it appear that she had failed to accomplish her purpose, that of dying.

These dark thoughts did not occupy much of her time. There were other things to think of. Camp sites, fuel, water, food. Once an idea was rejected, like that of wintering with Growers, it was gone. It did not exist. Deer had no clear idea of what preparations she would make for winter once they found a place to camp. She only recalled that when the People wintered in the scrub oak thickets it had been easier. There were natural windbreaks, there were nuts and acorns to gather. There were also deer, turkeys, and squirrels that came to share such a harvest.

In addition, it is difficult to remain in a dark mood when one's companions are a child and a playful young dog. Mouse was learning quickly, and already could carry on a conversation in the tongue of the People. Only occasionally would she resort to hand signs.

Running Deer soon realized that this was no ordinary child, but one of high intelligence and wisdom beyond her years. That, of course, accounted for her survival. With her parents dead, her world falling to pieces, her body fevered, her people abandoning her, the little girl had managed to find food and water, and to survive.

Sometimes Mouse would stare into the distance, lost in thought. At those times, Running Deer would avoid interrupting such flights of memory. Deer would move quietly, staying near until the child's attention returned to the present.

Oddly, perhaps, the girl seemed to be a happy child, too. She loved to watch the silvery minnows in still pools along the streams where they camped. She giggled at the antics of a trio of fox pups, rolling and biting in mock combat on a stretch of grassy bank across the stream. A scolding jay, a sunning turtle, all brought exclamations of joy.

Twice as they traveled, they encountered small bands of buffalo. These were scattered groups, strayed from the huge herds. Those would migrate through, following the dying grasses as Cold Maker began his push from the north. They would come later, and would provide the great fall hunts for the people of the prairie. These scattered bands were also moving south, drifting slowly, warned by the shortening of the days. An old cow or two, left behind when the main herd moved north . . . Maybe a young cow, late calving, had stayed behind with her calf . . . A young bull, chased away by the massive herd bulls. These loners, companionable by nature, would band together. Possibly they would rejoin the larger herd later.

For now, however, Running Deer was glad to see them. She did not want to try for a kill just now. It would be too difficult to care for the meat, and she wanted to reach a suitable winter camp site. But since these scattered buffalo were moving south, too, *aiee!* Let their winter meat furnish its own transportation! She thought that she could manage a kill among the scrub oaks when the time came. The pattern of patchy thickets and grass made for good hunting for a single hunter on foot.

Deer had not tried the bow that she had salvaged. She must do that soon. There was little doubt in her mind. In her younger days she had hunted well. Now, she knew that she did not have the strength to draw one of the stout hunting bows of a warrior. She had intentionally chosen one of lighter pull, that of a young man, probably. It would still hurl an arrow with enough force. Well, later . . .

They were now seeing patches of oak thickets, straggling along a sunny south slope, or up a rough gully. The groves of nut trees were more numerous and larger. But they kept on. Running Deer had in mind exactly the setting that she wanted. Not a specific place, but one with certain qualities about it.

Why does a nesting bird investigate several sites which seem identical, rejecting each until one seems right? Does she search for a place where the *spirit* is good, and start to gather twigs only then?

It was that way with Running Deer.

"Here, Grandmother?" Little Mouse would say eagerly.

"No, child. The thicket on the north is too narrow." Or, "No, we cannot see far enough to the south." Or, "It is too far from the stream."

One spot which nearly satisfied Deer was finally rejected because there were tall trees to the *east*. It would be mid-morning before the winter sun's rays would be able to reach the camp. They moved on.

Finally, they came to a spot that satisfied all the requirements. It was still early in the afternoon, but Running Deer shrugged off her pack and set it aside.

"Here, Dog," she called.

The animal, sensing her tone, ran to her. Deer loosened the straps of the harness and began to unload the *travois*.

"It is here," she told the girl, "that we will spend the winter. Its spirit is good."

Part Two

15
>> >> >>

In front of their lodge, the stream made an arc perhaps fifty paces across. At the upstream end to the west of the camp was a shallow riffle, where it was possible to cross easily. Beyond that, a wide grassy meadow stretched into the distance in the southwest, toward wooded hills a day's travel away.

To the southeast, a closer thicket of scrub oak sprawled across the hillside. That, thought Running Deer, might be a place where turkeys and deer would be likely to winter. For now, she would avoid it, to leave its spirit undisturbed.

Possibly the best feature of their winter camp was the thicket behind them on the north. It was a strip of dense scrub oak, perhaps two or three bow shots wide, which covered the south slope of the ridge. The slope was rather steep, and she realized that this would help with the warming qualities of Sun Boy's torch. Yet even better was the protection from the howling winds of winter's annual onslaught. Cold Maker would bide his time as the days grew shorter. Already she could tell at dawn and dusk that Sun Boy's torch was beginning to fade. When the time came for Cold Maker's traditional attack, it would be one of surprise. Maybe just a heavy frost at first, just a parrying thrust or two, but then . . . *aiee,* she did not look forward to it. Her aging bones reminded her in the morning chill that she had used them hard and long.

But here . . . Running Deer had already visualized how it would be. Cold Maker's thrusts always came from the north. That was where he lived. Sometimes he would veer in from the northwest, to try to catch the unwary by surprise, but that was little different. She had stood in various places along the stream through the meadow, sighting along the timbered slope and the ridge at the setting sun. She verified her opinion after dark by the position of the Real-star in the north, the star that never moves.

Yes, a winter thrust by Cold Maker would have to top the crest of the ridge before it reached them. That would expend effort, and the partially exhausted Cold Maker would pause to drop much of his snow in the brushy timber of the slope before it reached the place she had chosen to camp.

The spirit of the place seemed good, too. She walked along the edge of the woods, searching for just the right spot. There . . . an irregularity in the grassy border that abutted the thicket . . . It was cupped toward the south. There was some protection to the northwest, but the bulk of the scrub growth was directly north of her chosen site. She picked the spot for their fire, kindled it with great ceremony, offered tobacco as the flames licked upward, and it was good.

"Here we intend to winter," Deer chanted in the singsong ritual of the Song of Fire. "We ask the acceptance of our presence and of our offering."

Just to make sure, she added another pinch of tobacco.

Now there was much to be done to prepare for winter. The next morning Running Deer began to plan.

"We will make a lodge," she explained to the little girl.

"A big lodge, Grandmother?"

"No, no, child. We do not have enough skins for a big lodge. Or poles, either. And if we did, we could not set it up, just you and I, could we?"

"That is true." Mouse giggled. "Did you have a big lodge, Grandmother?"

Running Deer smiled sadly at the memory. "Yes, once . . . My husband, Walks in the Sun, was a great holy man. We had a fine big lodge. But he is dead now."

"Then how do you put up your lodge?"

"Ah! I did not have that big lodge any more. A smaller one, after the big one wore out."

"And you could lift that one?"

"No, no . . . It was too big for one old woman to put up."

"As big as mine . . . my mother's?"

"No, not that big. But I had help. My sons . . . You saw my sons, Mouse?"

"Maybe . . . when I was sick? Those men came on horses?"

"Yes, those are the ones."

Her heart was heavy . . . They must think her dead. She marveled at the resiliency of the child, who had lost both parents as well as everything else.

"Did you tell me once that you had a little girl, Grandmother?"

"Yes, maybe I did."

"How was she called?"

"Her name was Bird . . . Little Bird," Deer said thoughtfully. "Little Bird."

"Is she grown now?" asked Mouse.

"No, she is dead, little one. Long ago. She was not much older than you."

"My heart is heavy for you, Grandmother." The girl paused and then brightened. "Was she pretty?"

Running Deer had not talked with anyone for a long time about her daughter and the loss that she had suffered. There had been the boys, the busy days of helping her husband's work. Then her sons had grown up and set up their own lodges. She had seldom talked with Walks in the Sun about their lost daughter. It had been so long ago, and there seemed little point.

"Yes," she mused, "Little Bird was a beautiful child, like you."

Gray Mouse smiled. "Tell me more of her, Grandmother."

"Well, as I said, she was beautiful. But not only in face and form, but in spirit, too. She was kind and happy and loved all things. She could run and swim and ride, and . . ."

The feelings that had been held in for so long now came pouring out, and she found herself laughing and crying and recalling scenes that had not entered her mind for many years. *Aiee,* she thought, *I*

have never mourned her properly until now! There was a joy in sharing these things with this orphaned child, who had lost so much more
. . . Deer gathered the girl to her.

Finally she rose. "Come," she said. "We can talk of such things
later. Now we have much to do."

She had already been planning in her mind the sort of shelter that
she would be able to construct. In her lifetime, she had been in
contact with several different tribes of people, all of whose customs
differed slightly. Their dwellings did, too. In addition her own, the
People, used several makeshift shelters when they traveled. The big
conical skin lodges were normally erected only if they intended to
remain for an extended time.

Now she tried to plan a shelter for the two of them, using materials
that they had or could acquire. It must be soon, too. Nights were
already cool.

Her general idea was to build a sort of lean-to, open on the south.
She could cover the top and sides with brushy limbs and twigs, and to
make it windproof, with skins. She would need more skins, but a kill
or two . . . It need not be very big. In fact, the smaller the better, so
that their body warmth would help to warm it.

"What sort of lodge will we have, Grandmother?" Gray Mouse
asked.

"I will show you . . . Look, these two trees will be the back cor-
ners, these the front. Here I will chop out the brush between them. It
must be clear and flat . . . You can pick up the rocks, there. Then
we will cut some grass to make our bed soft."

"We sleep in it *tonight?*"

"No, no, it will not be ready. We sleep in our robes a night or two."

They began to lay aside poles for the framework. The leafy brush
was saved, too.

"We will pile some of that around the back and sides. Then maybe
pile snow around that," Deer explained.

By the day's end they were tired, and it was good to eat a little, sit
by the fire, and watch the sticks turn to glowing coals. Yellow Dog lay
near, exhausted from chasing squirrels, who clearly had the advantage. They could take to the nearest tree when pursued.

"Grandmother . . . a story?" Mouse pleaded, creeping into her
lap.

"It is good," agreed Running Deer. "Which story do you want?"

"A new one . . . one I have not heard," the girl suggested. "I know! Where did your people come from?"

For a moment, Deer thought that the girl meant this summer, but obviously, that was not it.

"You mean long-ago times?"

"Yes! How did they get here?"

"I see . . . Well, the People lived deep inside the earth, and it was dark and cold, and they wished for something better. So they sang and prayed, and finally, a god-man came, and he found a hollow cottonwood log. It was leaning, so . . ." She demonstrated with her hands. "The roots were still in the earth, and this Sun Boy . . . well, he still carries his torch . . . but that time, he took a drum stick, and sat astride the log. He pounded on the log, and a man crawled out into the light. He did it again and a woman came out. Then, each time Sun Boy struck the log, another, and it became easier, and they kept coming." She paused and waited.

"*Aiee!* Are they still coming, Grandmother?"

Running Deer smiled to herself. That was the desired response. It was a joke to be played on those to whom the story was new. Usually the listener would ask, if the storyteller was skillful. Then the standard answer:

"Of course not! A fat woman got stuck in the log, and no more could come through. They are still down there."

Usually there was laughter at that point, but little Gray Mouse seemed concerned.

"But what happened to Fat Woman?"

Running Deer could not recall that anyone had ever asked that before. At least, she had never heard it. But she could see the concern in the eyes of the girl. *What a sensitive child.*

"Well . . . I . . ." How could she answer? "Well, then the others, those still below, you know . . . They saw that they must help her. Two men took her by the ankles and pulled and pulled. Finally, she popped loose, so hard that the log was shaken loose, and the hole closed up. No more could come through."

Mouse giggled and clapped her hands. Once Fat Woman had been rescued, the child was quite happy with the rest of the story.

Deer wondered, though, about the changed ending that she had devised. Well, why not? She knew that the stories change sometimes, through generations of storytellers. She recalled one version that had the deity on the log a different god, even. The trickster, Old Man of the Shadows, wasn't it? It seemed likely. It would have had to be someone with a sense of humor to bring humans into the world, would it not?

And Fat Woman herself . . . One version said that it had been a *pregnant* woman instead. That surely would have bothered the sensibilities of Gray Mouse!

She stroked the girl's hair . . . Mouse was almost asleep now. There would be more stories later, through the long winter. Maybe Mouse could tell some of the stories that *she* knew. Maybe, even, Running Deer could learn more about who the girl's people might be, who came to and died in the Sacred Hills.

16

》》》

It was not long before the camp began to seem like home. Nomadic dwellers settle in quickly because of the nature of their lifestyle. When the first fire breaks the chill of the evening as darkness approaches, the camp site becomes home.

That was how it seemed to Running Deer and her orphaned foster child. It may have helped, too, that the spirit of the place was good, and that it matched theirs well. Deer had cut and trimmed poles for the small lodge that she had in mind, but did not begin to assemble it yet. Thongs of rawhide were needed, and they would come from a kill. She was not concerned about when that would occur. They had food enough for now. An opportunity would present itself. Deer or buffalo, either would do. She would prefer a buffalo. The skin, or part of it, could be dressed and tanned with the fur on, to make another warm robe for the coming winter. After she had cut the necessary thongs from it, of course. She was partial to the flesh of the buffalo, too. Its flavor was sweeter, and lacked the strong taste of meat from the deer.

It was a sacred thing, the bond between the People and the buffalo.

The herds furnished not only food, but clothing, shelter, tools . . . No other creature was so important to the life of the People.

Running Deer hoped to obtain two buffalo kills during the autumn moons. She did not want both at once, because she could not do the work involved with two skins and the vast amount of meat that must be processed. Meanwhile, a deer would furnish the thongs that she needed. There was much deer sign in the area. They tied the dog each night to prevent his chasing deer. She wanted them to stay near, undisturbed.

It was on their third day in what would be winter camp that she saw the turkeys. A flock of about thirty birds emerged from the thicket to the southeast of the camp, and worked their way across the meadow, moving almost straight northward.

"Stay here. Hold the dog!" Deer whispered to the girl as she picked up her bow and ducked into the thicket.

She had practiced a little, shooting at a hummock of soft dirt. She hated to risk the loss or breakage of an arrow, but she felt that she must test the weapon. The results had been quite satisfactory. The bow handled well. *You have chosen well, old woman,* she told herself. The prospects were exciting, beyond what she would have imagined. And now she would be able to try her skill on a real target.

The People had not often hunted turkeys, especially after the coming of the horse. Larger game was preferred. One does not risk the loss of a good arrow on lesser game when it might be used to kill a buffalo. Even so, sometimes it became necessary to try for turkeys or even squirrels. Running Deer had selected an arrow intended for this purpose. It lacked the carefully designed flint tip, which should not be risked on such a shot. To provide the weight needed on the point of the shaft, this arrow was equipped with a heavy wooden head. Carved as a larger portion of the shaft, sharpened to a cone on the tip, and hardened over the fire, this arrow point was less subject to damage, and was ideal for small game.

Deer nervously fitted the arrow to the bowstring as she moved through the oaks. She carried only one. It was not likely that she would have more than one chance. She was breathing heavily, both from exertion and from excitement. It had been a long time since she had experienced the excitement of the hunt, and it was good. She smiled, amused at herself. It was like her first hunt as a child, when she stalked a rabbit.

Now she could see through the foliage of the scrubby trees ahead, and into the grassy meadow. *Ah!* There were the birds . . . As always, she was startled at their size. And how *black* they appeared! They were moving slowly past her, catching insects in the grass. Always, two or three stood motionless, heads up, watching, at any given time. Then the watchers would hunt for a few moments, while others kept a lookout.

The flock was nearing a stand of real-grass, and soon she would no longer be able to see them. She must act before the birds finished crossing the open area, which was covered with short curly buffalo grass.

Suddenly a jay in a tree near where she knelt happened to notice the crouching figure and began to cry a raucous alarm. Instantly, every bird in the meadow was alert, head up, looking. She would have only the space of a few heartbeats . . . She drew the arrow to its head, leveled it at the large male bird nearest her, and released the string.

As the bowstring twanged, she knew that she had missed. Her shot was high . . . She knew that she had jerked the string as she released it, a childish mistake. But as the arrow flew, the great bird, alarmed at the movement in the thicket, rose in flight. A sweep of its broad wings, another, a third. Its heavy body rose ponderously into the air. The bird was perhaps half the height of a man above the ground when Deer's arrow reached that point, too. She could see the massive wing raised high, exposing the thinly feathered ribs above the breast. The most vulnerable spot, maybe, as if the deadly shaft knew, and sought it out. Transfixed, the turkey fell heavily, flopping aimlessly in the grass as life ebbed quickly. The other birds were disappearing into the oaks, running or flying low.

Running Deer leaped out of the thicket and ran toward her kill. She remembered well that her very first quarry had escaped because she was too slow. Her arrow had flown true, had struck the rabbit squarely, but had gone completely through and out the other side. She had been so elated at her success that she stood watching in childish glee while the doomed rabbit ran for some distance, crawling into a burrow with its dying struggles. No one else had been present, and her friends had laughed at her story. Worst of all, she had killed for no purpose.

This time, though, the quarry was beyond any effort to escape. It was a large gobbler, fat from the bounty of late summer's insects and autumn's nuts and acorns. It was heavy to carry, and she was breathing hard as she returned to the camp.

Gray Mouse ran to meet her, eyes shining with excitement.

"May I carry it, Grandmother?"

"No, no . . . it is too heavy," panted Running Deer. "Here . . . you carry the bow and arrow."

"The arrow is bloody. I will clean it off," said the girl. "I will call it 'Turkey Killer.' *Aiee*, Grandmother, you shoot well! No other could hit a bird as it flies! How do you do that?"

"I started long ago, child. It takes a long time." She was still short of breath.

"I will be a great hunter like you," Mouse babbled on. "Will you teach me?"

"Of course. When there is time . . ."

"It is good. You will make me a bow?"

"Yes, yes, child. Later."

"It is good. I will be a great hunter. You will be proud, Grandmother. Maybe I can be as great a hunter as you!"

Running Deer was pleased, of course. She saw no reason to explain that it was only a lucky shot, one that would have missed if the bird had not flown at that moment. Why spoil the child's dream? Anyway, it appeared to be a good omen, and she was grateful.

As she thought about it, maybe it would be a good idea for Gray Mouse to have a bow of her own. The child certainly showed indications of strength. Maybe she would be a warrior woman like the legendary Running Eagle, of the People. There were no major enemies just now, but there might be in times ahead. But for now, Gray Mouse wanted only to be a hunter. *It is good,* thought Deer. *It will help her to grow strong. I wonder if I can make her a bow.* Yes, surely she could devise something. Meanwhile, she would teach the use of a throwing club. Maybe Mouse already knew of that. And if she were unable to devise a small bow for the girl, probably Beaver Track could help.

But that would be next season. There was much to do before that time came. She turned to Gray Mouse.

"You can wash the arrow at the stream, Mouse. Then come right back."

The girl and the dog bounded away, and Deer turned toward the task of cleaning and plucking the bird. The wing feathers she would save to fletch arrows. Some of the others for ornaments. The beard . . . the stiff, hairlike tuft that grew on the front of the throat . . . That should surely be saved. Its spirit would be powerful.

Gray Mouse returned with the arrow, and Deer placed it on a nearby bush to dry. She must remember to look at it occasionally. If it seemed crooked she could warm it at the fire and straighten it.

Several days' travel away, Singing Wolf sat looking into the sunset. He could not remember when he had been so unsure of anything. Or of everything, maybe.

The world had been good when they left the Sun Dance. The People had felt the renewed strength, the patriotism, and the personal rejuvenation that always followed this most important celebration of the year. The return of the sun, the grass, and the buffalo, the basis of the People's very existence . . . And it was good.

Even when they had stumbled upon the Camp of the Dead, it had not seemed a problem that had belonged to the People. Such things happen to others, not to us. The People could have gone on, their hearts heavy for those less fortunate, but that was not to be.

First the thing of the child. That was a bad thing. As far as Wolf could see, there had been no right way to handle it. The band had moved on, with some misgivings about leaving the dying child, but what could anyone have done? At least, without sacrificing his or her own life?

It was still a hurt that made his heart heavy, that his mother had chosen such an action. Both she and the child were dead by now. He was alternately sad, angry, and even proud. It would have been a story to be retold for generations if it had not been for the other tragedy, that which struck the entire band.

The *poch* . . . How could No Tail Squirrel have known that when he had been honored by the finding of the horse that it was not really an honor but a curse? The *poch*-spirit must be one of great treachery, as well as great power.

Wolf was certain that the dividing of the band had been the only thing to do. It was like the action of a band of quail when a fox strikes into their midst. They scatter in all directions, sacrificing one or two. If they stay together, the fox could simply follow, taking one and yet another until all are eaten.

But it is not so. After the attack and the loss of one or two, the birds scatter and wait. When the fox is gone, they begin to call to each other, and gradually the survivors reassemble.

That was what he intended for the People. What he hoped for, anyway. There had been some effort to set up a plan to keep in touch, but it did not seem advisable until the threat had passed.

And how long would that take? They had no idea.

He wondered how the others were doing. His own lodge and that of Beaver Track, visible in the distance, were the only ones of which he was sure. The band had left the family of No Tail Squirrel behind, and surely some of those were dead. The next family that had been invaded by the *poch* . . . There was no way to know. And beyond that, he knew nothing. Were other families involved also? He was certain only of his own and that of his brother. None of either lodge had yet sickened. Might they do so, even yet? It was nearly four moons. Surely it would have happened already.

When the band divided, there had been a loose agreement. Those lodges that had no *poch* would assemble for winter camp on Sycamore River as they had previously decided. Those whose lodges had sickness would stay away.

Now they were soon to be forced into a decision. Should they go to Sycamore River, or try to winter alone, here? When it came down to it, which would be *least* dangerous?

17

» » »

There would be some, Singing Wolf was certain, who would feel that all the misfortunes of the People were deserved. Punishment, maybe, for some infraction of that which is expected of humans by the higher powers of the spirit world. It had always been so. Probably the older members of the band would shake their heads and cluck their tongues in disapproval over some action by the younger generation. He was made to feel that one of the objects of their disapproval would be the thunderstick. It was only in his own generation that the French trade guns had come into use. He himself had possessed one of the first, captured from a young Shaved Head of the woodlands to the east.

He could understand the dread of such a weapon by those unfamiliar with its use. It carried much power, and a great deal of mystery. The mystical black granules which burned with such destructive force were in themselves dark and dirty, and left a stain on the hands and garments of the user. It was inevitable that some disapproved its use.

It would be pointed out that the People had never encountered the *poch* until they began to use the thunderstick. Singing Wolf was not impressed by this logic. If it were valid, nothing new would ever happen. True, there were some of the old women who even now preferred a good flint knife to the modern implement of metal. Rubbing-sticks to kindle a fire were still used by some, rather than the steel striker which was now common.

Wolf himself was something of an anachronism. He used the striker and flint as a matter of convenience, but also the fire-sticks. For reasons that he could not have explained, he felt better about a ceremonial fire that was kindled with the traditional fire-bow and yucca spindle. His son, if he proved to inherit the gifts and the duties of the holy man, might feel no such pressure. Times change. He was certain that there had been those who opposed any progress. Glass trade beads to replace the traditional ornamentation by quills must have been scandalous to some. The use of the horse, even, must have met opposition. His father had once told him that maybe the warrior societies had been formed over such a disagreement. It was true that the paintings on the Story Skins showed the Bowstring Society always on foot.

Singing Wolf did not believe, however, that the *poch* was a punishment. He was not certain what it was, but doubted that theory. He intended to continue the use of the thunderstick. He could find no real taboo that had been broken by the People. That would be understandable.

The *poch* was more like an evil spirit that the People had encountered accidentally. It was apparent that it jumped from one to another. And, as the trader had told him, separating the healthy from the sick seemed to be the only way to stop its spread. But for how long, he was unsure. How careful must they be? He felt that he must talk to his brother. They had spoken a few words from a distance, but had had no closer contact. Now there were decisions to be made.

Wolf walked toward the distant lodge of Beaver Track, and stopped about a bow shot away.

"*Ah-koh!*" he shouted. "Beaver, I would talk with you!"

In a moment his brother emerged from the lodge and came a few steps toward him. Beaver Track held a spear.

"There is trouble?" he called.

"No, no. Come here. We must talk."

Beaver Track approached cautiously. "Is it safe?" he asked.

"I am made to think so. Let us talk of that. Sit."

The two men sat down, a few paces apart. It was hard to overcome the fear that had been instilled by this summer of death.

"What is it?" asked Beaver Track. He was inclined to follow the advice of his brother in matters of this sort. A holy man must have an understanding of such things.

"I am made to think," Wolf began, "that sometime we must rejoin the band. The problem is, when?"

"How will we know?" asked Beaver.

"That I cannot tell. But see if what I say sounds like truth."

Beaver nodded.

"You have no sickness in your lodge?" Wolf asked.

"No. None at any time. And yours?"

"That is true. Now, Beaver, think on this: the *poch* jumps from one to another. If two people, or six, or ten get close to each other, it jumps more easily, no?"

"Yes, maybe . . ."

"Now, if nobody has it, as in our two lodges, it cannot jump."

Beaver Track was cautious. "Maybe. But what about No Tail Squirrel? He was not even close to anyone with the *poch.*"

"True. But the horse blanket . . . *It* had been used by someone who did. Squirrel sickened only a little while after he found the horse."

"That is true. How long can the *poch*-spirit lie in wait?"

"Ah, that we do not know. But there must be a time when it has to leave, or it would kill everyone."

"It *did,* in that Camp of Death, Wolf!"

"No, not everyone. Some left, remember?"

"Yes, that is so. Did the traders tell you anything of this . . . How long, I mean?"

"No. I should have asked, but I did not know, Beaver. I am made to feel, though, that the *poch* passes through and is gone. Of this, I remember: the trader said that one who has it and *lives* is then safe."

"Forever?"

"Yes, I am made to think so."

"So, what are we talking of, Wolf?"

"Well, we must be planning for winter. Shall we go to Sycamore River?"

"Is it safe?" his brother asked again.

"It is as I said, Beaver. We do not know. But if both our lodges are healthy, we should be no danger to each other."

Beaver Track nodded, unsure.

"Then, if that goes well, we could rejoin the others," Singing Wolf went on.

"How soon would we know?" asked Beaver.

Wolf shrugged. "Who knows? Say, half a moon? We could hunt together a little, meanwhile, prepare a little meat for winter, then decide."

"It is good," stated Beaver Track, rising. "Will your family come to my lodge this evening?"

Wolf smiled and clasped his brother's hand. "It is good!" he said huskily.

There was no new outbreak of *poch* when the two lodges joined company. The theory of Wolf seemed to hold true. It was good to see the children at play, and the wives happily visiting again. And there was optimism. If this proved successful, they would seek out other families.

It was decided that when the moon was full, they would begin to travel toward the selected winter camp. Meanwhile, there was no point in moving the big lodges. That was a major undertaking, and not worth the effort for half a moon's time.

Each day brought more optimism. There were no signs of the return of the *poch*. The brothers, working together, downed a fat yearling buffalo cow, and the meat and the hide were quickly processed into pemmican, dried strips, and rawhide.

Finally, the moon signaled the selected departure. The lodges of both families came down, belongings were packed, and the horses rounded up. It was hard to travel with so few to do the work. Normally there were eager young men to drive the horse herd and to chase after strays. In this case, though there were no more than thirty animals, there were also no young men. Someone must lead the way, and this fell to Beaver Track, as the most experienced scout. Singing Wolf would bring up the rear and keep the horses together, while the two wives managed the pack horses and assorted youngsters. Dark Antelope, the oldest of the children, assisted his father with the horses at the rear. It was the most important task assigned to him in all of his eight years, and he reacted with pride and dignity. His mount, of course, was a great help, a veteran at this sort of work.

"*Aiee!*" exclaimed Wolf when they paused for a noon halt. "I had forgotten. Riding rear guard is not easy!"

"True," laughed his brother. "Especially when you herd horses too. Is it dusty?"

"Not too bad. The rain yesterday helped, maybe. What I really miss are the wolves."

"I, too! I have worried all morning."

Both men laughed. Under normal circumstances there would have been a scout or two ahead and behind, and another well out on each flank. There was actually little danger now. Enemies were few, and the task of serving as wolves was mostly that of an honor guard, and to gain experience for young warriors in case of trouble later. There was always a chance of newcomers into the area, whose motives might be questionable.

There were also those who might be opportunists. Horn People on the north, Shaved Heads to the east, even Snakes to the south, all wasted no love for the People. It had been one of the concerns when the band had split up, and it must still be so. Wolf hoped devoutly that the word of this troubled summer experienced by the People would not become widespread. Then another thought came to him. *Word of the* poch, *the spotted death, might keep others, potential enemies, away!* That was almost amusing. But not quite.

The noon halt over, the little column moved on. It was a good day to travel. A good day to be alive, really. The ripe freshness after the recent rain had intensified the colors and scents of the prairie. There was a profusion of color. The bright golden yellow of the sunflowers and other autumn plants mingled with several kinds of brilliant purple. Flocks of blackbirds, assembling for the migration to the south, wheeled and maneuvered in preparation. Quail and their summer's broods were beginning to join together in coveys of thirty or forty birds, their defense in sheer numbers.

Deer, too, were beginning to group together. It was not quite rutting season yet, so the does and their young were grouping together, while the males kept apart, also in small bands. Their new antlers, still fur-covered, were too fragile to be of much use.

A coyote watched the little band of travelers from a distant ridge as they passed. Singing Wolf wondered if the coyote was trying to decide whether this was a hunting party, worth following for his share of the kills.

Not today, Uncle, he thought with amusement. *But good hunting to you!*

When they stopped for the night, Beaver Track rode out in a wide circle around the camp. It would be good to avoid any surprises. He returned to report nothing of a threatening nature.

"There is a village of Growers over there. Shall we ride over after we settle in?"

"Go ahead," called his wife. "We will start the fire. We have food, water, and wood."

It seemed a good plan. It was wise to let the Growers know they were in the area, and they had talked to no one for some time. There might be useful news.

"Here," said Rain, handing her husband a packet of pemmican. "A gift, or maybe you can trade. We could use some beans."

Wolf reached down for the packet, and they cantered away. Both men were silent for a little while, and then Beaver Track spoke.

"What if they have the *poch?*"

Singing Wolf had been thinking the same thing. This season there was a different kind of danger on the prairie. It might be as hazardous to meet a friend as an enemy. All rules of etiquette had changed.

"If they have," said Wolf grimly, "we touch nothing, drop our gift, and leave quickly, no?"

18
» » »

"**W**e had heard of this sickness," the Grower chief said carefully. "It has struck your people?"

"Not our lodges. Mine, or my brother's here."

"Wait . . . How are you called?"

"I am Singing Wolf . . . Elk-dog People, Southern band. This is Beaver Track, my brother."

The Grower nodded, still cautious. Normally these introductions would have come first, but there was new urgency this season. Before the visitors had even introduced themselves, they had been challenged with questions about the spotted sickness.

"I know of you. You are a holy man," the Grower went on. "It is good. Now tell me of your People and the sickness. Yours is the band of Broken Lance, no?"

Briefly, Wolf told of the finding of the abandoned camp, and of No Tail Squirrel and his misfortune in finding the saddled horse.

"We are made to think that the horse or its blanket carried the sickness," he explained. "The man became ill, then his family, then another lodge. Our Southern band divided for safety."

He hesitated to state news of that sort. If their vulnerability became widely known, *aiee!* That would not be good. But the dispersion of the Southern band was probably already known anyway.

"Our two lodges have been spared," he went on. "Of others, we have not heard. Has the sickness been here?"

The Grower shook his head. "No. A trader was here, and he told that your people had sickened."

"All of them? Other bands?"

"I do not know. Maybe only yours. But the trader was frightened. He and his wife were leaving the hills here."

"They were not sick?"

"No, no. They did not wish to be, though."

"Where did they go? The sickness may be everywhere."

"South. We had heard of none there."

That news was likely to be as accurate as any. Traders talked to everyone, and had wide knowledge of happenings across the plains.

"Wait!" Wolf had another thought. "Was this trader a white man?"

"French? No, no. Arapaho . . . Trader People. The white traders stay in one place, no?"

"That is true," Wolf agreed. He had decided not to express his thought that maybe the whites were the source of the *poch*.

"Where do you go now?" the Grower asked.

"Sycamore River. Our band will winter there. But we do not know how many."

"Ah, my heart is heavy for your people. But your two lodges are healthy. There may be others. And surely, this too will pass!"

They offered their gift of pemmican and obtained a sack of beans and another of corn. The sympathy of the Growers was apparent as they parted.

"May your people winter well, Singing Wolf."

"And yours, Uncle!"

The two families moved on. Nights were growing colder now, and the colors of the trees beginning to change. Sumac thickets on the slopes flared to brilliant reds for a few days before dropping their leaves. The cottonwood leaves of shiny, fluttering green became golden yellow almost overnight, seeming to glow with their brilliance. Oaks reddened.

The prairie grasses, too, heralded cooler weather with more subtle changes in color. Tall spires of blue-green plume grass shot up to the height of a man in a few short days, and blossomed in golden feathery glory. The first frosts would change the blue stems and leaves to a pale yellow. By contrast the big real-grass, also tall and bluish in color, would become a rich burgundy. "Little" real-grass, shorter and softer, became a softer color also, a muted pink with curls of white seed heads along the stems.

Geese and ducks were becoming restless, seeming to know that there was something that they must do, but undecided yet. Small flocks of water birds began to gather, bands of a dozen or so honking noisily as they beat their way a short distance from one body of water to another. The beginnings of the long lines that would mark their migration could be seen. Young birds, still experimenting, formed, dissolved, and reformed the precise V-shaped lines that are the symbols of their kind.

The eaters of flying insects, the swallows and martins and flycatchers, were already gone. The first hard frost would eliminate their food supply. Long-standing instinctive memory reminded them of shortening days and hunger ahead, and they must leave.

With the other creatures of the prairie, the People became restless, too. Even in the comfortably warm sunlight of autumn, they too felt the restlessness that may be a frustrated migration urge. It whispers into the ears of the human race, as it does to the swallow or the geese, that the time is at hand: *there is something that you must do!* It has become less well defined in humans, perhaps. It has been dulled along with our other sensibilities. Humans draw farther away from the real world, that of the spirit, and into a complicated muddle that is known as progress. But they still hear the whisper, and feel the concern at certain seasons of the year. *There is something . . .*

For the two brothers of the People with their families it was more apparent. Migrate a little bit, move south a little way, hunt, *prepare for winter!*

Just how to do this had been a question, but it was now decided. They would go to the specified camping place on Sycamore River. It was well known to the People. They had used it before, only a few winters ago. They would winter there, whether any other families arrived or not.

As they moved in that direction, they had two main concerns. One, of course, was food. They had seen no great migrating herds of buffalo yet. There were scattered individuals and small bands, and there should be no problem. Of course, what *should* be . . . *aiee*, there should not have been the spotted death!

A more threatening concern was that of their vulnerability. A traveling group with only two warriors was at risk if they encountered a large body of potential enemies. Even a small war party of Shaved Heads or Horn People would badly outnumber the fighters of the two families. True, the two women were skilled in the use of weapons, but there were the children to think of. And the women themselves . . . two attractive young women of the People. There had always been enemies who desired young women of the People for wives. Tall, long-legged, women with spirit . . . *Our women are prettier than theirs*, the old saying went.

So the two brothers were concerned as they traveled. Nothing had been said. It was unnecessary. The women knew it, too. There was danger. For a little while, there had been a greater danger, from the *poch*, but now things seemed to be getting back to some semblance of normal, with the normal dangers of small-group travel.

"How far do you think it might be to Sycamore River?" asked Singing Wolf.

Beaver Track shrugged. "Maybe six, eight sleeps. You think so?"

Wolf nodded. "Something like that."

"Why have we seen no one else?" asked Beaver.

It was a question that both had been afraid to voice. For a while it had been good to see no one. They would have chosen not to do so. Any traveler might be either a potential enemy or some of their own people, carrying the *poch*. Either would not be good.

But now . . . In approaching winter camp, they were assuming that the threat of the spotted death was lessening, perhaps over. *Then where are the others?* Wolf thought.

He tried to convince himself that everyone was being cautious. Maybe some would choose not to winter together. It was even possible that in some of the widely dispersed families the *poch* was still rampant. He knew that his brother must have been thinking along these same lines. Now it was out in the open. There was another cause for concern. *Are we all that is left of the Southern band?*

There flitted through his mind the thought that they might find it necessary to join another of the bands. They could not do so this winter, but if they survived, it might come to such a move. Then yet another dread struck him. What about the other bands? Had the *poch* struck them too? *Are we all that is left of the People?*

He hesitated to mention that possibility yet, though he was sure that the others would have the same suspicion.

That question was partially answered two days later. Beaver Track, in the lead, approached a rise and suddenly jerked his horse around to retreat a few steps. With hand signals he motioned for a stop, and Wolf kicked his horse forward, his heart pounding.

"What is it?" he asked.

"Other travelers," Beaver said softly. "Only a few bow shots away."

"A war party?"

"I think not. They have pole-drags."

That was good. Families in transit do not seek a fight. Unless . . .

"How many?"

If it were a large band, a few young men might think it great sport to harass or attack as small a party as their two families.

"I only had a quick look, Wolf. I saw three or four *travois*. It may be three lodges."

"It is good. They may be our people."

The two men crept up the slope to look over the ridge. There in the near distance straggled a column of travelers much like their own. A little larger, maybe. A couple of young men pushed a herd of some sixty horses along behind. The party was heading southwest, and their route would join the vague trail followed by the brothers at some point ahead.

"Who are they?" asked Wolf. "Can you tell?"

Beaver Track lay on his belly and curled both his hands into loose fists. Then he placed them together and peered through the tunnel formed by his hands. With part of the unneeded light eliminated, a sharper image presented itself.

"I cannot . . . ah! The man on the left, there . . . Wolf, is that not the blue stallion of Yellow Bear? And yes, that is Bear! It is good! Our own people."

They rose and watched the procession for a little while. Rain came walking up the hill.

"What is it?" she asked, a little irritably. "I am made to think that you two would not stand up if there was danger. But you might tell us, too."

"I am sorry, Rain," Singing Wolf told her. "You see, there . . . We think that to be the family of Yellow Bear, no?"

She studied the distant column. "Yes, maybe. Those two on the flanks may be his sons. But Bear had three, did he not?"

"Maybe so . . ."

The doubt was there, dark and heavy, hanging in the air between them.

"Maybe one of them took his family somewhere else," Beaver Track suggested.

No one answered, but all were thinking the same thing. If the extended family of old Yellow Bear had been struck by the spotted sickness, how many had died?

Even more important, were any still sick?

"Will we camp with them tonight?" asked Rain.

The brothers looked at each other for a moment.

"Maybe," said Wolf slowly. "We must be sure . . ."

"Look, Wolf," Beaver Track interrupted, "I will go and see how it goes with them. Then we can decide."

"It is good," Singing Wolf agreed. "But I will go."

Beaver Track thought about it for a moment. "Yes," he said finally. "You know more of such things."

"Anyway," Wolf said as he swung to his saddle, "we will have some news today of the People!"

19

>> >> >>

The meeting with the families of Yellow Bear and his sons was as cautious as that of the brothers earlier.

Wolf had ridden forward to overtake the column and initiate contact.

"*Ah-koh,* Uncle," Singing Wolf called as they approached.

Yellow Bear rode to meet him, flanked by one of his sons.

"It is Singing Wolf, and my brother, Beaver Track," Wolf called out. "Beaver is back there with our families."

Yellow Bear drew his horse to a stop some twenty paces away.

"I see who you are, Wolf. How is it with your families? Do you have the spotted sickness?"

"No, no, Uncle. Have you?"

"We did have. My son Hunts Antelope is dead. Two of his sons . . . The wife of my other son Lame Wolf, and her baby."

"*Aiee!* My heart is heavy for you, Uncle. Are any still sick?"

The old warrior shook his head. "No, that was three moons ago. We have mourned, and it is behind us. Things happen . . . You have had no sickness?"

"No, not in Beaver's lodge or mine."

"It is good. You are moving to winter camp?"

"Yes. We did not know how many will be left. Have you heard? We talked to Growers who said the band is scattered," Wolf answered.

"But we knew that. What of the other bands?"

"We have heard nothing."

"Nor have we."

"May we join you, Uncle?" Wolf asked respectfully.

In normal times the question would not even be asked. But these times were not normal. With lives at stake, one becomes quite cautious. However, Yellow Bear did not hesitate.

"Of course. How far . . . ?"

"Just over the hill. Go ahead. We will join you at night camp."

"It is good," said the old warrior.

Singing Wolf turned his horse, but Bear called him back.

"Wolf!"

"Yes, Uncle?"

"My heart is good," Yellow Bear said clumsily. "It is good to see our People again."

"That is true, Uncle. May we soon find more."

It was two days later that Beaver Track, scouting ahead, saw the trail of another party on the move. He dismounted to examine the signs left by the unknown travelers.

Horses . . . many of them. They had followed or perhaps were driven over a trail left by *travois* poles. It took a little time to decipher the complicated mixture of sign. The grooves made by the pole-drags were partly obscured by the hooves of the horse herd which followed. Several *travois*, it appeared from the deep grooves in the prairie soil. "Deep" translated instantly in his mind to heavy loads, probably lodge covers. Several of them, at least three.

One final piece of information that might have seemed trivial was most important of all. It was a strip of soft-tanned leather less than a hand's span in length, dirty and worn. The very fact of its condition spoke to Beaver Track of what it was, the ornament from the heel of a warrior's moccasin. It was a sort of symbolic thing, originated by the Elk-dog Society when the People first acquired the horse. It identified the wearer as a horseman. The dangling decoration, in principle, states that the wearer is a *rider*, a man of dignity, and not one who walks in the dust. It is apparent that even a horseman also walks in the dust sometimes. The proud decoration drags behind his steps, and becomes worn and disheveled. It is frequently lost and must be replaced.

One of these lost ornaments was the object which brought a special smile to the face of Beaver Track. Only a few nations in the tallgrass prairie used such a decoration. And the only man who would be likely here, in a party of this size, would be a member of the Elk-dog Warrior Society of the People.

Beaver swung to his saddle and turned on the back trail.

"Some of our people are ahead," he reported to his brother, waving the leather thong.

"Ah! Elk-dog warriors . . . How many? Did you talk to them?" Wolf asked.

"No, no. They are maybe a day ahead. Three, four lodges. Many horses. The horses covered the pole tracks, mostly."

"A party much like ours, then? Of the People . . . They must be Southern band, too, no?"

Beaver Track nodded. "I was made to think so, Wolf. They must be heading to the winter camp, too."

For the next day or two there was much speculation as to the identity of those ahead. Ashes of the cooking fires left by the party ahead indicated more about them. There might be five lodges. Some children, maybe an infant, judging from the yellow color of the excrement on a piece of soft moss that had been used to wipe a small behind. This was an encouraging sign. There were survivors, possibly born after the spotted *poch* sickness had passed.

It was a joyful reunion when they arrived at the designated camp. There were at least ten of the big lodges already in place up and down the broad meadow. All doorways faced east, and each family had chosen a sheltered site, protected by trees and brush from the winds that would soon howl out of the north.

There were tearful cries of joy at the discovery that a friend or relative still lived. Mingled with such cries were wails of anguish as someone learned of a loss. The Song of Mourning echoed along the river. Nearly every lodge had been visited by death at the hand of the dreaded *poch.*

But life is for the living, and goes on. Already there were changes. The widow of No Tail Squirrel had moved into the lodge of her sister as a second wife to the sister's husband, Crooked Horn. Another pair of sisters, both widowed, were being avidly courted by a handsome young man of the Blood Society. It had already become a ribald joke in the camp. No one was certain . . . Either he could not decide between the two sisters, or they would not be parted. He might have to take both . . . A lodge with two wives and three children, already established. That would be quite a change for a young man still living with his parents. There were many chuckles, and mock wagers about the young man's ability to handle the situation.

"Let him try!" giggled an old woman. "They can teach him. Or I can! He looks good to me!"

Only a day or two later the extended family of Broken Lance arrived, also with some empty places around the fire. The chief sought out Singing Wolf.

"*Ah-koh,* Uncle," Wolf greeted respectfully. "It is good to see you."

"And you! How does it seem now?" The old leader was direct and to the point.

"It is hard to tell yet, Uncle. Have you seen any of the spotted *poch* in the last moon?"

"No. Maybe it has passed."

"I am made to think so," Wolf agreed. "We talked to some Growers. They had escaped it, but were afraid."

Broken Lance nodded. "We, too. Yet I have heard of no new sickness."

"Nor have we. Do you know of the other bands?"

"Oh!" the chief exclaimed. "There was a trader . . . He had been with the Mountain band. They had none. Red Rocks, I cannot say, but they are far away."

"The Northern band?" Wolf asked.

Broken Lance shook his head. "The Growers we visited said they are not sick. But that was only a story from someone else."

Wolf nodded. "But generally true. What of the others?"

The old man was quiet for a moment, and finally spoke. "I fear for them, Wolf. Both the Eastern band and the New People are closer to the traders. If the *poch* comes from there . . . *aiee!*"

"Well, we will learn later."

"Yes . . . maybe."

. . . . .

By the time the moon was full again, it appeared that all of the families of the scattered Southern band had returned. All that would . . . There had been mourning in nearly every lodge, and there were brief episodes of mourning for a little while as people learned of the loss of a friend or relative.

It appeared to Singing Wolf that the band had lost about one in three. There were nearly as many lodges as before, but some sheltered the remains of two or even three families who had combined.

Another thing occurred to him as he watched the preparations for winter. Usually, in a time of sickness, those who were stricken had been the young and weak, or the old and infirm. This time it was not so. The deaths had occurred without regard to age or status. Young, old, wives and mothers, children, the elders and the youths, even warriors in the glory of young manhood.

Among those who had survived, most were severely marked. The bright red spots, round scars the size of a thumbprint, could be seen on the faces of fully half the people in the band. Wolf supposed that they would fade in time to be the color of normal skin. It was already apparent, however, that the scars would be visible. Nearly all showed a deep circular depression, a pit with clearly marked edges. It would long be a reminder of the Year of Spotted Sickness.

That would be the theme of the painting which Wolf must place on the Story Skins. The annual depiction of the history of the People was intended to represent the most important event of the year. Surely there had been no more important happening for some time. Certainly not since his father, Walks in the Sun, had handed down the office and the responsibility at the time of his death. He gazed at the silver dangles on the Spanish bit, the Elk-dog Medicine emblem of the People. He had inherited the custody of that talisman at the same time.

It was not used in a horse's mouth any more . . . It had not been for many generations. According to the legend and the paintings on the skins, it had been worn by the First Horse. And that in turn had been ridden by an ancestor of Singing Wolf, an outsider who had heavy fur upon his face. Heads Off, he was called, according to the story. The reason for that was rather vague, at least in the mind of Singing Wolf. Was the ability to remove his head and replace it some sort of a trick or illusion? Wolf had studied the Story Skins and was inclined to believe that what Heads Off had removed was a hat or headdress of some kind. It appeared round and smooth in the pictographs . . .

His thoughts were interrupted by the approach of his brother.

"*Ah-koh!*" greeted Beaver Track. "Wolf, I have been thinking. The buffalo are coming, and we will have the hunt in three days, maybe. Our wolves are watching them."

"It is good."

"Yes . . . but Wolf, we have fewer hunters. Are there enough to carry out a proper Fall Hunt?"

It was a question. A number of mounted hunters would be needed to surround a part of the herd and force the animals to run where they could be pursued and killed. Would there be enough riders?

"I . . . I am made to think so, Beaver. It will be a smaller hunt. But we have fewer mouths to feed this winter. I will talk to Broken Lance."

"It is good. You will sing and pray for the hunt, too, Wolf?"

"Of course!"

Beaver Track stooped to leave the lodge, but then turned back for a moment. He appeared uneasy.

"Wolf . . ."

"Yes. What is it, Beaver?"

"Wolf, there are many who wear the tracks of the *poch,* no?"

"Yes . . ." He was unsure what his brother was suggesting.

"Well, I was thinking . . . Many have sickened and then survived."

"That is true."

"We have mourned our mother, but . . ."

Wolf saw his brother's thought now, before it was spoken. *Aiee,* why had they not thought of this before? They had assumed that Running Deer would have been a victim of the spotted death. There had been nothing else there, at the Camp of the Dead.

But what if she had survived?

"Wolf, we have to go and look for her," Beaver Track said.

20
» » »

It was true. They must know, must find out if she lived. It would probably infuriate their mother when they came searching, if she *had* survived, because her action had been a suicide gesture. But that had been hers to choose, as it should be.

Now it was different. If she had survived the *poch*, she might have changed her mind. And certainly it was unlikely that she could survive the winter alone. Wolf doubted that she would do such a thing as seek shelter among the Growers. Running Deer's pride would make her starve before she was reduced to begging. *Aiee*, to be blessed with so stubborn a parent!

But before they could even try to consider such a thing, they must be sure whether she *had* survived the sickness.

"We must go back there," Wolf said thoughtfully.

"What about the hunt?"

"We should help with that," Wolf agreed, "but be ready to leave as soon as it is finished. How long will we have to travel, Beaver?"

"I do not know. We can go fast and light."

"It is good."

He knew it was not. It was dangerous . . . It would be a tough, demanding journey, with the threat of the first winter storm hanging over them. But he could see no other way. He explained the situation to Rain, who agreed.

"Let us make you a pack of food for traveling. Green Heron and Beaver will do the same. Then you can leave as soon as the hunt is finished. I will talk to her."

Wolf nodded. "It is good. But we will help with the heaviest part of the hunt."

Rain dismissed the offer with a wave of her hand. "Do you think we are helpless? Heron and I can do it."

"But the skinning . . ."

"Look, Wolf! You roll the carcass over with a horse to finish skinning the other side, no? We can do that. The butchering is ours, anyway."

He had to agree. The management of processing the bounty of the Fall Hunt, or any other hunt, was organized by the women. Among the People, whose women were held in high regard, their men often helped with physically demanding jobs. The heavy chore of lifting the massive lodge covers was assisted by the husbands, under direction of the wives.

It was true also of the butchering. The sheer physical effort of positioning a heavy carcass, including the use of a horse, was quite often done by a husband at his wife's request. There were good-natured jokes about their allies, the Head Splitters, whose women did not enjoy quite the same status. A woman whose husband was less than cooperative might chide him with a sarcastic remark: "*Aiee!* Did I marry a Head Splitter?"

As a result of the cooperative attitude of their men, however, the women of the People were quick to do what was needed in emergencies such as this.

"Do not worry on it," Rain urged. "You and Beaver must go as soon as you can. Heron and I will manage for our lodges."

She began to fill a rawhide pack with strips of dried meat, light and easy to carry, but nourishing.

The hunt, which had been questionable because of fewer hunters, was good. Everyone knew that its success would be critical to the winter food supply. Therefore, the planning had been meticulous.

Each ceremony, every prayer, and every offering of tobacco to the spirits were carried out with heartfelt reverence.

The wolves carefully manipulated the herd to the desired area. A rider would show himself, approach slowly at a walk, then turn and ride away when the great beasts began to move. They would ride to a position slightly upwind, letting their smell drift across the herd to keep the buffalo moving, maneuvering, until they were in the right location, a broad level meadow. It was surrounded on three sides by a wooded slope, a rocky hillside, and the stream. It was apparent that when the herd began to run, they would break for the open prairie on the unencumbered side to the southwest. On that side the hunters would be stationed.

The portion of the herd now being maneuvered by the wolves of the People was probably fewer than two hundred animals. There was no purpose to large numbers, and they would be more difficult to manage. Slow, careful work had separated this smaller herd from the main migration, and moved it toward the lush meadow that would be the scene of the hunt.

It must be admitted that one may as well expect things to go wrong in such a situation. Large numbers of people and animals in interaction produce unpredictable results. Yet this time it was not so. It was as if the powers that supervise such things smiled on the effort. *It has been a hard season for the People,* some higher authority may have decided. *Let them not be faced with starvation, too.*

The animals moved as if directed, and nearly every hunter counted a kill. There was plenty to share with the few who were unsuccessful.

Wolf, hunting with a bow, rode into the hunt and almost immediately found himself approaching a yearling bull from the right side. It was like a dream, placing an arrow just behind the short ribs to range forward into the heart and lungs. He would try for another . . . a fat cow crossed in front of him and actually turned to present an easy shot. Two kills!

Wolf turned, looking for his brother, to see Beaver's quarry go down kicking. Other buffalo were falling before the lances and arrows of the hunters. He could see that the hunt was good.

In a short while the herd was gone, thundering out into the open prairie to rejoin the main herd. Wolf looked around quickly, counting the bodies of buffalo lying scattered across the meadow. Yes . . . enough. Plenty for each lodge. It would be a winter without hunger.

Wolf rode back to his first kill, the yearling bull, and dismounted to perform the necessary ceremony. Never had the words of the apology been more sincere, as he addressed the lifeless buffalo.

"We are sorry to kill you, my brother, but upon your flesh our lives depend, as you depend upon the grasses. May your people prosper and be many . . ."

He remounted and looked around for Beaver, who was now riding toward him.

"Aiee, what a hunt!" Beaver chortled. "Shall we go now?"

Wolf glanced at the sun. It was still high overhead. Why not?

"I want to change horses," he said.

"I, too."

They headed back toward the camp, and met the butchering parties heading toward the meadow. Most of the women were leading pack horses. They located Rain and Heron and paused to tell the women their intention.

"It is good," agreed Rain. "Your pack is ready. How many kills, and where?"

"Two for our lodge," Wolf told her. "A yearling bull, there . . ." he pointed, "a cow beyond."

Beaver Track was giving Heron similar information. The wives would identify their kills by the painted patterns of ownership on their arrow shafts.

"You might talk to the wife of old Pale Elk," Wolf suggested. "I did not see him make a kill. Maybe . . ."

"Of course," Rain nodded. "We will take care of it, Wolf. Now go!"

He dismounted for a quick embrace, spoke to the children, and stepped back to his horse.

"Dark Antelope," he addressed his son, "you are the man of the lodge. But do what your mother says."

The boy nodded. "It is good, Father."

The brothers took only a little while at the horse herd. Each had already decided which mount he would use. An entirely different animal would be required for this long but hurried journey. One would never use a buffalo runner for such a purpose.

Wolf threw the saddle on his roan gelding and drew the girth tight. Beaver Track approached now, leading a rangy dun.

"Not your bay?" asked Wolf.

"No. He is sore-footed."

Wolf nodded in understanding.

They rode back to the camp, where they picked up their packs and robes, and turned their horses northeast on the back trail. It was just past midday, and they would be far away by the time darkness fell.

It was many days later before the two brothers approached the area they sought. They had pushed their horses and themselves to the limit of endurance. The animals were thin and gaunt, not having had enough time to graze. The men, too, had lost weight and were sore, tired, and irritable.

They had no clear idea of what they might find. The body of their mother? It had been three moons . . . How long ago would she have fallen ill? They talked very little. Even then, it was mostly short and to the point, relating to camping sites, water, and their dwindling food supply.

Two nights when the moon was nearly full they continued to travel. Much distance was covered, but the toll on the horses was too heavy.

"They need to graze nearly half the time, Wolf," Beaver Track protested. "If we push them too hard, we will have no horses."

Wolf nodded. He was embarrassed that he had not realized how hard they had been pushing the animals.

"We will go more slowly," he agreed.

Eventually, after what seemed an eternity, they sat on their horses, overlooking the scene of the spotted death.

"The Camp of the Dead," said Beaver Track softly. *"Aiee!"*

The place was eerie to look at. It was deathly quiet. Not even a bird or an insect dared to speak in a place so heavy with the presence of spirits crossed over. Many of the lodge covers had fallen away and lay rotting on the ground. Some of the poles had collapsed, but most were still standing. The wood was turning silvery gray from the sun, wind, and weather, and resembled the bleached ribs of a man who lay outside his tattered lodge. Some of his bones were scattered, but the ribs were mostly intact. A tall seed head of grass grew up directly through what had been his chest not many moons ago. Wolf wondered if there had been anyone to mourn for him.

"Let us look for our mother's camp," said Wolf in a voice that did not sound like his own.

The crisp autumn wind sighed through the bare lodge poles.

"It was over here, was it not?" asked Wolf.

"I am made to think so."

They found the frame of the lean-to, and ashes and bits of charcoal from the fire. Nothing more.

"This is the place, no?" Wolf questioned.

"Yes."

"She is gone."

"Yes. But alive or dead? Let me look." Beaver dismounted and began to circle the area on foot.

Wolf stepped down also and waited, staring at the place where their mother had last stood. The horses grazed eagerly.

Beaver Track returned, a strange look on his face.

"Wolf," he said. "I am made to think she is alive!"

"You cannot tell, Beaver. Any sign is three moons old!" Wolf snapped irritably.

"I know, but look . . . There is nothing at her camp here. *Nothing*. Not even a scrap of the hide that we wrapped meat in for her. So she took it, to use."

"But if she was dying, would she not try to prepare herself?" Wolf asked.

"I thought of that. Maybe she would go to join those on the scaffolds," he pointed. "But there is no sign of her there. No, Wolf. She was alive . . . she left here, because she took her things. Her knife, her ax, her robe!"

"Someone else may have come by and taken them."

"Why?" Beaver demanded. "There were better tools in the camp below, there. Better robes, too, but think on it, Wolf. No one would take a robe from the dead. No, she is alive."

"Yes," agreed Wolf finally. "Or was, when she left here."

21
>> >> >>

They discussed the situation. Should they start back to the winter camp of the Southern band? What else could be done?

"She must have gone willingly," Beaver Track observed. "Otherwise, there would be *something* left at her camp."

"But with whom? And what happened to the child?"

"Yes . . . we saw nothing of the girl. Our mother may have wrapped the body for burial."

"Where?" Wolf demanded. "Beaver, she would not place it on one of the scaffolds with others. Maybe she left it in one of the lodges. Or buried it among the rocks."

"Maybe we should search."

"No . . . There is nothing to be done anyway, if we did find the child's body."

"That is true."

"But, back to our mother. We are made to think that she is alive. Or was when she left here. How long since her little camp there has been used?"

Beaver Track shrugged. "That is hard to say, Wolf. It has rained since then. The ashes of the fire . . ."

"Yes . . . it has rained . . . when?"

"Two or three times, the past moon. But maybe it rained where we were, and not here."

"We cannot tell then," Wolf mused.

"The ground is dry, though," Beaver Track noted, touching a crack in the ground. "There has been no rain here for maybe half a moon."

"Ah! That helps. She left more than half a moon ago, no? And because she chose to leave."

"It seems so."

"And she could have been with friends . . . Head Splitters, maybe. Could she have been a captive, Beaver?"

The tracker pondered for a little while. "I am made to think no, Wolf. Think on it . . . No one would carry off an old woman. She has no value as a wife or as a slave. They would kill her or just leave her. There would be no honor in killing an old woman."

"That is true. Then she left because she wanted to go with them. But with *whom*?"

The two men looked at each other for a moment and both came to the same conclusion.

"Alone?" suggested Beaver.

"Maybe. Let us think now. She knew where we would be, on Sycamore River. Would she try to join the band?"

"I am thinking not, Wolf. It is far, for an old woman on foot."

"And she is stubborn. She would try to winter by herself, Beaver."

"Yes, I think so. She would head south. Could she do it? Maybe we should go and look for her."

"I am made to think," said Wolf, "that it is too late to try. We have to wonder when the first snows will come."

"That is true. By now, she has found a place to winter, no?"

Singing Wolf nodded. "Unless," he mused, "she intends to die fighting Cold Maker in the open."

"But if she planned to do that, Wolf, why would she bother to go anywhere? Why leave here?"

They talked longer, but kept coming back to the same theory: their mother was alive, and had made plans to winter, either with friends and allies, or alone. And probably, far from here.

There was nothing more to be done. It might be that they would never know the fate of Running Deer. That possibility was not spoken aloud by either of her sons. To do so might bring it to pass.

Singing Wolf glanced at the sky. In the intensity of their discussion, they had not noticed the approach of a heavy blue-gray cloud bank from the northwest.

"*Aiee!*" exclaimed Wolf. "We must find shelter!"

"Let us use the camp of our mother here," suggested Beaver. "A little repair, some fresh brush on the top, a fire . . . Then when this storm is past, we must travel hard!"

Running Deer sat under the shelter a few sleeps to the south, and thought on the change in the weather. She had been expecting it, of course, but there is a difference. Such a thing can be expected, but one is never really ready. When the wind turned, and Cold Maker came howling across the hills and scrub oaks, she wondered if she could really survive a winter. She looked at the sleeping girl, and tucked the robe more tightly around her. *Sleep well, little Mouse,* she thought.

She drew her own robe around her shoulders more closely. It was not quite dark, but she had seen the storm front and prepared for the worst. There had been a few cold nights, a few mornings with crusted ice around the edges of the stream. Frost had replaced many of the fall colors with its intricate patterns of white, lasting only a short time each morning until the day began to warm.

But this was different. The chilling cold seemed to strike clear through her body, even through the woolly robe around her shoulders. She had felt this coming in her aging bones, a half day ago. As a child she had wondered at the older ones of the People. How did they know of a coming storm? "I feel it in my bones," her old grandmother had told her. "They tell me the storm is coming." Deer had thought that remark odd and funny then. She did not understand how her grandmother's bones could tell her anything.

But now she knew all too well. The bone-deep ache, made worse by remaining too long in one position, was a constant reminder. She shifted a little, trying to draw her left foot into a more comfortable position. No . . . that would not do . . . Maybe she could extend it toward the fire for a little while and warm the ache out of her knees. Both legs . . . Yes, better . . .

The fire would soon need more fuel, to reflect into the inside of her little lodge. She would wait a little for now, until her legs needed to be repositioned again. Then she would get up and move around, bring a little more wood within reach.

Gray Mouse stirred in her sleep, and Yellow Dog, curled next to her for mutual warmth, tapped the ground with his tail two or three times. He did not even lift his head. It was good to have the dog, Running Deer thought. Initially, she had thought of the creature as a potential food supply if they were not wintering well. It seemed unlikely that Yellow Dog would serve that purpose now.

He had been no problem at all. Deer had been fortunate enough to kill a fat cow when a band of buffalo wandered through the area. It had been almost more than she could handle, to skin and butcher a substantial portion of the meat. But Gray Mouse had proved a willing helper. One heavy load may be divided into many small ones, with more trips. Fortunately the kill had been only a bow shot from their shelter, and many trips were possible. Yellow Dog, recipient of many scraps from the butchering, was therefore constantly near. Running Deer had managed to utilize his effort, too, in carrying bundles of meat. She would tie a pack to his back and hand one to Gray Mouse, then shoulder her own, the heaviest, for the carry back to the lodge. Across the meadow, cross the riffle of the stream . . . *aiee, the water grows cold* . . . Leave the packs and return for another load.

After enough weight was removed from the carcass she was able to turn it to finish skinning. She had to cut the hide up the back and remove half, then turn and finish the skinning of the other side. No matter. It was easier to handle the heavy fresh skin that way. If she needed to do so she could sew it back together. With that in mind, she stripped out most of the sewing sinew from along the back and loin as she butchered. It would dry without attention, and she could split it later after softening in water. Or in her mouth as she worked, after it was stripped.

Two days' hard work moved most of the buffalo carcass that Deer thought worth salvaging. She waved to the pair of coyotes waiting on a distant rise.

"The rest is yours, my brothers!"

For several nights the sounds of the coyotes, making good their claim, echoed across the meadow in chuckling laughter or yipping quarrel. Yellow Dog was concerned at first, but soon ignored the sounds of his distant kinsmen. They disappeared at dawn, to return each night for more feasting.

But that was behind her now, the tedious tasks of drying and storing the meat finished. She felt good about her winter supplies, and the halves of the robe had tanned well. She had not even considered bothering the deer herd that was preparing to winter in the timber to the east of her camp. She had been careful not to let Yellow Dog bother them. It was good to have them for emergencies.

She noticed now, as she replenished the fire, that the wind had died with the daylight. It was calm, dead calm, and she understood. Cold Maker had driven his line of invasion past them, and now paused before his next onslaught. Deer looked up into the darkening sky expectantly . . . Yes, here they came, the first fluffy breath-feathers of snow, floating with utter silence to land softly on things below. This sort of quiet snow always reminded her of the soft silent flight of *Kookooskoos,* the owl, hunter and messenger. It made her feel his presence, whether physical or in spirit. It was the season of hunting for *Kookooskoos* as well as for his human counterparts. She had seen a pair of owls often, had wished them "good hunting!" and had wondered whether they would bring a message. And if so, good or bad?

The snow was heavier now, falling thickly, and beginning to whiten the earth. At least, that in the circle of the firelight. Beyond that she could not see, but knew that it was so. There was an occasional hiss now, as the heavy melting flakes survived long enough to challenge the fire. She wondered idly if it could ever snow hard enough to kill a fire. Rain Maker could do that on occasion, but snow . . . She thought not. She *hoped* not!

She was becoming drowsy now. She must think about this . . . A person freezing to death becomes sleepy, and she must decide whether it would be safe to sleep. No, she decided, that must be different. It is said that such a sleep comes on with a longing just to rest a little while and then go on.

Surely this was not the way she felt. There was no desperation here, but confidence. And the cold . . . not too bad. Uncomfortable, true, but much better since the wind had died. The warmth of the fire was good. Maybe later she could build a reflector, to turn more heat into the open side of the lodge. She would think on that. Yes, small logs and sticks on a frame of stakes . . . Stacked like the sticks of a willow backrest . . . Peeled, probably. That would reflect more heat into the lodge.

An owl sailed in out of the snow-filled darkness and perched on a nearby oak. Three times *Kookooskoos* called his own name, then sat for a little while.

"Do you want to talk to me?" asked Running Deer. It was unusual for the bird to be active in a snow storm.

The owl did not answer.

"Do you have a message?" she asked.

As messenger for the People, *Kookooskoos* might carry a message either good or bad. Deer was uneasy about this.

Soon the owl spread silent wings and sailed into the darkness.

"Good hunting, Grandfather," Deer called after him.

Had there been a message, and if so, *what?* Her husband, the holy man, had often said that one must be ready to *listen.* Singing Wolf was much the same about it. It was not a matter of listening with the ears, though, but with the *spirit.*

She tried to open her mind to that. She had been somewhat fearful just before the owl came. Could she tell whether she was about to freeze or was merely drowsy? How did she feel now about the owl's visit?

Good, she decided. There was a calm, a satisfaction about the visit of the messenger. So it must be, then, that the message had been neither bad news nor warning. It must be *good.*

Relieved, she lay down next to the sleeping child, with the warm dog between them. Yellow Dog thumped his tail a time or two and went back to sleep.

Somehow, she felt that the owl's message had been not just for tonight, but for the winter ahead.

"Thank you, *Kookooskoos,*" she murmured as she drifted into an untroubled sleep.

22
» » »

It was the Moon of Snows now. The Moon of Long Nights had passed, and on some days Running Deer thought that she could actually see the difference. Every season the war between Cold Maker and Sun Boy was repeated. Since Creation, likely.

Cold Maker would initiate the combat, pushing from the north as Sun Boy's torch began to fade. Sun Boy would wisely retreat. There is a time for heroism, but it is not at the first skirmish. Through the Long Nights Moon and that of Snows, Sun Boy would always retreat to the south, avoiding a confrontation. Sometimes it seemed that his torch must have gone out entirely. There were days at a time when the dark pall of Cold Maker's clouds hung low over the earth.

Maybe Sun Boy's torch does go out sometimes, Running Deer thought. *Maybe that is when he is making a new one.* This was a possibility that she had never heard spoken. Maybe there was a reason, though. If that were true, such a time would be ideal for Cold Maker's final push, and it would be over. Without the return of the Sun Torch, there would be no return of the grass or of the buffalo. The world would be dead, along with all its creatures. And the People . . .

For that reason, she had never mentioned her thought, even to her husband, who had been wise in such things. The idea that maybe Sun Boy's torch *does* go out sometimes was so threatening . . . What if it did, and Cold Maker discovered his opportunity to finish the age-old war permanently? But if Cold Maker does not know exactly when to strike, the danger is lessened. Therefore, if we do not speak aloud of it, there is still some protection. Maybe . . . At least, *less* risk.

This had not been an unusual winter. An average number of storms sweeping through. A push by Cold Maker, a retreat by Sun Boy, an attempt to hold his torch high and proud. Another push . . . Sun Boy was far to the south now. On some mornings, even when his torch did burn, its rays were pale and watery. There was barely any heat to beam down on the snow that covered the earth like a tossed blanket. This, Deer was certain, was the time when Sun Boy was making his new torch, lighting it from the old, fanning it to get it started. It was the critical time in the age-old struggle for fire. The time, of course, when Cold Maker *must not know*, because he would push his advantage.

So she tried not to think about it. Cold Maker might overhear her thoughts. Patience . . . Let Sun Boy get his torch going. Then begin the push back, crowding Cold Maker, forcing him back to his icy lodge somewhere in the always frozen mountains in the unknown north country.

Then would come the Moon of Awakening, the melting of snows, the tiny bits of green revealed beneath.

But that was not yet. Cold Maker still held his authority. Ahead was still the most dreaded time, the Moon of Hunger.

Running Deer could remember a few times in her life when there had been snow on the ground from the Moon of Madness until the Awakening. Fortunately, this was not one of those. And her camp was pretty far south. She was pleased at her foresight in choosing this camp. Sometimes Cold Maker's first push came as early as the Falling Leaves Moon, too. That made for a long winter.

Even in a good year, food would run low before the return of spring, and the opportunity to hunt. It had been much worse, the old stories said, before the coming of the horse. Sometimes the People had a Fall Hunt that was less than successful. Then they had gone into the winter moons knowing that someone would die before the

Moon of Awakening. In fact, the old name for the Moon of Hunger, it was said, had been the Moon of Starvation.

She shook her head to clear it of such gloomy thoughts. This was not a bad winter. She had seen many that were worse. Much of the time the ground had been bare of snow. There was still plenty of dried meat in the storage area at the back of the lean-to shelter. And the days did seem to be getting longer. At least she thought so.

But it was a tiresome thing. It was late afternoon just now, nearing the end of another uneventful day. Snow, cold, pale sunlight, darkness. Eat, sleep, bring water, wood, keep up the fire . . .

There *had* been pleasant times. The child, Gray Mouse, had probably enabled her to keep her sanity. The legends of the People included stories of persons who, isolated and alone, had gone mad in the moons of Long Nights and Snows. She had never understood that. To Running Deer, it had always been pleasant to be alone. Time to think, uninterrupted by the necessities of living. Time to be with the things of the spirit. Like the quest ceremony. She had never taken a vision quest. There had always been other things in her life that required attention. She should have, maybe, after the death of her husband, she had thought later. At the time, it had never occurred to her. Vision quests are for the young anyway, she had convinced herself afterward. Not for an old woman.

That attitude, she realized now as she looked back, had been part of her bitterness. *Aiee*, how hard she must have made it for her sons! During that time she had refused to even think of anything that might be pleasant, or exciting, or *fun*. The memory embarrassed her. And she knew now that she had, for a while, lost the joy of being alone.

Gray Mouse had proved to be an intelligent child, one filled with the joy of seeing, hearing, and learning. Their days were filled with endless questions. "Why is grass green? What makes the sky blue? How high is it? Who teaches the oriole to weave her basket nest?" Sometimes Running Deer would throw up her hands in frustration. "Because it is so, child. That is the way it is!"

And Mouse would laugh. Maybe that was all the answer she required, when all was said and done. Upon one thing, Deer could depend . . . Stories. Every child loves stories, and this one was no exception. Deer had forgotten the joy of a child in her lap or at her knee, the shining, eager face and bright eyes as the story unfolded. She realized now that she had missed much joy in her preoccupation with sorrow. Her grandchildren would have listened to her stories. Dark Antelope, the oldest, had done so when he was small. But soon after, the loss of Walks in the Sun had shattered her world.

Through the autumn moons, as Gray Mouse learned the tongue of the People, Deer had regained the joy of the storyteller. The stories had helped the little girl as she began to use the language that was new to her.

Even with all this good, the depressing darkness of winter began to gnaw at the senses of Running Deer. She began to see how hunters or trappers, cut off from others for a long time, would be reduced to madness. There was a difference. It was one thing to be alone to think, meditate, and pray. It was quite another to be forced to be alone.

She had *felt* alone at first, because the girl could speak only a little. Soon, however, it was apparent that Gray Mouse was a person. Sometimes a quiet and introspective person, it was true, but who would *not* be? The child had experienced more horror in her short years than many do in a lifetime. Under it all, the quiet times and times when Mouse whispered restlessly in her sleep, there was a calm strength. A strength, maybe, that lay in her basic curiosity about all things, and her joy in learning them.

For Running Deer, then, it was a fortunate thing to winter with the girl. Each time she began to feel glum and irritable, Mouse would do or say something that would make her smile. When it seemed that the aching in her old bones was more than she could tolerate any longer, there would come a distraction that would cause her to forget. The girl would bring a pretty leaf or a feather and show it with an eagerness that made a small thing like aching knees only a minor nuisance. The childish laughter at the antics of a brood of young foxes, the fascination with the beauty of a snowflake on the dark fur of a buffalo robe . . . And it was good.

Even so, her spirits were low, and wearing thin. Deer felt that this winter would never end. How many times can one tell the story of how Bobcat lost his tail before it begins to sicken?

"Not that again, child!" she had snapped, only this morning.

She had immediately felt sorrow over the cutting remark, and had tried to repair the damage.

"Maybe later . . ."

But the damage was done, and the hurt hung between them like the ugly green-gray cloud that carries the storm.

"It is nothing, Grandmother," said Gray Mouse.

Running Deer knew that it was not true. She had seen the hurt in the child's eyes. Why had she been so sharp with her refusal? There was no need. She could tell the Bobcat story again, or tell it a hundred times. What did it matter? Well, she would try to make it up this evening, with a story of some sort as they prepared for sleep. She watched the girl and the dog playing along the stream a stone's throw away.

Gray Mouse would make a snowball and toss it toward the water. Yellow Dog would bound after it. Sometimes he would retrieve it and bring it back to her. Other throws would land the ball of snow in the stream, where it would promptly disappear. Then the dog would splash around in mock confusion. Either way, the rippling laughter of a happy child at play would ring across the snow-covered meadow.

Yes, she must try to think of a special story tonight. Just now . . . the blue shadow of the ridge to the west was creeping across the valley. She could see it move. The sun on snow could be a painful thing to tired old eyes, but the blue shadow was restful in appearance. It would soon be dark. She built up the fire and called to Gray Mouse to come home.

It would be a moonlit night tonight. Not quite full, but a silvery night, crisp and cold. She checked her fuel supply. Maybe she should try for some fresh meat tomorrow. The deer in the grove there? *Aiee*, a few bites of fresh liver would be good for her spirit! For now, though, dried meat and pemmican.

"Mouse, could you hand me a bundle of pemmican, there?"

The girl reached for one of the rawhide packs in the rear of the shelter, and then stopped in surprise.

"*Aiee*, Grandmother! Somebody has been eating our food!"

Running Deer hurried to see, her heart racing. This could be a real threat.

It was true. Some wild creature, possibly a raccoon, had discovered their cache. In the deepening darkness she could not tell yet how serious the loss might be.

They ate, more sparingly than she had planned. She did attempt a story, but her heart was not in it. She slept little that night. Her peace of mind was not helped by the distant song of a pack of hunters who might compete with them for the deer that she had been saving. It was the first time she had heard the sound since they had been in this winter camp.

Wolves.

23

>> >> >>

Gray Mouse had settled into her new life with the resiliency of childhood. It was not without problems, however. The language barrier was quickly overcome, with the help of hand signs. But the major task of the young at her age is that of learning, anyway. It was a small step to learning in a different tongue.

The difference in the stories which she had noticed was merely a matter of pleasant diversion now. Sometimes she would share her own version of a story, and this seemed to please Grandmother.

By the time Cold Maker's first serious thrust had come and gone, their relationship was well established. Sometimes Gray Mouse had to stop and think, to remember that there had once been other people in her life. Her mother and father, many others . . . a camp with many lodges . . . Such thoughts always led to unpleasant memories, which her mind tried hard to block out. Sickness, fever, dead and dying all around, the spotted death. Sounds of mourning, the smell of death . . .

But memory is kind. That which is good is retained much more easily than the unpleasant. Sometimes it was hard to remember the horrors of the summer, and how she came to be with this grandmother. Her memories of the previous life were those of her mother, holding and rocking her, singing softly . . . Her father, strong and handsome, playing with her, letting her ride on his back. These memories were good. When Grandmother became impatient with her, she would withdraw into that pleasant part of her past, and as much as she could remember of the happy times.

Some of the grandmother's actions were completely beyond her understanding. There had been that time when the owl came and sat in a tree near their little camp. It would have been an easy shot, yet Grandmother did not even reach for her bow. Mouse watched in astonishment as Grandmother looked at the evil thing calmly, and even talked to it like a friend. It had been a ritual, almost, like the apology over a kill.

She had said nothing at the time, but later, when Grandmother seemed relaxed and in a pleasant mood, Mouse brought up the matter.

"Grandmother, why did you not kill it?"

"Kill what, child?"

"The owl. It came and sat on the tree, there. An easy shot, no?"

"But one must not kill the owl. He is the messenger from the Other Side. He carries news of the spirit."

"But Grandmother, we must kill owls. They are bad."

"No, no, child. They are to be *honored.*"

"But my father . . ." Gray Mouse began.

Suddenly, she stopped. There was something wrong here. Had she misunderstood? No, surely not. She clearly remembered the dead body of an owl hanging in a tree where her father had placed it. *It will be a warning,* he had said. *Other evil-doers will see and fear that I will shoot them, too.*

But now, this grandmother, the most important person . . . no, the *only* person in her world, looked on the owl as a creature to be *honored.* Why would one honor something evil? A gnawing doubt rose. Mouse hardly dared to consider it, but she could not escape the reality. Grandmother had honored something evil! Was that to say that Grandmother, too, was evil? Fear gripped her.

Mouse seriously considered running away, before Grandmother could do her harm. She could take some of the supplies, hide them, and then sometime as Grandmother slept, leave silently with Yellow Dog. *He* would take care of her.

The plan did not really get very far, because Mouse had no idea where she would go. Her own people had threatened to kill her. Those others, who had been with Grandmother, were people she did not know. She knew that there were other people, those who planted crops. Growers, Grandmother called them. They were different, somehow. And since the unknown breeds more fears than a known danger, she hesitated to look for refuge among Growers. They might be more dangerous than Grandmother. She did not know where to find them anyway.

Gradually, the idea of running away faded and was forgotten. From time to time Mouse would think of it and then postpone her departure. After all, if there seemed to be any threat, she could leave then, no? Meanwhile, she would have Yellow Dog to protect her from overt harm.

It helped, maybe, that Grandmother had never shown her anything but love and kindness. That is not to say that Grandmother was not quick to correct. Her tongue could be sharp. A thin sheet of ice had frozen across one of the still pools in the stream during one of the cold onslaughts of early winter. Gray Mouse, curious and full of interest, had started out onto the smooth surface. That had unleashed such a tirade from Grandmother that tears rose in Mouse's eyes. But even then, the girl knew that the scolding was for her safety.

Little by little, the conflicting customs of two traditions were forgotten. Owls do not visit a camp every day. When they were not seen as a reminder, she did not think of the problem. All her life, though, when Gray Mouse saw an owl or heard his hollow call in the night, she would experience a chill of fear, a doubt for her safety.

It is probable that Mouse did not fully understand the real threat for her safety when it came. The empty or damaged storage packs spoke silently of danger to the lives of both of them. Mouse, who had never really known hunger, assumed that Grandmother would merely shoot another buffalo. Even Running Deer was not concerned at first. It was for such an emergency that she had planned on the deer in the brushy timber to the southeast of their camp. It was a nice, healthy herd. She had watched them carefully, always from a distance and well downwind. Seventeen animals. About seven were small, this season's young. The does could be identified by their closeness to these. At least one big doe had apparently borne twins.

They had watched the strutting and challenge of the bucks when rutting season came and went, in the Moon of Madness. It was only then that the males, seen very little during the summer, became conspicuous by their behavior. They fought, paired off and mated, and began to band together to winter with the does.

Their flamboyant behavior was over now, abandoned with the loss of their antlers in the Moon of Snows. Running Deer thought that she should have little trouble obtaining a deer now. They would stay close in the shelter of the oaks, especially with snow on the ground. Maybe tomorrow, she would try for a kill.

That was the day the wolves came, and filled the evening with their hunting song. Running Deer was concerned. She did not have an unreasonable fear of the wolves themselves. Caution, yes. It would not be wise for a lone person to be out in deep snow when the pack was hunting. That would be asking for trouble. The real danger from the wolf pack, however, was indirect. If the wolves discovered the band of deer in the oak thicket, they would find it as welcome as the humans did.

Running Deer was faced with a dilemma. She did not want to be out while the wolves were hunting. Yet she hoped to kill a deer and drag it to camp before the wolves scattered the little herd.

Yes, she must try, at least. She could tie the dog, leave fuel for Mouse to keep up the fire, and make a quick hunt in the morning.

She settled in for the night, restless and uneasy. Several times she woke, hearing the distant wolf song and wondering . . . Could she do this?

At dawn she rose, built up the fire, and tested the wind. Yes, it was favorable for her purpose. She tied the dog, explained to Gray Mouse what she was doing, and cautioned the child to stay near the fire. Then she started a circuitous route to take advantage of wind direction. She had heard no song of the wolves for a while now. They had quieted as the moon set. She wondered if they had made a kill.

It took a long time in the heavy snow to maneuver into the position she wanted. She was almost there when she saw the tracks. Quickly she examined the trail left in deep snow . . . Tracks of two or three deer, running hard for their lives. Alongside were the paw prints of several large wolves. Her heart sank. Why had she seen or heard nothing? It must have been while she slept. And the hunt would be a quiet one. The song is stilled when the chase begins.

The deer, it appeared, had come from the shelter of their winter home, trying to escape into the open where their speed would be effective. She doubted that they would have been successful. She squinted against the glare of the sun on the white distance, but could see nothing. Yet somewhere, there must have been a kill.

And now the deer were scattered. Even if any were still in the area, they would remain alert and alarmed for some time. It would be useless to hunt now. Tired and depressed, she turned back toward the camp. It was remarkable, how much farther it seemed on the back trail than when she had started on her hunt with excited enthusiasm.

The wolves stayed in the area for half a moon. She could hear them in the distance. They must have made several kills, but it was a pack of eight or nine. She had seen them occasionally. A family of that size would need a lot of meat. The thought was depressing, because that was the meat she had counted on for emergencies.

This was rapidly becoming an emergency. Even carefully hoarded, the sticks of dried meat were dwindling. Their corn was gone, and most of the beans. A few more days . . .

There came a day when Running Deer realized that she had not heard the hunting song of the wolves for several nights. Cautiously, she circled the area, looking for tracks. A light dust of new snow helped in that respect. She found old tracks with powdery new snow in each, but no fresh ones.

That was good. She could see no sign of wolves since yesterday's snow. The bad part, however, was that she saw no sign of deer either before or after the snow. The herd must be gone, chased away or killed by the hunting pack.

Her heart was heavy as she hurried to the patch of oak timber that had been the shelter for the deer. The snow was trampled and packed, with the recent dusting of new snow on top. It had been a good shelter, she saw. Even now, she could feel the warmth of the protection from the wind. There had been no protection from the hunters, though. Here and there, gnawed bones and bloody snow told the tale.

She turned to go and tripped over something buried in the snow. Irritated, she reached for the offending object. It was an antler, shed by what must have been a magnificent buck. Five well-shaped points and a small spur near the base. But since it had been already lost before the wolves came, it would have been ineffective in defense anyway. Protection was found in flight. She wondered if even that had been successful.

"I am sorry, my brother," she murmured. "I needed your flesh worse than the wolves did, too!"

24
»»»

Running Deer waited and watched for deer to return, but there were none. She rationed the remaining food even more meagerly and gave most of it to the little girl. There were constant pangs in the pit of her stomach. Her buckskin dress hung loosely on her bony frame. There had been a time when that body had been one to flaunt with pride, she recalled. But that was a long time ago. It did not seem to matter much now.

She risked a shot at a squirrel in an oak behind their camp, and lost one of her precious arrows. Even worse, she missed the squirrel, and the hunger continued. She tried to estimate how long they could survive, and how long it might be until the Moon of Awakening. That would bring the thaw, and the creatures would begin to move around. Then the hunting would be easier.

Day after day, she tried to think of something that could be used as food. She watched the squirrels. They were said to store nuts, were they not? By this means she discovered a cache of acorns and hickory nuts in the hollow of a tree, and cleaned it out, down to the last shell. The nuts were hard to crack and to pick out, and the acorns too bitter to eat. Running Deer remembered, though, that some of the forest people to the east of the Sacred Hills used acorns.

She shelled the acorns, pounded the meaty kernels inside as she would pound corn, and then leached the bitter acid out by repeated soaking and boiling. The resulting mush was certainly not to be compared to broiled buffalo hump, but it would keep body and soul together a little longer. She found herself wishing that they had gathered acorns during the Moon of Falling Leaves. But how could she have known?

The wolf pack had effectively cleared the area of deer. Even the other hunters were ranging far. One night the cry of a cougar split the darkness like the scream of a woman in torture. It made the hair stand on the back of her neck. Gray Mouse crept close and the dog, every hair erect from nose to tail, tried to crowd between them.

There are no deer to be hunted here, she directed her thoughts at the great cat in the distance. *But come to look for us! Your flesh would be as good for us as ours for you!*

They did not see the cat, but the next day she found tracks near the stream. It was not heard again. Running Deer was somewhat disappointed, and was made to think that maybe she had warned the cougar by her thoughts about trying to kill and eat it.

She did kill one turkey, shooting it out of a tree where she had seen it go to roost. The night was moonlit and she maneuvered under the roost to drop the big bird with an arrow. It furnished food for several days.

But then it too was gone. She began to think of the last resort, the one she had hoped not to use. The People had always used dogs as a food supply, and even raised them for the purpose. Originally the dog had been a beast of burden as well, before the horse. Many families still kept dogs just for the change in diet. A long winter on just the dried flesh of the buffalo created a hunger for fresh meat. In this case, any meat would be welcome. It was no longer a matter of hunger, but of survival.

Yellow Dog . . . The girl had become quite attached to the animal, and would miss him. She, Running Deer, would miss him. He had furnished warmth at night during the coldest part of the winter. But now his flesh was needed to sustain life in another way.

She pondered whether to try to explain to Gray Mouse before the slaughter of the dog. That would be a hard task. Maybe it would be better simply to go ahead. While Gray Mouse slept, perhaps. A quick and sure blow with the small ax . . . skin and butcher quickly. Yes, that might be best. She could have meat broiling when Mouse awakened, and then explain the need for such action. But she was not happy about it, and would never be.

The day came. Yellow Dog was off making his daily rounds in a big circle around the camp. He stopped at each of his usual places to lift a leg and mark his territory. A rock by the stream, a tuft of grass in the meadow, a tree . . . At that point he always disappeared to circle around or through the patch of oak timber behind them. He would appear from the east to complete his circle.

Running Deer knew exactly where the dog would emerge from the bushes. It was always the same. She knew how long his circuit would take. With a bit of sadness she picked up the ax, tucked her skinning knife in her waistband, and cast a glance at the sleeping child.

Sleep well, little one, she thought. *We will eat today.*

Her shrunken stomach rumbled at the thought, and she moved toward Yellow Dog's path in the snow. He would come out of the bushes there, by the rock, and she would be waiting. He would come to her, and . . . She hoped that she could be quick and efficient. High on the head, between the ears . . . She was puzzled at her attitude. It had never been a problem before, and the traditional apology had sufficed to make her feel that . . . Well, everything has to eat something else, does it not?

She could hear the dog coming now, along his private trail through the thicket. He was moving more slowly than usual, it seemed. Maybe it was only because of her own concerns for the reaction of Gray Mouse to what was about to happen. Running Deer concealed the ax behind her and prepared to extend her left hand in greeting. Then, as Yellow Dog neared the opening in the thicket, she saw that he was carrying something.

The dog, man's first domestic animal, is a social creature. He has, through the ages, developed a complicated relationship with man, which often reveals itself in strange ways. Old instincts run strong. This includes that of bringing meat to the young at the den, or retrieving a part of the kill to share with the family-pack.

Maybe the sounds and smells, or the spirit of the wolf pack's presence had been felt by this, their distant cousin. Yellow Dog had been kept tied during the presence of the wolves, to protect him against any inclination to join them. That would probably have been a fatal mistake.

Now he ran free. He stepped into the open, saw Running Deer, and ran happily toward her. The object in his mouth was a fat, freshly killed rabbit. Proudly, the dog dropped it at her feet and stepped back, tail wagging as he waited for the expected praise.

Tears came to the old woman's eyes. She dropped the ax and fell to her knees in the snow, circling the neck of Yellow Dog with her arms. How could she have thought . . . ?

In a little while she rose, picked up the gift, and they started back to the camp. Deer was thinking busily, planning how she would use the unexpected kill. They could broil the rabbit, sharing the head, feet, skin, and entrails with Yellow Dog. The bones would be used for soup . . . Not much, but better than nothing.

This in turn gave her an idea. Maybe she could find some marrow bones from the leavings of the wolves in the deer thicket. They would have been frozen, and could be cracked and boiled for soup. Yes, she wondered why she had not thought of that before. Maybe they could survive after all.

"Wake up, little one," she called cheerfully. "Yellow Dog has brought us a gift, and we will eat!"

It was as if this incident provided a turning point. Things were better. It helped that her outlook was better, of course, and events began to fall into place. The wolves had left the area, and it was not long before the deer began to return. Running Deer stalked and killed a young buck and the three of them feasted.

With the first bite of warm raw liver as she butchered, the world seemed to come alive. Her body, starved for the life-giving juices, reacted with such joy that all seemed right. Gray Mouse, too, responded to this springtime ritual, smearing her cheeks with the fresh blood. They laughed at each other's "painted" faces. Yellow Dog gulped whatever scraps were tossed his way with enthusiasm.

After the first orgy of fresh liver, they began to slow down, and Running Deer placed some choice cuts of venison to broil.

"It is not as sweet as buffalo," she told the girl conversationally, "but it is good!"

The next day, as if it were planned that way, a soft warming breeze began to ease its way from the south.

"Ah!" Deer muttered. "Sun Boy *is* coming back, after all."

Gray Mouse giggled. "That is good, Grandmother, no?"

"Yes, very good."

"What will we do now?"

"Wait for the snow to melt. Then, travel."

"Where?"

The little voice was anxious, and Running Deer realized that they had not talked of the future at all. Since the two of them had been together, there had been little hope for a future. But now they had survived the spotted death, and the Moons of Long Nights and Starvation. She was made to feel that they could accomplish anything.

"We must find the People," she said.

"Your people, Grandmother?"

"Yes, child. Your people are dead or gone, remember?"

The girl nodded soberly. "Will your people hurt me?"

"No, no, of course not!"

"They did not want me, before."

Running Deer spread her arms and Mouse crept into her lap.

"That was different, little one. They were afraid."

"Of *me?*"

"No . . . well, yes. Of the *poch*, the spotted death that killed so many. They were afraid of me, too, remember? Those two men who came back and brought us meat? My own sons. Even they were afraid."

"I do not remember that, Grandmother."

"No, child, you were very sick. But now we are alive, and it is good."

"Where are your people?" the girl asked.

"Ah, that we will not know. They have wintered on a river we call the Sycamore. But they will move, when the Moon of Greening comes. I am made to think that we should try to join them at the Sun Dance."

"Where is that place, Grandmother?"

Running Deer laughed. "Not a place, really, Mouse. A time and a celebration. It takes place in the Moon of Roses, two moons from now. This is the greatest time of the year for the People. You will like it, Mouse! It celebrates the return of the sun, the grass, and the buffalo. There will be singing, dancing, feasting, races . . ."

The eyes of Gray Mouse were shining with the excitement that she saw in Grandmother's face.

"Where will it be?" she asked eagerly.

Running Deer chuckled, half to herself. "Ah, child, that is why I laughed. I do not know. I let myself forget. I did not expect to be alive, so it did not seem important!"

25

》》》

It might seem that finding the People at the site of the Sun Dance would be a virtually impossible task. If the entire expanse of the vast prairie, stretching from the woodlands east of the People to the great mountains in the west . . . The width would be a whole season's travel for an old woman and a child, even if they knew their destination. How could Running Deer hope to locate and then reach the camp of the Sun Dance by the time the whole nation gathered for the annual festival?

Several facts, however, would be of great help. The five bands of the People, now six with the joining of the New band, had long ago established the areas where they preferred to range. The Mountain and Red Rocks bands were expected to winter in those respective areas. The Eastern band favored the fringes of the woodlands to the northeast as a place to winter. There were French traders in that area, so the trading of furs was much easier. It was a dangerous area, with many different tribes of forest people moving in from the east. But then, the Eastern band had always done foolish things.

The Northern band, traditionally one of the two strongest, ranged as far north as the river the French now called the Platte. They wintered farther south, of course, often in the valley of the Kenzas. Her own, the Southern band, was probably the closest to where she had wintered with the girl.

While all of this knowledge would seem to be of little help, it was invaluable to Running Deer. She did not even think about such basic facts. They were just there. The fact that all of the scattered bands would assemble annually in the Moon of Roses was assumed. The site was selected each year for the next celebration. *Aiee,* she thought. *I should have been giving attention when the Council was talking of it.* It was a bit embarrassing to remember how ridiculous her attitude had been. She must have caused much pain for her sons and their families.

But back to the present with its own problems . . . She knew that the gathering place would be somewhere in the middle, where no one band would face the hardship of extra long travel. Usually the two western bands complained anyway, but if they chose to live in the shadow of the mountains, so be it. Sometimes the People decided to humor them, and held the Sun Dance farther west. They had done that only two years ago, so probably that would not be the case this season. Besides, she would remember, would she not? There would have been much talk and the Eastern band would have complained bitterly at the long trip that they would have to make.

So, Deer had concluded, the site would probably be fairly central, maybe in the Sacred Hills. And in all her lifetime, there were no more than ten sites where the Sun Dance had been held in that general area. It required special facilities. Plenty of good water, enough level space for the scores of lodges, and grass enough for the hundreds of horses that the People possessed. Fuel was less of a problem. The prairie would be littered with thousands of dry buffalo chips from last season's migration of the great herds.

But which of the sites that the People used would it be? She could not guess, but there would be ways to find out.

"We will start north," she explained to Gray Mouse. "Maybe northwest, a little. We know that much. Then we will ask as we travel. The Growers will have news."

Along most of the rivers of the prairie country there were villages of people who raised crops. By virtue of their way of life, they were usually peaceful. Crops are vulnerable to destruction by an enemy, and difficult to defend. How can one prevent the burning of a field of grain if there are those who would want to destroy it? It was easier and safer, usually, to trade with all comers, but become allied with none. So the various farming tribes had a great tendency to remain neutral as their nomadic neighbors carried on widespread hunting and warfare.

The People, even knowing that there were many different tribes whose main activity was farming, had adopted the term Growers to include them all. There were exceptions. Pawnees, aggressive and warlike, were to be avoided. But they were farther north, Running Deer knew. She might encounter Kenzas or Wichitas, but no matter. Any of them would probably answer questions, especially if she had a small gift of dried meat.

Yes, they could follow the old trails that crisscrossed the prairie, and head generally northward, asking as they went. There were places where travelers had camped before, probably for generations. A source of water and fuel was all that would be needed by a small party. These traditional stopping places would be found about a day's travel apart. Sometimes they would be located next to a cluster of Growers' lodges. It was in that way she could gain news of the People.

It was the third day before they saw another human. The day was late, and she was glad to see a plume of evening smoke ahead. It had been a long time since she had spoken to another adult. A Grower village, maybe? No, only one smoke. The camp of another traveler?

She could see the couple as they approached, the man seated and smoking. The woman was tossing a couple of sticks and a buffalo chip on the fire. Packs were piled nearby, and a horse grazed beyond.

Running Deer strode in boldly, making the sign for peaceful greeting. Her next sign was that of identification.

"I am of the Elk-dog People."

The man looked her over, nodded, and gave the sign for trader. That could be either his occupation or his nationality.

"Arapaho?" Deer asked aloud.

The man nodded and drew a pipeful of smoke into his mouth.

"How are you called?" asked the woman in the tongue of the People.

"Ah! You speak my tongue!" Deer answered. "I am Running Deer. This, my daughter Gray Mouse."

"Yes, we speak many tongues," the trader's wife said . . . *"Daughter?"*

"Well, granddaughter. Her parents died with the *poch.*"

"Aiee, it has been bad," the woman agreed. "Your people . . ."

"My people?" Deer interrupted. *"They* have the *poch?"*

"How is it that you do not know?" the woman demanded. "What is this?"

Quickly, Running Deer explained.

"Ah, I see," the other answered, her suspicion subsiding. "My heart is heavy to tell you then. Your people were hard hit, last season."

"All bands?"

"That I cannot say. The Southern band the hardest, though. I remember that."

Running Deer's heart sank. She wished now that she had been with them. It could have been no worse. But *how?* Could her sons have carried the sickness back when they brought her the buffalo meat? If they did, then *they* must have fallen sick . . . maybe, dead.

"Do you remember any names?" she asked eagerly. "Singing Wolf? Beaver Track?"

"Ah, Mother, I do not know. We did not see them, we only heard of the sickness, you know."

"Do you know where they will have the Sun Dance?"

"No, no. Or *whether* they will have it. But tell me, Mother . . . Do you not fear to travel alone?"

Running Deer shrugged. "What is to fear? What can happen to an old woman that has not happened already?"

"But you might be killed by someone."

Deer laughed, a sardonic chuckle. "Why? I have nothing worth killing for. And there is no honor in killing an old woman."

"That is true. But you have the girl there . . . Would you sell her? She will make a good wife someday. She is pretty."

Deer tried not to appear as offended as she actually was.

"No, no. She is mine. To take her, one would *have* to kill me."

"See? It is as I said. I only offered . . ."

"No!"

The subject did not come up again. They camped together, exchanged small talk and provisions and comments on the weather. It was good to talk to adults, despite the haunting fears about what might have happened to the People. And, of course, the unfortunate remark about the child. But maybe the woman *did* only intend to be helpful.

Deer slept little, but by morning was convinced that there had really been no evil intent.

As they parted, the trader asked yet another question that bothered her.

"What about the dog? Would you trade him? He looks strong."

Deer thanked him, but refused. *Aiee! A trader must trade anything,* she supposed.

Gray Mouse clung to her hand as they watched the couple and their laden pack horse move on down the trail.

"Grandmother, you would not trade Yellow Dog to them?"

"Of course not, child. Nor you, either!"

Mouse relaxed.

Then another thought came to Running Deer. "Wait!" she called. "Are there Growers ahead?"

"Yes," the woman called back. "Two sleeps. A big village. They are friendly."

"It is good," Running Deer answered. "May your travel go well and your trading prosper."

It was good to know about the Growers. Maybe they would have some news of the People. She picked up her pack and they traveled on.

26

»» »» »»

"We have not seen them," the Grower said. "A Head Splitter . . . are they not your allies? Yes, so I thought. One of them told us that he planned to attend your Sun Dance. Where is it to be, Mother?"

"Ah, that is what I do not know. But they *will* have it?"

"So the Head Splitter said. But I do not know whether he knew."

"And you do not know whether all of my people, all bands, had the spotted sickness?"

He shook his head. "I do not know one band of your people from another. We see mostly your Southern band, is it not?"

"Yes. They were to winter on the river we call the Sycamore."

"Ah, yes, *those.* They wintered there, we were told. Someone . . . the Head Splitter . . . No! A trader . . . A trader told us that your Elk-dog People had been hit hard by the *poch.* My heart is heavy for you, Mother."

Aiee, Growers! thought Running Deer. *If they know the answer to your questions, they tell you. If they do not, they tell you anyway.*

"Then you do not know where they will hold the Sun Dance?" she asked.

"No . . . no, I am made to think not."

The little party moved on, still heading north. Maybe if she could be in familiar territory, the Sacred Hills, their spirit would help her.

They had gone only a little way when there was an odd, short bark from Yellow Dog. He had stopped and was looking along their back trail.

"Someone is following us," said Gray Mouse.

"Let us stop to rest," Deer suggested. "We can sit in the rocks over there."

It was a puzzling thing, a lone rider. Not too skilled a rider . . . He was sitting too far back and bouncing a lot, Deer noted. A Grower? She readied her weapon. In a situation that makes no sense, it is wise to prepare for the worst. She tried to appear casual, but to be alert for anything.

It was the Grower to whom they had talked. He drew the horse to a stop and sat there for a moment, breathing heavily from the unfamiliar exercise.

"You do not need the bow, Mother," he said with a chuckle. "It is only that I have learned . . . My wife thought of something you should know. The Head Splitter I spoke of, you remember? His woman and mine talked. She says the woman told her of your Sun Dance. It is to be at Medicine Rock."

"Ah!" Deer exclaimed with glee. "It is good! I should have known, but I had forgotten. May your crops grow well, Uncle!"

The man turned back toward his town, and the heart of Running Deer warmed toward Growers. It had been a kind gesture. Maybe Growers were much like real people. At least sometimes.

Medicine Rock! This was one of the most powerful of the spirit-places of the People, and of their allies the Head Splitters as well. Gray limestone, a sheer bluff that dropped off into the river below. There were crevices and caves in its face, and the past of the People had been deeply influenced by the events there. The legends and stories of strange happenings were many.

Eagle, father of the legendary warrior woman Running Eagle, had wintered there, it was said. He had been injured and was thought to be dead. Eagle had never been quite the same, but was noted ever after as a man of the spirit. One who understood . . .

It was at Medicine Rock that the People and the Head Splitters had become allies, to defeat a more powerful enemy. The magical powers of the place and the combined powers of holy men of both nations had helped them to stampede a great buffalo herd over the bluff, pushing the enemy Blue Paints to their deaths. It was said that bleached bones of buffalo, horses, and men could still be seen in the deep crevices.

White Fox, a kinsman of Walks in the Sun, had taken his vision quest there, and had encountered spirits that seemed threatening and evil. He had also discovered a strange wild girl who had been unable to speak except in animal sounds. She had become his wife, and a respected woman of the People.

Medicine Rock was feared by some as a place of evil. The usual attitude of the holy men of the People was that it was a place of great spiritual power. Neither good nor evil, or maybe both. To some, there might be evil there, to others, not. The ways of the spirit are strange, and it may depend much on what one *seeks*, no?

The Sun Dance had been held at Medicine Rock before. Running Deer could remember twice . . . maybe three times in her lifetime. The most recent had been ten or twelve seasons back. It was considered a special site. To be perfectly accurate, the Sun Dance was not actually at the Rock itself, but within sight of it. It was actually forbidden by the Big Council to climb the bluff or to approach it too closely while the People were camped there. It would not be good to disturb the spirits that dwell there. Any who chose to risk that danger could stay behind when the People moved out. Then their vision quest or prayer or communion with the spirits would plainly be a personal act, and would not reflect on the entire Elk-dog nation.

It was seldom that anyone did stay behind. It was left to the occasional young holy man on his vision quest, or an older one seeking to understand more of the power of his gifts. The spirits of Medicine Rock were very powerful. It was said that the vision quest of White Fox had been a terrifying ordeal. Walks in the Sun had considered, however, that part of that may have been due to the interference of the evil that had hovered over the wild girl, South Wind. *No matter,* Deer thought. *I will not go near the place!*

Still, it was exciting to be in the vicinity and imagine that one was seeing the same places that were looked upon by such as Eagle, Sees Far, Wolf's Head of the Head Splitters, and White Fox, the holy man of the People. It was exciting.

Deer's excitement was tempered by concern, however. What of the Southern band, her sons and their families? She had learned, at least, that there were some of that band alive. There must be, because the Growers knew where they had wintered.

They pushed on.

She knew that they were on the right trail when a broad track joined their path. A large band, many lodges, with pole-drags digging furrows in the prairie sod. This group had been traveling from the east, it appeared. *The Eastern band, maybe?* she thought. *No, they would come from the northeast. Besides, they are always late.*

That left only the New band, the group who had joined the People just in this generation. These outsiders spoke a similar tongue, and their ways were much the same. Despite early misunderstandings the newcomers had been well accepted. Some of the People even believed that these were the descendants of the Lost band, whose seat in the Big Council had remained vacant from early times. Most of the People did not think so.

The acceptance of the strangers, the New band, had been helped along by the perpetual need for hunters, trappers, and warriors for defense in case of attack. Already they had been granted a place in the Council circle. Not the empty place of the missing band, but a space between that and the seat of her own, the Southern band. Likewise, that was the segment of the camp circle that would be theirs at the Sun Dance encampment.

Maybe that had been part of their reason for choosing the same segment of the whole vast territory over which the People roamed. The southeast brought some danger of contact with the Shaved Head forest people, but what better area was there? The Northern band was large and wide-ranging across their area. The Mountain and Red Rocks bands were far from the others. The newcomers had likely wanted to avoid too close an identification with the foolish Eastern band. So their logical range had become an area to the east, but well south of that band. Yes, these must be the tracks of the New band, headed for the Sun Dance.

Not far ahead, either, Running Deer thought. The horse droppings were less than two days old.

"It is good," she told Gray Mouse. "These are the tracks of our people. Now we just follow them."

That night they could see the points of light from the campfires of the band ahead of them. Their excitement grew. It was useless excitement, of course. They could never close the gap, could come no closer until the other travelers stopped. They would not likely do that until they reached Medicine Rock. However, this country had begun to look familiar to her, and she felt that they were only a few days away.

The Sacred Hills . . . how restful to the eyes! Rolling grassland, now brilliant green with the Moon of Growing. (Grass-growing, some of the older of the People called it, to distinguish themselves from the Growers.) The paths of streams as they snaked through the hills were marked by the darker green of willows and cottonwoods. In the deeper gullies and canyons, great groves of hardwoods flourished. Walnut, oaks, sycamores, and maples.

Running Deer looked across this expanse of grass and sky and knew that it was home. The closest of the flat-topped ridges in the distance was a day's travel away, and was bathed in a misty blue. Beyond that, another, and another still, each a slightly different shade, marked by the blue of distance. Each succeeding range of hills, more blue than the last, finally blended into the distant blue of the sky, and the world was complete. Running Deer took a deep breath of the clean prairie air. She had not realized how much she had missed the tallgrass prairie. *But I always do,* she told herself with a smile.

Somewhere out there now was the Medicine Rock, and the People, gathering for the Sun Dance. Deer felt good about it. Life was good, the world beautiful. She felt better than she had for years. Since the loss of her husband, maybe. Strange, she had not thought of that for a while . . .

She could see the misty fog of smoke from the campfires of the People for a day before they drew near. It was a gray-white cloud that seemed to hover over the broad valley. The tracks of the New band were heading that way, so that must be the place.

She remembered the thrill of each band's approach. The young men of the bands already there would ride out as newcomers were sighted, mounting a wild mock attack. The young warriors of the approaching group would join them, yelling the full-throated war cry of the People, waving weapons and, in recent years, firing thundersticks. The joint company of warriors would then circle the entire camp a time or two. Or maybe, until the women began to complain about the dust in their cooking.

Often young women, unmarried or still childless, would join the mad charge. Deer had done it a time or two herself, before her marriage. It was a good way to attract the attention of young men, for the men of the People held great admiration for a "manly-hearted woman." She recalled with pleasure the experience, wind in her ears, hair streaming behind, yelling with the others, screaming the war cry. *Aiee*, it had been good! She had not thought of that for years, either.

It had been exciting, even, to watch the younger ones with this informal introduction to the more structured days of the Sun Dance. She would enjoy it, this year! With some regret, she realized that no great charge of young warriors would mount a mock attack on an old woman, a little girl, and a dog.

And it was so. Two men, acting as wolves, rode out to see who might be approaching, alone and on foot. They reined in their horses and studied the travelers without speaking. Finally one, the older of the two, spoke to the other.

"Let us go and find the holy man, Singing Wolf," he said. "I am made to think that this is the ghost of his mother!"

27
>> >> >>

It was a strange experience to rejoin the People, not knowing what to expect. When Running Deer and Mouse arrived at the site of the Sun Dance, the Southern band was still in the process of regrouping. Word had gone on ahead from the wolves, and they had come to meet her.

There was a tearful reunion, and then the questions . . . Who had survived, who was missing? All of the other bands had arrived intact, each as a group. The families of the New band who had been just ahead of Running Deer were even now lifting the heavy lodge covers and establishing their presence.

But in the area assigned by custom to the Southern band, something was obviously amiss. Deer could see that where there should have been at least forty lodges, there were fewer than thirty . . . The light breeze shifted, and above the sound of activity that hums constantly around a big camp, she heard a voice or two raised in the Song of Mourning. She had known to expect this, but had not been ready. So many lodges . . . each a family. She could remember specific families. The lodge of No Tail Squirrel, with its distinctive designs in red and yellow, was nowhere seen. Others . . .

"Is this all?" she asked Singing Wolf, her voice husky.

"We do not know, Mother. We had split up for safety, after the first became sick."

"Your families?" she asked, dreading the answer.

"All here. We were spared, Mother. Most lodges have been in mourning, though. And we do not know how many are still out there."

"But we have to think, Wolf," she observed, "that any who could, have already come."

"That is true," Beaver Track agreed. "We have talked of this, but not much."

To speak of an evil event might encourage it to happen. Deer nodded in understanding.

"But it makes our hearts good to see you, Mother!" Wolf exclaimed. "We did not know . . . we mourned . . . and the child, too!"

Gray Mouse stood timidly behind Deer, clinging to her buckskin skirt and peering around at the strangers.

"Here, Mouse, these are your uncles. This is Singing Wolf, the other, Beaver Track. They are your family, as I am."

Family relationships among the People are sometimes strangely defined. Any adult male older than one's self should be addressed as Uncle, to denote respect, regardless of blood relationships. In the same way, a child would regard as Mother or Grandmother any close relative of appropriate age. Even close friends of the family . . . A child might easily have several grandmothers and many uncles.

"You will come to my lodge?" Wolf asked.

That was already assumed. As the oldest son, he was responsible for the support of his mother, under these circumstances.

"Of course," she agreed. "But the mourning . . . there is still sickness in the Southern band?"

"No, no. There has been none for several moons. But we have not been together. Some are only now learning of their losses."

She nodded. "And the other bands?"

"None have had the sickness, Mother. Their hearts are heavy for us, though."

For days, people inquired, gave sympathy, and adjusted to the changes in the structure of the Elk-dog People as a nation. Some broken families now readjusted by joining relatives in other bands.

In one notable instance, a handsome young widow with three children took a visiting Head Splitter as her husband. There was gossip, because hers had been a family of great respect and prestige. Many thought that she remarried beneath her, but there were those who supported her strongly.

"So her husband was a subchief," an old woman observed. "A leader in the Bowstring Society. But he is dead! This young man has a good reputation. He respects our ways. Did he not come to honor our Sun Dance?"

"Because Head Splitters have none," her friend retorted. "But he can never be a leader like her husband was."

"There are things besides politics," the other snapped. "His heart seems good. I am made to think he loves her and will be a good husband. How many men would leave their own people for a woman?"

"But he will have to *earn* respect. He cannot take that from her dead husband."

"Of course. Does not anyone have to earn his own respect?"

It would be a long time before such matters were smoothed out and the Southern band was able to see the changes objectively. Meanwhile, there were major political changes under way. Prestige shifts constantly, as new leadership rises and the old declines.

For many generations, the Southern band had held a position of great respect among the People. Even though the Real-chief of the entire nation was usually elected from the Northern band, the prestige and the wisdom of the Southern leaders were always strong. The other bands listened carefully to the voices of the Southern band's leaders when they spoke in the Big Council.

But here was a new situation, one that might have a profound effect. The Southern band had been badly weakened. Broken Lance, their respected chief, had escaped the *poch*, but was not growing any younger. Several of the strongest and wisest who might desire Lance's seat in the Big Council had been struck down. In effect, then, the tragedy had created an empty space into which aspiring leaders might move.

Band loyalties were flexible. A band with a dynamic young leader might attract several families from other bands. People with vision, maybe, who saw in the charisma of this leader the possibility of gaining prestige. A two-edged weapon. Those with vision might strengthen a band and add to its prestige. Many times, however, those who shifted from one band to another were the misfits. There were always a few who seemed to jump from one band to another from season to season. Some minor quarrel with a neighbor, a jealous wife . . . There are many reasons to change bands. Some are good, some not.

It would remain to be seen, the composition of the Southern band after the Sun Dance. For this, naturally, would be the time when the shifting and repositioning would take place. When the bands separated for the season, those who had decided to shift loyalties would merely follow the band of their choice.

There was much behind-the-scenes discussion, some persuasion by friends and relatives. All of this political undercurrent, quietly taking place, almost unnoticed by many, would shape the course of the People for generations. Not only the Southern band, but the entire Elkdog Nation, for good or bad . . .

There was a quiet struggle of a different sort taking place in the lodge of Singing Wolf and his wife, Rain. Not of the sort that one might think. Rain had always gotten along well with her husband's mother. Deer was simply a part of the extended family.

True, there had been a time these last few years when the old woman was virtually intolerable. But that had not been a personal thing. Running Deer had been intolerable to *everyone,* not just her son's wife. Privately, Rain had always admired the old woman's spunk. She, Rain, had hoped to be as energetic and forceful as Deer.

Now it was with pleasure that she recognized the old spirit. Running Deer was herself again. There was none of the bleak, dark sadness and helplessness. There was defiance of ill-fortune, with an energy and enthusiasm not seen for several years. The tragedy and the coming of the child had actually been good for Running Deer. The disagreeable, crotchety old woman was gone, and in her place had returned the wife of Walks in the Sun, the mother of Singing Wolf and Beaver Track, whom Rain sincerely admired. The bad times seemed behind them. *For which let us all give thanks,* Rain prayed silently.

A more complicated matter was the addition of another child to the lodge. Gray Mouse was timid and afraid at first. She preferred to avoid contact with the family whenever possible, drawing aside with her doll or with her big yellow dog.

"Do not bother her," Running Deer quietly told the other children. "Mouse has suffered much, but she will do well. Give her a little while."

There were apparently two incidents that occurred which provided the impetus for the change. The first involved Deer.

Gray Mouse was quite reluctant to allow Running Deer out of her sight. Fear could be seen in her face, and she would cling tightly to the hand or the fringes of the skirt of her protector.

They were gathering sticks for fuel along the stream one afternoon and chanced to meet an old acquaintance of Deer's.

"Ah, Running Deer! I had heard you were back," the woman cooed. "And this . . ."

Gray Mouse was trying to hide from the woman's prying gaze, slipping behind Deer's skirt, but the woman kept peering around to get a better look at this curiosity. Mouse instinctively disliked her.

". . . this must be the Child of the Dead! Well, she is a pretty little thing, except for the scars, of course."

Running Deer felt her temper rising to a boil. The woman was talking about the little girl as if she were not even there. As if this were a non-person, an amusing object for diversion, but not to be taken seriously. With great care, Deer held her wrath in check.

"Pretty Bush," she said with a tight smile, "she is not dead, she is alive and she is of my family. This is my daughter, Gray Mouse." The smile remained, but the tone of her voice stiffened now. "You or anyone else who calls Mouse such a thing as you just said will have me to face! Is it not so?"

Pretty Bush took a step backward and the color drained from her face. Deer stepped toward the woman.

"*Is it not so?*" she demanded.

"Yes . . . yes . . . it will be as you say, Deer," the woman mumbled as she retreated.

"And what is her name?"

". . . Mouse. Gray Mouse. That is her name. Yes . . ."

"Then remember it!" Running Deer called after the retreating figure. Yellow Dog gave a short growl and would have run after the woman, but Deer called him back.

The other incident was not so climactic, but perhaps even more significant in the long run. Dark Antelope, a few years older than the new inhabitant in his parents' lodge, seemed to take a great proprietary interest in the little girl. He brought her bites of choice food, made little playthings from cottonwood leaves, and helped her to begin to play with other children.

"Come, little one," Deer heard him say gently to Mouse. "We will go to play with the others. I will take care of you. Here, hold my hand!"

Besides, Yellow Dog seemed to approve. Running Deer smiled.

When the bands separated after the Sun Dance, Singing Wolf watched carefully and then went quietly to talk to the band chief.

"*Ah-koh,* Uncle."

"Yes?" Broken Lance said eagerly.

"Thirty-eight lodges," Wolf reported.

"*Aiee!* We only had forty-one before, no?"

"That is true."

"It is good. Now, how many are *truly* good?"

"It will be hard to tell, for a while. I see two, maybe three that are no help. They have joined three different bands for a season or two. Two lodges, brothers from the Eastern band."

The chief chuckled, but Wolf went on.

"They may be our best newcomers, Uncle. You know how it is with the Eastern band. They produce leaders, sometimes, but they have no one to lead."

Both men chuckled, and Wolf went on.

"The others, in between, probably. A few good hunters, a few opportunists. We will see."

"It is good. Thank you, Wolf."

"My honor, Uncle. Now, if I can keep my mother from fighting anyone who looks at Gray Mouse . . ."

Both men laughed again.

Part Three

28
>> >> >>

Antelope had sensed a certain restlessness in his friend this season. Gray Mouse was sixteen or seventeen summers old, no one was sure. It was no matter anyway. The question was only there because of the manner in which Mouse had joined the People.

Ten seasons it had been, maybe more. Again, it did not really matter. Mouse barely remembered any life prior to that time, though Antelope did. He remembered it well. To this day, the scent of decaying flesh gripped him with a panic. His memory leaped back over the years to a time when a whole village of skin lodges lay before the People. Those in that Camp of the Dead had been strangers, struck down by the *poch*, the spotted death. No one except Antelope's father the holy man and one or two others had been allowed to go near. That had made it even worse, because what fear is greater than the fear of the unknown? The smell, though, had been a powerful thing to young Antelope. That had pounded the incident firmly into his memory, to bring it back at unexpected times.

He was embarrassed to admit that he did not even remember that there had been one survivor of the Camp of the Dead, a small girl. He first remembered Gray Mouse when she turned up at the Sun

Dance at Medicine Rock. Mouse had been in the company of Antelope's own grandmother, who had been thought dead. That was an unforgettable summer.

First, there was the disruptive change of two more people moving into the lodge. One was the small girl who belonged to Grandmother. The boy's heart had gone out in sympathy to the frightened girl, and she quickly became like a sister to him. There were a few incidents in which other children thoughtlessly or even cruelly inflicted hurt on the little girl. There was a short while when it appeared that she might become known as the Child of the Dead. That possibility was short-lived. Few of the People had the courage to face the wrath of Running Deer. Even then, it might have been a hidden joke among the children, except for Antelope.

From the very first day, he felt a responsibility to his new sister. There was a need for the girl to be protected, and the youngster seemed to assume that it was his duty. They were an odd couple, some four years apart in age. About right, as it turned out, for the purpose. Any children who were cruel or thoughtless enough to torment Gray Mouse were a year or two older than she. By the same token, three or four years *younger* than her protector.

In a short while everyone in the Southern band was aware of a simple fact of life: anyone who showed disrespect for Gray Mouse had to face the wrath of Running Deer or of Dark Antelope, or both. In addition, the large yellow dog which always followed her was yet another protector.

This is not to say that Mouse was pampered. Running Deer was a strict parent, as she had been with her sons. It was amusing to see the change in Deer after her "return from the dead." *(Do not say "dead,"* someone would warn sometimes. *You may have to fight her.)* From a tired and bitter old woman, she had become a vibrant and active person. She could, and did, work as hard as anyone in the band.

Deer had insisted that she wanted her own lodge again. It would be better for Gray Mouse. This was actually a clumsy social situation. A widow with the status of Running Deer would normally have been taken into the lodge of her oldest daughter, but Deer had none. That had been part of her reluctance to live in the lodge of one of her sons.

On her return, Running Deer, even though she had mellowed some, still had strong opinions. She and her new daughter would have a small lodge of their own. They would camp close to the lodges of Wolf and Beaver Track. Thus, the relationship of Dark Antelope and Gray Mouse was something like that of a brother and sister, but different. The People understood it, and there was no need for discussion. Besides, comment might rouse the ire of Running Deer, and that was certainly to be avoided. Deer seemed not to change at all now. She was ageless. Energetic, active, hard-working. A visitor from one of the other bands had once commented on it to Rain.

"That is odd. I remembered Wolf's mother as a somewhat older woman."

"I, too, at one time," Rain agreed.

The children had grown up together in this strange yet comfortable extended family relationship. Some people may have thought of them as a couple. Many of the children of the People paired off as friends quite early. Mostly, though, they were regarded as brother and sister. At least they were in the early years.

Other changes were taking place in the band, ones which did not really concern Mouse, Dark Antelope, and Running Deer. There was considerable political shifting for a year or two. A family who had recently joined the Southern band to move into a politically empty spot found that there was none, and moved on, as they had before and would again. There was no loss there.

Other, more stable lodges joined actively in the affairs of the band, and were respected. The prestige of the Southern band wavered and recovered, as strong as ever. Much of the credit for this was due to the statesmanship of Broken Lance. The aging leader seemed destined to go on forever, becoming more capable as he went.

With young couples establishing their own lodges, the size of the Southern band was nearly back to strength now. Their prestige, too, had not suffered, only wavered.

Dark Antelope had reached the age of puberty first, before Mouse. Had they been of the same age, the girl would have matured earlier. It was not uncommon for a couple of childhood friends to stay together through this difficult time, even though she might be taller and more physically mature for a season or two.

In this case, Antelope's advancing maturity seemed to make little difference. He was, naturally, drawn to girls whose physical characteristics showed development. But he and Mouse discussed such things, and basically thought nothing of it. It is doubtful that either of them even considered the possibility of a romantic relationship. Still, no girl seemed right for Antelope. He had not married, and still lived in the lodge of his parents.

He proved himself as a hunter, and was accepted into the Elk-dog Society. He had considered the Bloods, but some of them had radical ideas. There were many of the available girls who would have jumped at the chance to establish a lodge with Dark Antelope, but nothing happened. Some wondered if he would become a woman-man, but it did not seem likely. He did not seem romantically interested in boys, either. He had not decided yet whether to aspire to his father's status as a holy man.

"Do not worry about it," Singing Wolf told Rain. "I matured late, too, you know."

A change began to be noticed with the body changes of Gray Mouse. Mouse had been thin and gangly as she grew. Then overnight, it seemed, there was a difference. Mouse had always been a pretty girl, but *aiee!* She suddenly grew taller. Her face and hair began to glow with a new radiance. The stick-straight legs began to show attractive swells at the calves, with corresponding trimming at the ankles. The shirt portion of a new buckskin dress was found to be too tight. It was necessary to resew the seams at the sides of the chest to accommodate the gently bulging breasts.

An even bigger change was in her attitude. It was a difficult time. There were times when Gray Mouse seemed calm, quiet, and helpful. At other times she was uncooperative and defiant. There seemed to be no pattern, and it was completely unpredictable. Sometimes Running Deer was at her wits' end. About that time, Mouse's mood would change and all would be well again.

"*Aiee,* I see why it is the young who are made to have the children," Deer confided to her daughter-in-law on one of these occasions. "Have you had such problems, Rain?"

Rain laughed. "It is the way with girls, Mother. You have had only boys before!"

There was an obvious difference in the attitude of the girl toward Antelope, too. It, too, was a variable thing. Sometimes it manifested as a coy, blushing sweetness. At others it was a fiery jealousy toward any other young woman who even looked possessively toward the young man.

Running Deer viewed this with mixed emotions. She was not ready to have her child thinking of a lodge of her own. Yet, if Mouse were to do such a thing, Dark Antelope would make a great husband and provider. But was this acceptable? Was he not her brother?

Deer approached her son, the holy man, with the question.

"I, too, have thought of this, Mother," Wolf told her. "I am made to think in this way: Gray Mouse is an outsider."

"No, no!" Deer's temper flared. "She is not! She . . ."

"Wait, Mother! About this, maybe it is good for her to be. True, she has become one of the People, one of our family. But by blood, she is *not* the sister of our Dark Antelope. They are not brother and sister, and there would be no question."

Deer nodded, only half convinced.

"Would the council have to decide?"

"Maybe. But Mother, they have said nothing, the two young people. Let *them* tell us what their desires might be. Maybe they are not interested except as brother and sister."

"Yes . . . *Aiee*, Wolf, I thought that raising boys was hard."

Her son laughed. "And so it was, Mother. But let us see what happens now. Maybe there is no problem."

"What is it? What is the matter?" asked Dark Antelope.

The two were sitting on the hill behind the camp of the Southern band, watching the sunset. That should have been a serene moment of sharing, but there was the restlessness that came between them.

They *had* talked of marriage, but Mouse was not ready.

"I have waited this long," Antelope told her. "I can wait a little longer."

Somehow even that irritated her, but there was nothing to say that would not be misunderstood. She did not want to hurt him. Not really . . . And now this question. *What is the matter?* She wanted to yell at him, to tell him, *If I knew, there would be no problem!*

She sighed, and Yellow Dog raised his head, thumped his tail, and sleepily returned to his rest. He was growing old. The dark yellow along his muzzle showed many gray hairs now. A glum feeling came over her. She knew that the dog was older than most of the dogs of the People already. Most had either been eaten by this age or had met with a misadventure with some wild creature. But she hated to see this happen to *her* dog, this creeping of age upon him. Yellow Dog seemed to be part of her problem, and she was not sure why.

She had been a secure and happy child, feeling safe and loved. At least, most of the time. She no longer had the night-visions, the dreams of death that had plagued her for a long time.

Maybe it was that she was unwilling to give up the safety of her childhood for these new feelings. It was exciting to be a woman, to feel the stirring in her blood, the need for a man . . . But to become a woman meant to leave behind the safety she had known since she had been with Grandmother.

And Dark Antelope . . . He was her protector, brother, teacher, friend. Could he also be her husband? Or would it be better to look for another?

She suspected that some of the young men more nearly her own age might be interested. She had even flirted a little. But they all considered, probably, that she belonged to Antelope.

Maybe I do, she thought. *How do I know?* She resented his attempts to bring up the matter, and had told him so. "I will tell you when I am ready," she had snapped at him, and then regretted having hurt him. And she was no closer now to knowing how she felt.

An owl called in the growing shadows downriver.

"Good hunting, *Kookooskoos,*" Antelope murmured.

She had heard it all her life. *No, not all my life,* she thought. There was a time . . . an owl should be *feared!* Dimly remembered, her first winter with Grandmother, all alone . . . There were things that were different, and it had worried her that what she thought she knew was not the same as what Grandmother told her. *Which is right?*

A wave of resentment rose in her. Her grandmother had stolen her identity, and left her confused.

"Sun Boy chooses his paints well tonight," observed Antelope, interrupting her thoughts.

The traditional story of the People, where Sun Boy paints himself to prepare to spend the night on the other side of the earth . . . *Is it really Sun Boy?* her mind demanded. Maybe for *my* people it is some-one else.

She looked at Dark Antelope as if she had never seen him before. Was this her problem, that she was trying to be something that she was not, something never intended?

"Antelope," she said dully, "I do not even know who I am."

29
>> >> >>

There was a time that season when Gray Mouse and Dark Antelope drew apart. Mouse refused to accept it for a while, but finally was forced to the inescapable conclusion. There was a barrier between them.

"No, Antelope," she tried to explain to her friend, "it is nothing you have done, or *not* done. It is not you, it is my own problem. I must do this alone."

"Do *what,* Mouse?"

Anger rose in her. "How do I know?" she snapped irritably. "Let me alone. I must do this myself."

The bewildered youth retreated. He still had no understanding of *what* the girl must do, but one thing was clear. He had no part in it.

The heart of Gray Mouse ached as she saw the hurt in his eyes. She wanted to try again to tell him, to try to explain, but she did not know how.

She also longed to confide to someone else. A woman . . . Her only woman confidante, though, was Grandmother, who was even *more* a part of the problem. Likewise, there were no girls of her own age to whom she could talk. She had made friends very slowly because of the Child of the Dead circumstances. *Aiee,* how angry that had made Grandmother! The few girls who had been close enough to call friends now had other interests. Largely romance, of course. Yellow Leaf had already married. Singing Doe was so preoccupied with her young suitor of the Blood Society that she could not see beyond the tips of her fluttering eyelashes. *Aiee!*

So there was no one to talk to, and this caused an even greater feeling of isolation. *I am alone,* thought Mouse, in a mixed mood of panic and resentment from which there seemed no escape. *Why do I feel this way? There are those who love me, but are no help. They do not understand.*

Tears began to flow. She had gone alone to the hilltop to think, and was finding that it did not help much. Again, she had the lost and lonely feeling that she did not even know who she was. Why did she feel so alone, so *different?*

As she pondered that thought, another began to take shape. It was not exactly comforting, but it was something. A place to begin her understanding, maybe. Even then she had not yet begun to realize the importance of such a thought: *I feel different because I* am *different!*

The idea began to take shape and grow. *I know nothing of my people,* she thought.

Each time she had asked the question when she was small, it had been brushed aside.

"That is all behind you, child," her grandmother would croon as she took the little girl in her arms. "You do not need to worry. You are safe here, and you are one of the People now."

Now Mouse's resentment began to rise. *She had no right to take that from me!* Mouse thought. She pushed aside the twinge of guilt over all that Grandmother *had* done for her. But she must face this.

"Grandmother," she began that evening as they returned to the sleeping robes, "I would talk with you."

The lodge was dark, with only a glow from the coals of the dying fire. Nights were becoming cool, and the cooking had been moved inside for the season.

"Of course, child. What is it?"

Mouse shoved aside the ripple of resentment over "child" and resolved to maintain her calm.

"I would know of my people."

"What would you know, Mouse?"

"Who I am . . . Where did my people come from, where did they go?"

There was a long silence.

"Grandmother?" Mouse wondered if the older woman had fallen asleep.

"Yes, yes, child, I heard you. You mean your parents, no? Those of the Camp of the Dead?"

Gray Mouse was astonished to hear Grandmother use the hated words, those which had so infuriated her long ago.

"Yes . . . I do not know who I am."

"You are mine now, a child of the People, Mouse."

The girl stifled her anger. This was the old answer. More properly, the old *refusal* to answer. She tried to keep her voice calm.

"Grandmother," she began, her voice trembling a little, "I am made to think that I must know. You must tell me what you know."

Again, the silence. Mouse was about to speak again when Running Deer gave a deep sigh of resignation.

"Ah, I knew that someday . . . Mouse, my heart is heavy, because I cannot tell you."

"You *will* not!" accused the girl angrily.

"No, no, not that. Once it was true, maybe. But child, you must understand. We had no contact with them. They were already dead. Besides, there seemed no need to know. It was thought that you and I, both of us, were already dying. Then, it was that when we lived instead, there were more important things. Food, shelter for the winter . . . You needed *me*. Aiee, we needed each other, Mouse."

"But you might have told me!"

"There was nothing to tell, child. We did not know."

"Know *what*?"

"Anything! We knew nothing at all about those who were the Dead."

"But you must have known *something!*"

"No . . . Remember, child, we were afraid. Afraid of the *poch*. They were strangers."

"But *who*? Arapaho? Pawnee? Head Splitters? Cheyenne?"

"No, no. None of those. We would have known them. Someone from outside."

"From where?"

"Again, child, we did not know."

She tried to talk to Singing Wolf.

"Uncle, what can you tell me of my people, those who died from the *poch?*"

The conversation was a little easier, but the information equally scant. The holy man shook his head.

"We knew very little, Mouse. There was danger, you know. You were the only one alive, and you were dying, or so it seemed. We only wanted to get away."

The girl nodded. "This I can understand. But was it known . . . they were not Growers, so what nation . . ."

"Again, we did not know. They came from the north or northeast."

Instantly, Mouse was alert to this new information.

"Ah! You knew that?"

"Not exactly, Mouse. But we knew who they were *not.* To the south are mostly Comanche . . . Snake People. Some Caddoes who hunt, but their lodges are different. To the west, the finger-cutters, the Cheyennes. But mostly, I am made to think that the *poch* came from the French. They are only north or east of the People. Not Arapaho or Lakota . . . we just did not know."

"I . . . I do not remember, Uncle. Were their lodges nearly like those of the People?"

"Yes. I did not study them closely, but I am made to think so. Some of the smoke flaps were blowing loose . . . Yes, they must have been much like ours. Why do you ask these things, Mouse?"

Gray Mouse shrugged. "I cannot explain, Uncle. It is a need to know. I do not even know who I am. My mother was a pretty woman who sang to me, but that is all I remember."

Wolf nodded, understanding. "It is good."

"*What* is good, Uncle?" the girl asked, frustrated.

"That you wish to know. You might want to take a vision quest, when you are a little older. *Aiee,* but you are grown now! Well, talk to some of the Growers when we camp near them. They hear news from all."

Mouse started to turn away, not completely satisfied, but the holy man stopped her.

"Wait! I am made to think that you were wearing a little ornament

when we found you. A pendant . . . Ask your grandmother. I wonder what happened to it?"

"Yes . . . maybe . . ." Running Deer rummaged among the
things in the storage space behind the lodge lining. "I think so. I had
forgotten."

She drew out a small ornament on a thong. It was round, about two
fingers broad, and consisted of beaded geometric designs in yellow,
red, and black. The beads were sewn to a soft piece of buckskin.

"You were wearing this when we found you," Running Deer said.
"I had forgotten."

A moment of irritation flashed through the mind of Gray Mouse.

"You took it off?" she demanded.

"Yes, child. You were covered with sores around your neck and
shoulders. I took it off so that you could heal. I saved it for you, but
then I was sick."

Mouse's anger cooled slowly.

"I had always intended for you to have it when you were older,"
Deer went on. Her eyes seemed to look back into the past. "The
years have flown . . . You *are* grown now."

There was a vague sense of familiarity as the girl took the pendant
in her hand. It was part of the answer. The rest was out there, just out
of reach. Carefully, she recovered her composure.

"Thank you, Grandmother." She placed the thong around her neck
and again felt a familiarity as the beaded circle swung gently against
the front of her dress. The soft skin that held the beads had a musty
smell about it, mixed with the smoky odor of the tanning fire. Even
after all these years, the scent stimulated memories of her childhood.
Fragmentary thoughts, fleeting and dim in the cobwebby recesses of
her mind. She could almost put the scene together, but not
quite . . .

In a way, the finding of the pendant was even more of a frustration.
Somewhere out there, someone must know the answers she sought.

She asked anyone who might know, at every opportunity.

"Yes, I remember them," a Grower woman told her. The Southern
band had paused to trade for corn and beans and pumpkins on the
way to winter camp. "It was ten seasons ago, maybe. They had come
from the north. We heard later that they died from the spotted death.

Too bad. And they were your people? You are not of these, the Elk-dog Nation?"

"They found me. I have been raised by a grandmother of these. But now I seek my own."

"Yes. Well, I know no more. Those who died came from the north."

"Does this design mean anything to you?" Mouse asked, lifting the pendant to show.

The woman looked long and hard. "I do not know," she admitted. "I have seen one like it, maybe."

"And this hand sign?" asked Mouse desperately.

She gave the almost forgotten sign, preceding it with the sign for nation. *"The nation of . . ."*

The blank look in the eyes of the Grower woman told the story. The sign was completely unfamiliar to her.

"I saw it then, maybe," the woman admitted, "but I do not know. My heart is heavy, but I cannot help you."

30
>> >> >>

Gray Mouse was restless as she thought over what she had learned. Her information was still quite scant, but that only made her more determined. The beaded pendant dangled at her breast, a taunting reminder that there was much that *could* be learned if she only knew how.

But there was an excitement in it now, a challenge that seemed mixed with the thrill of the season. The migrating geese high overhead, the hurry of squirrels storing nuts, the Moon of Falling Leaves. The restlessness would continue, she knew, through the strange influence of the Moon of Madness. There were times when she considered leaving the security of the lodge that she shared with Running Deer to follow her quest. These times did not last long, of course. To follow the call of the geese would take her search in the wrong direction. She must search to the north, not the south.

It was in that way that a plan began to form in the girl's mind. In the Moons of Awakening and of Greening, the geese would be moving again. This time, their call *would* be to the north, the direction in which her quest pointed. And had not Singing Wolf himself suggested a quest for her?

She realized that this was not what the holy man had had in mind. He had been thinking of the more traditional vision quest to be undertaken by a young person. Usually by the young men, but there was nothing to *prevent* a woman of the People from seeking visions.

Mouse's quest would be different. The search quest, which usually required travel to unknown places, was far less common. Many times it was a result of the vision quest. The vision would demand a journey to accomplish a specific purpose. Such a quest was told of in the story of Horse Seeker, a young man of the People. He had been called to a faraway place by a vision of a great horse, the Dream Horse. That was long ago, but there were still those among the People who pointed with pride to horses whose blood was that of the almost supernatural Dream Horse. True or not, the story was a part of the tradition of the People.

The quest of Gray Mouse was to be different. It was demanded not by a vision, but by a need to know. The entire situation was different, she thought. Different from any in the history of the People, because she herself was different. More and more the idea kept nudging her. *These are not my people.* The need to find her own was growing within her, and the plan began to take shape.

The timing had been decided by circumstances. The quest would be to the north, so it would happen in the spring. All things would move northward then. The retreat of Cold Maker, the migration of the geese and the buffalo, the sun, the greening of the grass . . . Even the People would be moving a few days' travel to the tallgrass prairie of the Sacred Hills for the Sun Dance and the summer camp.

That would be the time. Her plan must be completely secret, or they would try to stop her. But the Sun Dance . . . yes, that would be the time. There was always such excitement then, such confusion, so many distractions. *Aiee,* if she handled it well, she could be gone a day or two before anyone missed her at all. The thought was quite satisfying. She would begin to assemble the things she would need and prepare for her departure in the moons ahead.

Supplies would be acquired during the first spring hunt. A few days' rations of dried meat would be easy to prepare and conceal. A horse . . . she already had a good horse, a gift from Beaver Track, her uncle. Beaver had always seen to it that his mother was supplied with horses for her needs. Running Deer seldom rode now, but Mouse had no doubt that Grandmother could if she wished. And with the horses of Running Deer, there grazed two that were set aside for Gray Mouse. One was a stolid old pack horse, the other a young gelding. She would not need the pack horse.

With her plan in mind, Mouse began to ride more, sometimes riding on a small hunt with some of the young men. This was not uncommon among the People. A young married woman with no children might accompany her husband on a hunt. Or a single woman seeking a man . . . What better way to catch the eye of a young bachelor? Her real motive would not be suspected, and she could condition both herself and the horse during this autumn and winter.

This part of the plan proved to have one thorny problem. Dark Antelope became her constant companion. Ah, well, she could contrive a quarrel when the time neared, to make him back away. There was a pang of guilt, but she firmly pushed it behind her. She must not let a thing like this dissuade her from her purpose.

Autumn suddenly became winter with the first probe of Cold Maker into the camp of the People. A heavy frost blackened vegetation and there was a thin crust of ice along the edges of the stream one morning. It was apparent that the season was changing. The morning was sunny, but all through the day there was a steady flutter of leaves from the elms, willows, and sycamores. Most of the nut trees had already shed their summer garments. In a day or two only the oaks would retain their leaves.

Mouse always hated to see the change in the oaks, from bright reds and yellows to a dull dry brown. That would mark the oak thickets for most of the winter until the buds of new leaves pushed last year's stems free. *No matter*, she thought. This season, such changes marked the passing of time, and brought her nearer to her quest.

Winter dragged on, nothing unusual. In open weather some of the young men trapped for furs. That had not been a tradition of the People until a generation ago, it was said. The coming of the French traders had brought changes. It was possible to trade furs of good quality for many things. Metal knives, fire strikers, powder and lead for the thundersticks that were now coming into common use. Fully half the lodges now boasted a musket.

Bad weather, usually only a few days at a time, meant activity of a different kind. Friends would gather for a smoke in one of the lodges.

The pungent fragrance of tobacco mixed with a variety of other plants would fill the lodge with a bluish haze as the pipes passed from one man to the other.

In some of the lodges there was gambling. The stick game and the rolling of the plum stones were popular among the young men. Usually, however, Mouse and Running Deer would join the lodge of Singing Wolf or Beaver Track, listening to the stories of the visitors while Cold Maker howled outside. In this way, the winter was finally over, and Gray Mouse began to look forward to the excitement of the plan which lay ahead.

The swelling of the buds, the tiny sprigs of green under the melting snow, held a special meaning for Gray Mouse this season. These things heralded not only the Awakening but the season in which she would begin to carry out her plan, her personal quest.

Days seemed to pass at an incredibly slow pace, and the girl tried to conceal her impatience. Eventually the time came to move from winter camp and start toward the summer range.

The Spring Hunt was always a special event. The food of the People had been largely dried meat, pemmican, and dried vegetables from the Growers for several moons. There was a craving at this season, a need for fresh meat.

Buffalo, horses, all animals that graze have a similar need for fresh green grass in the spring. In the Moon of Greening they rush greedily into an area of lush new grass, gorging themselves to replenish their vital needs. All winter they have eaten dry standing hay and what browse may have been available from low-growing cottonwoods and other shrubs and trees.

The People of the Southern band burned a large section of the dried tallgrass prairie in the Moon of Greening. It was the usual way. Singing Wolf, to whom fell the responsibility for the proper timing of the ceremony, had studied the emerging sprigs of green for many days. There were other factors, too. Direction and strength of the wind, and the feel of the air. A ritual ceremony to verify his impressions . . . There must be no mistake, because the burning ceremony could be dangerous. Not only was the prestige of the holy man at stake, but the camp of the People as well. A shift in the weather could send the roaring flames in the wrong direction faster than a horse could run.

"Today is the time of burning," Singing Wolf finally announced.

Selected men of the Bowstring Society proceeded to the chosen area, carrying hot coals in containers of ashes. Those watching from the camp could see the rising threads of white smoke at each point of fire. The air was still, and each column grew as it rose high against the clear blue of the sky, to flatten and spread at some unseen upper level.

The burn lasted for two days. At night the fire, now merged into a single long line of flame, could be seen for a long way. Like a fiery snake, it crawled across the distant hills, a day's travel to the north. Behind the fire the prairie lay blackened and bare. The fire would burn on until it met with an impassable barrier such as a river or heavily wooded strip along a smaller stream.

But the black surface drew warmth from the returning sun more efficiently. Sleeping root systems far below began to stir and waken. Within a few days the black of the rolling hills was tinged with green, and in another day or two there was no black at all, only the lush green of new, life-giving growth.

Then came the buffalo. The wolves reported the first phalanxes of the great herds as they came from the south, following the greening. It has always been so. When Sun Boy is finally able to drive Cold Maker back to his ice caves in the northern mountains, the cycle begins again. The return of the sun brings the return of the grass and the buffalo.

And the Spring Hunt. Buffalo, growing fatter as they moved northward with the new season, would provide for the needs of the People. As the animals were starved for the lush green of the returning grass, so were the People in need. Their craving, similarly, was for the life-giving juices of fresh meat. Where pemmican and dried meat may keep one alive through the long winter, there is a hunger that grows. One dreams of the smell of fat hump ribs broiling at the cooking fire, with the rich juices trickling down to drip with a hissing sound on the coals. Or of fresh liver, warm and rich, all the goodness of the new grass concentrated in its powerful medicine.

The People waited. By custom and by order of the council, no individual would hunt before the formally announced Spring Hunt. To do so might frighten the herds away without a sufficient kill to supply the needs of the entire band. If necessary, the order would be enforced by the Bowstrings. It was seldom necessary, though. The penalties for breaking the custom were severe.

So the People waited, and the announcement finally came. The wolves had located a herd of appropriate size in a favorable place. Tomorrow would be the Spring Hunt.

31
>> >> >>

The hunt went smoothly. The wolves had done well, planning the approach and the killing charge. The goal was to induce the buffalo to circle, instead of breaking away in a straight run to the freedom of the far horizons. With this in mind, the line of mounted hunters approached quietly, moving upwind to avoid the telltale breeze that would carry the scent of man.

They were within a bowshot when the first cow raised her head with a questioning grunt. The eyesight of the animals was not very acute, but their keen sense of smell and motion compensated well. The old matriarch sensed something unusual in the figures that moved toward them, and now gave a snort of alarm as she turned to run.

In the space of a few heartbeats the herd was running, pushed by the riders. An animal fell, the fatal arrow jutting from its rib cage. Another . . . A young hunter with a lance approached from the left of a fat young bull, made his thrust and withdrawal, and moved on after the herd.

Now a selected trio, young men of the Elk-dog Society, emerged from a fringe of sumac to the left. Riding hard at the leaders of the

running herd, they would try to turn the animals in a circling direction. It was a dangerous move. A misstep or a stumble could throw a
rider beneath the thundering hooves of the herd. Yet even one circle
of the broad meadow would allow the hunters another few kills.
There were always young men willing to show their bravery by making the try. If they lived, it was with great honor. If they died, the
same. How could one lose?

The circling herd was beginning to break up now. Individual animals or twos and threes would manage to break out of the circling
mass. Dust rose, obscuring the vision and choking the lungs.

"Let them go!" called Yellow Moccasin, leader of the hunt. It was
too dangerous to continue to circle in the uncertain visibility. "We
have enough!"

The air began to clear as the breeze carried the dusty pall away
from the hunt scene. Dark bodies lay strewn across the little valley.
Here and there a rider hunted down a crippled animal and finished it.
Men identified their own kills by the markings on their arrow shafts,
and motioned to the approaching butcher parties.

Gray Mouse had considered joining the hunt as a hunter. It would
have been permissible, and she nearly decided to do so. The day
before the hunt, however, she rejected the idea. It would draw attention to her, and that was something she wished to avoid. The more
she could be unnoticed, the less chance she would be missed quickly
when she left the Sun Dance.

So she joined the butchering parties. That would give her more
unnoticed access to the drying meat, anyway, so that she could assemble supplies.

The apologies were performed.

"We are sorry to kill you, my brother, but upon your flesh our lives
depend. May your people be strong and many . . ."

Then the work began. Skinning, butchering, rolling the heavy carcasses to give access to the necessary portions. It was hard work, but
a time of joy for the resulting bounty. As the internal organs were
exposed, a bite or two of the raw liver was a prized delicacy. Still
warm from the animal's body heat, this spring tonic was a means to
satisfy the craving for life-giving nutrients not available from winter
stores. As the buffalo and the horses hungered for the lush green of
the spring grasses, so the People were starved for the bounty of fresh

meat. The longing was now satisfied, and in every way, the hunt was a success.

Gray Mouse tried to remain as inconspicuous as possible. In this she had little difficulty. There was so much excitement and so much to be done that it was unlikely anyone would pay much attention to one teenaged girl. She was busily engaged in scraping hides, slicing meat, attending to the drying strips on willow racks near the fire . . . All of these were normal, expected actions, so no one noticed.

It was nearly a moon before the Southern band struck the big lodges and moved on toward the site of the Sun Dance to meet the other bands. Mouse's little cache of provisions, unknown to anyone, was wrapped and tied in her extra dress and stowed in a rawhide carrier pack.

At last she was heading toward her own people. Sometimes Mouse felt that she could hardly refrain from showing her excitement. The plan was taking on more form in her mind as the time neared. She had been asking questions of any people they encountered. Cautiously, of course. It must not be apparent what she was doing.

A casual question to a woman of a Grower village . . . A conversation with the wife of an Arapaho trader who stopped with the People for a few sleeps and a little bartering.

"Have you seen an ornament like this?" she would ask casually.

Mostly she had been met with blank looks and negative shakes of the head. It was the trader's wife who nodded, but still in an uncertain manner.

"Do you know this sign?" asked the girl eagerly, making the hand signal that she had retained through all the years. "The nation of . . ."

Recognition dawned on the face of the other woman.

"Those? They are the ones you seek? Yes, we know them. We visited them last season."

The woman turned and shouted something to her husband in their own tongue.

"No, no," Mouse said quickly. "Do not trouble your husband. It is not important." She must avoid the attention which would surely be drawn to her if this conversation persisted. "The ornament was given to me," she hastily explained. "I only wanted to know from where it came."

The trader's woman nodded, looking a bit puzzled. "So that is where. They are far to the north."

"It is good," said Mouse, smiling politely. "Thank you!" She slipped away.

The following morning she made occasion to encounter the woman at the stream.

"Mother," she began politely. "I would know a little more of those people to the north." She gave the hand sign.

"Yes, I was made to think so, child," the woman said. "They are your people?"

"I do not know. I was found by these. My own were dead."

"Ah! A war?"

"No, no. The *poch.*"

"Oh. We heard that your Elk-dog People . . . Yes, this band, was it not? Seven, eight summers ago?"

"No . . . well, yes. Ten, maybe."

"Ah, how the seasons fly!" The woman shook her head.

"But I was with my own people then, Mother. They died, and a woman of these took me, became my grandmother."

"Ah, I see! And you wonder about your own!"

"Yes, that is it," Mouse said eagerly. "Can you tell me?"

"Ah, let me remember. A small nation . . . They fear the Lakotas, but everyone does there."

"*Where?*"

"Ah, I cannot . . . north. North of the river, the *Miss-ouree,* maybe."

"What others are there? Who would know?" Mouse demanded. "Lakota?"

"Maybe. But why do you ask, child? You do not want to *go* there?"

It was more of a statement than a question, and Gray Mouse realized that she might have gone too far. If this woman talked to others of the Southern band, her secret plan would become common knowledge.

Mouse laughed. "I? *Aiee,* Mother, how could I do that? I am not that foolish!"

The woman chuckled, looking not quite convinced. "Of course. Well, I cannot tell you much more. Yours is a small tribe. Two or three bands. They camp with the Crows sometimes. Bird People." She gave the hand sign for the Crow Nation. "That, to protect them from Lakotas, maybe."

A couple of other women were approaching, and Mouse was anxious to terminate the conversation.

"And you are leaving today?" she asked in a clearly audible tone.

The woman studied her for a moment, and Mouse felt that the gaze was filled with unspoken meaning. *She knows!* the girl thought, her palms moist from the tension of trying to guess what the woman might say next. *She knows that I will go there.* The other women were only a few steps away now.

"Yes, we must be traveling," said the trader's wife pleasantly.

She lifted her waterskins and waded across the shallow riffle toward the shore.

"May you travel well, Mother!" Mouse called.

"And you!" the woman called.

There was a moment as the other women began to fill their skins when the trader's wife was passing close to Gray Mouse. Only a moment . . . The woman looked straight into her eyes and again Mouse had the feeling that her innermost thoughts were visible.

"Be careful," the woman said softly yet casually. She walked on up the slope and out of sight.

Gray Mouse watched her go and felt somehow that here was a kindred spirit. The woman understood that Mouse *must* do this thing, no matter how dangerous. She could not rest until she did so. She was tempted to run after her, to thank her, but that would not be good. The woman did not turn back to look, and Mouse did not see her again.

She filled the waterskins and made her way back to the lodge. People were rising and activity was increasing. Another day in the lives of the People was under way. But for Gray Mouse, the most important event of the day had already occurred.

Maybe the most important of my life, she thought. *I know how to find my people!*

32

»»»

It was a strange feeling of familiarity with which Gray Mouse approached the Sun Dance site. *This has happened before,* she thought, in a moment of confusion that was almost panic. *I know this place!*

The gray face of the distant cliff seemed to cry out to her with a mixed message. There was a dark warning that reached her spirit with a hint of danger. Yet there was also a call to adventure, to go and seek and learn. It seemed to fit her mood perfectly.

But why the feeling of familiarity? It did not take long to understand. Mouse was intentionally trying to remain inconspicuous. She had found that in doing so, there was a certain advantage. She could listen and learn. It was in this way that she began to realize . . . She *had* been here before, as a confused, frightened child. It was the site of her meeting with the People when she and Grandmother had first rejoined them.

She had been distracted by many things. The People had been curious. Some had been kind, others had talked of her as if she were not present. And to the end of her days, Mouse would never forget the wrath of Grandmother over the "Child of the Dead" name. *Aiee!*

And it had been *here,* at this place. It now struck her as quite fitting. Her life with the People had begun here. Let it end here, as she departed quietly in the search for her own heritage. There was sadness in it. She knew that Grandmother would grieve. It was too bad. Mouse would miss her, too. But after all Mouse had not asked for this relationship. It had been a thing that happened. A chance meeting along the trail, where the paths of two lifetimes had happened to cross.

Three, maybe. Her relationship with Dark Antelope had been good. He had been a brother, a protector, many things to her. She had felt a romantic urge toward him as she matured physically. For a while she had even been quite comfortable with the thought of her own lodge, shared with Antelope. That was still a warm, exciting thought. And maybe . . . *No!* She thrust that thought aside. Before she could even consider such things, she must know. She must find her own people and recover the heritage that had been taken from her. She clasped a hand around the beaded pendant that bobbed against her breast.

Singing Wolf . . . The holy man would feel sorrow at her leaving. Mouse felt it too, as if she were betraying his trust. He had been a kind and dependable figure to a fatherless child. Yet she knew that of all the People, Singing Wolf was probably best able to understand the urgency of her quest. *After all,* she thought almost defiantly, *was it not Wolf who suggested it?* There was a nagging thought that this was not really what Wolf intended, but she thrust it aside. He *would* understand her need to know, she was certain.

Now, with the preparation for the ceremonies of the Sun Dance in full swing, her plans became more specific. Those who might have noticed her activities were distracted by other duties and interests. The brush arbor that would house the ceremony was under construction. Open-sided, built of poles and lashings, oriented to the east.

The family of the Real-chief was responsible for the procuring of the symbolic buffalo bull. Ever since their arrival at the site, young men of the extended family had been riding out to search for that special animal. Already, others were constructing the effigy at the end of the rectangular arbor. It could be seen taking shape as willow sticks were skillfully interwoven and tied to represent the great bull. Then at the proper time the kill would be made. The skin and the head would be placed in a lifelike position over the frame, to be left as an offering after the Sun Dance had ended and the People departed.

The day came when the keeper of the sacred bundles made the circuit of the camp, announcing the coming ceremonies. Four dawns this pre-dance ritual would continue, as the priest circled the area, chanting the announcement and blowing his eagle-bone whistle while his assistant kept cadence on a small drum.

That was good. Gray Mouse knew that now the entire sequence for the next ten days had been set in motion. There would be no diversion from the prescribed ritual. It was on this preoccupation that she had based her plans for departure.

There was another part to her deception, too. Through the seasons, she had become acquainted with young people in the other bands. There were numerous relatives of the family of Running Deer, especially in the Eastern and Northern bands. There were close family friends, too, such as Caddo Talker, an adopted Head Splitter of the Red Rocks band. He had been an almost-brother of Running Deer's late husband, it was said.

All of these relatives and close friends had children or grandchildren of about the age of Gray Mouse. She had known them through the years, playing together as children each season during the Sun Dance gatherings.

This time, she had gone to great pains. It must be apparent that she was associating with the young women of the other bands. Yet it must not be *too* noticeable. She did not wish to draw attention to herself.

It was not too difficult. She had contrived a quarrel with Antelope, which would justify her spending more time with the other young women. That had been the hardest part, seeing the hurt in his eyes. She fought down the urge to run to him, to explain. Maybe he would understand and forgive her someday. It was painful to think that it did not matter. She would be far away, and Antelope might never know . . .

She spent an afternoon with White Rose of the Northern band, another playing with the children of Otter Woman, a cousin of Wolf and Beaver Track. It did not matter who, as long as she established the pattern. But she found that it was pleasant to visit so. She enjoyed talking with Rose, who was about her own age, and to be married in the fall. They exchanged ideas about decorating garments, and the desirability of the new glass beads of the traders versus the more traditional quill-work. The plans of the other woman for her own lodge caused a pang of regret in the heart of Mouse. She tried to find joy in the happiness of her friend, but it was hard. Mouse tried not to think of what might have been.

The first day of the Sun Dance would be the time to depart. The first day would be so filled with emotion and excitement that no one would notice anything. Then, though the ceremonies would go on continually day and night for several more days, there would be a growing emotional draining, an exhaustion. People would begin to notice again.

She had no idea how long it might be before her absence might be noticed. Maybe a day, maybe more. But the longer it took, the greater the chances that she might elude those who would try to stop her. With this in mind, she initiated her plan the afternoon of the day before First Day.

"Grandmother," she said, as casually as possible, "I am going to visit White Rose tonight. I am helping her with her dress."

"It is good," Running Deer smiled. She was pleased that Mouse was involved with thinking of marriage and the establishment of a new lodge. Even though it was the marriage of another, this appeared to be a step in the right direction. She knew that Mouse and her suitor had had a lovers' quarrel, but that was to be expected. Maybe this contact with the happiness of another young woman would put things right.

Mouse had picked up her sleeping robe and a small bundle.

"You are staying with Rose tonight?" asked Deer.

"Yes, Grandmother. She has many things to talk about, no?"

Both women chuckled.

"Yes, child. It is good. Remember, though, the Sun Dance is tomorrow."

"Of course, Grandmother. We will come to the ceremonies together."

Running Deer nodded, pleased. There had been a time when the girl seemed almost unsociable . . .

Gray Mouse made her way through the camp by a circuitous route, trying to act as normally as she could. No one seemed to notice her. People were coming and going constantly. Even carrying a robe and a bundle, she attracted little attention. A pair of old women noticed her, and one nudged the other and smiled.

"That one goes to meet a lover," she chuckled.

The two laughed softly at their understanding of the girl's secret.

"She is pretty," one said. "Who is she?"

"I never saw her before," the other replied. "Another band, probably."

"Yes. She leaves the camp through another band than her own, to escape notice."

"You talk as if you know about such things, Pine Leaf," her companion teased.

"Well, I have some memories, you know," the other retorted. "And I remember a time when I helped you and Broken Shield . . ."

"Hush! That was a long time ago."

"Ah! And your husband does not know . . ."

"Hush, I said!"

The two old women giggled again and watched the girl as she disappeared in the trees along the river.

Gray Mouse had chosen the specific places that she needed for her plan. First, she went to a well-hidden spot in a plum thicket some distance from the camp, and deposited her pack and sleeping robe. It would be safe. Anyone who chanced to find it would recognize it as the property of another and respect it. She picked up her saddle, previously hidden here, and hurried on.

Mouse threaded her way through the heavy growth to emerge into the open at another point, near the horse herd. She waved to a distant youth who was acting as herdsman, caught her bay gelding, and quickly saddled.

It must appear, now, that she was merely going for a ride. Since she had done so before, that should not be difficult. The previous rides, however, had served a multiple purpose. She knew exactly where she would picket the horse. A quick glance at the sun's position . . . Yes, it was going well. Now to leave the horse tied in the gully she had selected, and spend some time with Rose . . . It would help if her story was as close to the truth as possible.

Shadows were growing long when Mouse left the lodge of her friend's parents. She headed directly toward the area of the Southern band's camp, but when she was out of sight, altered her path. Dusk was falling when she reached her cache. It took only a little while to assemble her equipment, including a small ax and a short bow and quiver of arrows that she had hidden previously. Even so, it was nearly full dark when she approached her horse, some distance downstream.

She rode to the top of a rise and paused to look down on the camp of the People. Hundreds of tiny sparks in the darkness marked their cooking fires. Here and there, a lodge cover glowed with the warm light of a fire inside. Mouse had always loved that sight, more noticeable in winter, when all lodges had fires inside. *Where will I spend this winter?* she wondered. *With my own people?*

The moon was just rising as Mouse drew rein and dismounted at Medicine Rock. She must not be too long . . . She did not *want* to be. There was no way to explain her wish to pause here, except that it seemed appropriate. Here there must be such powerful spirits, such strength. Power that she would need in her quest.

Above her, the cliff towered, grim and forbidding. She fought down the urge to run, to mount and ride away as fast as the bay could carry her. She had never been this close to the Rock, and its spirits seemed to reach out at her from the darkness.

Deliberately, she turned her back on the threat and drew out the little handful of twigs and tinder that she had prepared. It took only a moment to strike a spark and blow it into flame. She laid the fire carefully on the sand bar, added a few sticks, then a pinch of tobacco to honor whatever spirits might dwell here.

Then she stood, looking up at the flickering firelight on the gray stone. She raised her arms . . .

"Help me," she prayed. "Help me to find my people."

Her tiny fire was already dying when she remounted and turned the horse toward the place where a narrow path led up and around the rock and would enable her to travel to the north.

They reached the top, and she reined in the bay to let him catch his wind for a moment while she sighted her course by the Real-star. A rustling, shuffling noise caught her attention, and fear gripped her heart. Someone or some *thing* was following her along the narrow trail up the cleft in the bluff.

Mouse was instantly ready to dig heels into the flank of the bay and flee across the prairie. Only the reaction of the horse prevented her from doing so. The animal pricked up his ears, turned to look in the direction of the trail he had just ascended, and gave a friendly snort.

The creature that lifted itself over the rim was no fearful spirit-being. It was Yellow Dog.

33
»»»

Dark Antelope was troubled. He was still smarting over the quarrel that had marred this Sun Dance celebration for him. It was beyond understanding, how that could have happened so suddenly. He had thought that he and Gray Mouse were on good terms. They had not actually talked of marriage, but there had been broad hints. Somehow he had assumed that soon they *would* discuss it.

He knew that his father, Singing Wolf, had discussed the propriety with Running Deer. True, there was some confusion about their friendship. It was like a brother-sister relationship, yet that was not true. He and Mouse were not related by blood at all. They had grown up in different lodges. So when the question arose in the minds of the parents, it had been discussed and the decision made. Antelope's father had informed him that it had been decided. A courtship was permissible.

That had surprised the young man, because he was not ready. He was still enjoying the friendship. But yes, as he had begun to think about it, there was a great attraction. Little Mouse was turning into a strikingly beautiful woman. As the transformation continued, he found that he could not tolerate the thought of this beautiful girl in the arms of anyone else. He could see no man worthy of her. Since Mouse had not seemed interested in any of her various suitors, it had not become a problem. In fact, they had laughed together in secret over the bumbling attempts of some of the young men. This being the case, Antelope had not felt the need to push a courtship.

Maybe that was the problem, he pondered now, on this first day of the Sun Dance. *Maybe she wished* . . . But there was no use worrying about that now. The quarrel had been several days ago. He had not seen her since. Not to talk to, anyway. He had avoided Mouse because of the hurt, which he had no desire to experience again.

How strange it had been. He and Mouse were simply talking, making light conversation, when he noticed that nothing he said was accepted. A comment on the beautiful day was challenged by the curt remark, "It will probably rain!"

This was so completely unlike Gray Mouse that he was caught off guard. Then it had happened quickly. Maybe he should not have been so impatient.

"Mouse, what is it? What is the matter with you?" he had demanded.

As if that were a signal, the girl had seemed to fly into a rage.

"If you do not know," she screamed at him, "I will surely not tell you!"

She whirled and marched away, anger showing in every motion, in the swing of her hips and the length of her stride. Antelope was crushed and bewildered. The incident had taken place in public, with many witnesses. Some of these people were laughing at him and he retreated quickly to be alone and try to remember what he had said or done.

Antelope could think of nothing. He must talk to someone, a man. His father was too busy with his responsibilities as a holy man, preparing for the Sun Dance. He sought out his uncle, Beaver Track.

"Uncle," he began, "I would speak with you."

"Of course, Antelope. What is it?"

"It is about Gray Mouse." Quickly, he blurted out his story of the public quarrel . . . "And then she walked away!" he finished.

Beaver Track's first reaction was a howl of laughter.

Antelope's face burned with embarrassment, and he turned to go. "Forgive me, Uncle, for asking your help!" he shot back over his shoulder.

"No, no!" protested Beaver Track. "Wait. I had no cause to laugh. Let us talk of this."

Antelope turned back, still ruffled.

"Now, let us consider," Beaver Track said seriously. "You can think of nothing you said or did to anger her?"

"No, Uncle. I have tried to remember. It seemed that suddenly, I could not say anything that was to her liking. I said that the day was good, and she said no, that it would rain. *Aiee,* if I had called the grass green, I am made to think Mouse would have said it was red."

Beaver nodded thoughtfully. "You know, of course, that it is often so with women."

"That is true, Uncle. But I know Mouse well. This is something else."

"Yes . . . Antelope, this is sometimes . . . *aiee,* how can I say this? When a woman is with child . . ."

"No! I would know of that, Uncle."

"But . . . she has other young men who would court her, no?"

Antelope's anger rose, and he started to retort, but Beaver Track raised a hand calmly.

"No, no, Antelope, you must know that I had to ask."

The young man struggled for control. "That is true, Uncle," he said evenly, "but again, I would know. Mouse has talked to me, told me of her suitors. I am made to believe there is no one."

"That is good," Beaver agreed. "And you are probably right. After all, your grandmother is very strict with her."

"Could you talk to Grandmother?" Antelope asked.

"Yes, of course," his uncle agreed. "She may know."

But Running Deer did not know.

"No, I have seen no other young men," she told Beaver. "I knew about the lovers' quarrel, but those happen. She has been spending much time with your cousin, White Rose, talking of girl-things. No, I am made to think there is no problem. Give her time. After the Sun Dance, it will be as nothing."

Beaver Track relayed this to his nephew, but Antelope was not convinced.

"Something is not right about this, Uncle. I will talk to Mouse myself."

But it was easy to postpone such a conversation. He dreaded a

repeat of the tirade, and the excitement and distraction of the pre–
Sun Dance festivities continued. It was not until this, the first day of
the actual ceremonies honoring the return of the sun and the grass,
that Antelope determined to talk to Gray Mouse.

She was nowhere to be found.

"I have not seen her today," his grandmother told him. "She stayed
with our cousin last night."

"Cousin? Which cousin?"

"Rose. White Rose, Northern band. Rose is to be married, you
know, and Mouse was helping her sew . . ." But Dark Antelope was
gone.

"Yes, she was at my mother's lodge," Rose told him. "We talked
and sewed, and . . ."

"But where did she go this morning?"

"Today? I do not know, Antelope. I have not seen her."

"Since this morning, you mean?"

"No, today. I did not see her today."

"Wait! Mouse did not spend the night at your lodge?"

"No, no! When the light became too poor to sew, she went home."

"I see . . ." In truth, he did not understand at all, but he was
becoming quite concerned. He thanked his cousin and hurried to talk
to Beaver Track.

But his uncle was otherwise occupied, dancing with his warrior
society in the Sun Dance arbor. That might go on for a long time, and
Antelope felt that he could not wait. He walked outside the camp,
away from the noise of the drums and rattles and the chanting of the
songs. What could be going on?

He thought about what little he really knew. Mouse had left the
lodge of their grandmother a full day ago. She had been prepared to
spend the night, so she would have been carrying her sleeping robe.
Yet White Rose had not mentioned it. Jealousy and anger rose in him
as the next question struck him squarely. *With whom did she spend
the night?*

He was crushed, and his heart was very heavy. Mouse must have a
secret lover. That was her privilege, of course, but *why?* Why secret?
She was an eligible young woman. There were no taboos for her that
would prevent a relationship with any man of the People. She was kin
to none except by her adoption. That had been decreed. Even if her

lover were already married, there was nothing to prevent a second wife, or a third.

Somehow, that did not seem to be an answer. Young women sometimes allowed themselves to be courted by an older man with an established lodge. But those were girls who were attracted by the wealth and position of their lover. They were also quite likely to flaunt the courtship, to make it as public as possible. That would not be the way of Gray Mouse. He knew her well, since childhood. Mouse would not be likely to engage in that sort of courtship anyway.

But why, then, the secrecy? There must be something that he was missing here. Was his head confused by his sorrow over Mouse's secret lover? He tried to think who it might be, but came up empty. There was not one young man in whom she had shown any interest. No real interest, anyway. He must try to think, then, what else . . . ?

His worst fear was that Mouse had met with some accident. Or could she have been stolen? There was always talk of such activity, though he could not remember such an incident. True, she was a very beautiful and desirable woman. But she had planned this, had she not? Her sleeping robe . . . but she had not arrived at the Northern band with that robe. *What else did she take?*

He sought out Running Deer.

"Grandmother, what did Mouse take with her last night?"

"Afternoon. She went over there about this time. You are worried . . . what is it, Antelope?"

"I do not know, Grandmother. No one has seen her. She did not spend the night with Rose."

"*Aiee!* My baby! Wait . . . she did not go to our cousin's?"

"She did, but she left before dark. Grandmother, do you think she has a lover?"

"No, no, I am made to think not."

"Then what else did she take? Food?"

"Let us look!"

The two rummaged around the lodge and behind the lodge lining.

"I can see no food missing," Deer said. "She had a bundle . . . Ah! her new dress!"

"But why?"

Deer shrugged. "I had thought maybe she wanted to show it to Rose. The quill-work, you know."

He nodded, but another idea struck him now.

"Could she have gone on a hunt or a vision quest?"

"Surely she would have told us. Let me see . . . *weapons?*"

Neither had thought of that, but a search brought a quick answer.

"Her bow and quiver, her little ax. Her knife, of course," Running Deer stated. "What does this mean, Antelope?"

"I do not know, Grandmother. I will see if she took a horse. She would ride her bay, no?"

"Probably. Or my gray. But she has been using the bay."

"She *has?* Since we came here to the Sun Dance?"

"Yes. Almost every day, Antelope. Since . . . well, since your quarrel. I thought you knew."

"Grandmother, I will tell you if I find anything," he said as he hurried away.

There were many bays in the horse herd. Far more than he remembered. The young herdsman was able to help, at least a little.

"Your sister's gelding? She took it."

"Took it? When?"

"Yesterday. No, maybe the day before. But either way, she did not bring it back. I suppose she traded it, no? A good horse, that one!"

"Then you have not seen her?"

"Ah, would I not remember seeing a woman like that? Tell me, Antelope, is she spoken for?"

But Antelope was gone. He hurried back to the Sun Dance arbor. Yes, the Bowstring Society had relinquished the arena to the Bloods, and Beaver Track was nowhere to be seen. Antelope hurried to his lodge.

"Uncle, I must speak with you!"

The older man appeared exhausted from the rigors of the dance, but quickly came alert as his nephew blurted out his story. He glanced quickly at the sun.

"*Aiee!* We have not much light left. Come."

Beaver rose quickly, picked up his bow, and led the way.

34
>> >> >>

It was some time later that the first track was located, on a sand bar near the water. Beaver Track had quickly described the procedure he would use.

"No horses would be moving *away* from the camp, except hers," he explained. "If we can find a track or two, maybe we can tell which way she went. Oh, yes . . . is her dog with her?"

"I do not know, Uncle."

"We will find out. Now, first, we will look for tracks along the stream."

"But there are many . . ."

"That is true. But look, Antelope, if you start to travel, and want no one to see you, you would stay in the timber, no?"

Of course, now that it had been pointed out, it was easy to see. At some point, Mouse would have led or ridden her horse through the thin strip of timber along the river and would leave tracks.

"There it is!" exclaimed Beaver Track, pointing. "Now, stay back a little. Let me look."

He squatted, studying the depressions in the sandy surface. Finally, he rose.

"Yes," he mused, half to himself. "It is her horse. See how he paddles a little on the left front foot? And she was leading him, here." He pointed to a slender footprint. "She went that way."

"Toward Medicine Rock?"

"Maybe so."

"Then let us go there, Uncle."

Beaver Track thought about it for only a moment. "You are right, Antelope. There is not enough time before dark to track her there, but if we hurry, we may find something there."

The two men mounted and rode to the Rock, arriving just before dusk.

"Be careful," Beaver cautioned. "Let me look around. We do not want to spoil any tracks."

It was only a moment, however, before he called out.

"She was here," he stated. "Her footprints . . . a fire."

"A fire?"

"Yes. A ceremony. Just a few sticks, maybe tobacco."

"But why, Uncle?"

"Who knows? This was a prayer fire, though. Let me look for horse tracks."

He waded across the riffle to study the other bank, a narrow strip along the base of the bluff. "Nothing," he said, returning. "But I am made to think . . . Yes, I remember . . . A path up the cliff. Was it not downstream?"

They hurried in that direction, and Beaver quickly discovered what he sought. "Yes, she crossed here. That is the trail to the top."

"Then let us go up."

"We should wait, Antelope. It is nearly dark, and the moon will not rise until later. We know she went this way, but at the top, we do not know, and we cannot track in the dark. We will come back in the morning. Oh, yes . . . her dog is with her now. There are tracks . . ."

They found the tracks at the top of the bluff the next morning as soon as it was light. Tracking was more difficult here, because the grass that covered the earth beneath did so more completely. It was short buffalo grass here, in contrast to the assortment of tallgrass species on the slopes and in the gullies. Finally Beaver Track found that which he sought, and rose with a grunt.

"She went this way," he pointed. "North. See, the horse tries to choose the best footing, so he chances on a trail, here. Other animals have found it the easiest way, too."

He pointed to a barely visible strip of black earth which meandered across the flat between and among the patches of gray-green buffalo grass.

"See, her horse's footprint . . ." He touched the edge of the circular mark, testing its texture. "Sometime early yesterday, maybe," he concluded.

"Then let us hurry," Antelope urged. "She has traveled a whole day!"

"That is true," his uncle agreed. "But let us think on this, Antelope. If we move too fast, we will miss something. Besides, are you ready for a long journey? It may take many days just to catch up to her."

"I have some meat," Dark Antelope pointed to his pack. "A few days."

"And I, too," Beaver agreed. "So be it. Let us go on a little way. Maybe we can learn more. Do you know why she would do this?"

"No, Uncle. I . . . we quarreled."

"Yes, I heard. That was odd, too. And her prayer fire, down below. One does that to start a quest or a journey."

"You think she plans to travel far? But *why?*"

"I do not know, Antelope. Maybe she only seeks solitude to fast and pray. A vision quest. But if that is it, we should be able to tell in a day or two, by how she travels."

They moved on, following the dim game trail. To one unaccustomed to the plains, there would seem to be no trail at all. But the passage of elk, antelope, buffalo, and the predators that follow them has worn shallow grooves in the prairie sod over the centuries. An animal, headed in a given direction, will chance upon and follow these dim paths. It was only necessary for those who sought the missing girl to determine her general direction and then follow the lay of the land and their horses' inclinations.

They found a spring gushing forth from a hillside, where Mouse had dismounted and walked around for a little while.

"She rests her horse and lets him eat," said Beaver Track, pointing to cropped grasses nearby. "Many dog tracks in the mud here, so she was here for a while."

"That means . . ." began Antelope hesitantly.

"Yes. She plans a long journey. For a vision quest, she would hurry there and stop."

Antelope agreed, still confused. They drank and watered the horses, then hurried on.

It was late in the day when they came to the place where Mouse had camped for the night.

"You tell me what you see," Beaver suggested.

Antelope nodded. "Her fire, here. She rolled in her robe and slept, there, south of the fire a little way. The dog beside her, maybe. Her horse grazed there, below the spring."

"It is good," his uncle agreed. "You will be a tracker yet."

It was high praise, from one as skilled as Beaver Track.

It was mid-morning when tragedy struck. They had stopped at a narrow stream to let the horses drink and to stretch their own legs for a few moments. Beaver Track's horse had wandered a few steps downstream. Suddenly the animal jumped wildly and ran a few steps, shaking his head and pawing at his nose with a forefoot. The men had hardly turned to look when the unmistakable buzz of a real-snake's rattle reached their ears.

Beaver Track hurried to his horse, deeply concerned, while Antelope went to look at the snake.

"Be careful," Beaver called. "Its mate may be near."

Cautiously, Antelope explored the area, but found nothing. Even the snake which had assaulted Beaver's horse had disappeared into a rocky crevice.

"He is bitten," called the tracker. "*Aiee,* what a poor time!"

A single fang had left a puncture on the soft part of the horse's nose. It was swelling rapidly, and the horse seemed half crazy with the pain. Beaver Track drew his knife.

"Here, you ear him down," he called to Antelope, "while I make the cut."

It was quickly done, a crossed gash over the wound. Blood and serum gushed out.

"What else can we do?" asked Antelope.

"Nothing . . . Wait and see. *Aiee,* this is bad! If we had a fresh liver of buffalo or deer . . . anything."

"I will go and see what I can find," Antelope offered.

"No. It would take too long. We can try a mud pack. Yes, it is warm enough."

Beaver was already scooping up a handful of mud to pack over and into the wound. The horse now stood, head drooping, back humped, listless. It was obviously a very sick animal. They led it to an unobstructed area to lie down and the horse half fell to a recumbent position.

"Let us build a fire," said Beaver. "To warm the mud pack will be good."

When they had gathered sticks for a fire, heated mud, and repacked the wound, there was little else to do.

"I could take your horse and go on," Beaver offered. "Or you can go on."

"I am made to think," Antelope said slowly, "that this means *I* must go on. I am meant to look for Mouse. I can do this, Uncle."

Beaver nodded as if only partly convinced. "Yes, maybe. We might leave this horse and try to find another. There may be a Grower village downstream."

"But their horses, Uncle . . . not as good as you need. Besides, it would take time."

"That is true. You go ahead. I will see how this horse does. Maybe I will look for another and follow you."

Antelope swung to his saddle. "Thank you, Uncle, for your help. May it go well with you."

"And with you, Antelope."

"We will come back this way, to see how it has gone with the horse," Antelope said as he turned his mount away.

"It is good," Beaver Track called after him.

Both men knew that it was not. Beaver Track, alone and on foot in an unfamiliar country, was not in a good situation at all. Even if his horse lived, it would be many days before the animal could travel. There might be a day when his decision would be to abandon the dying or useless horse and rejoin the Southern band on foot.

Likewise, Antelope was heading into unknown country. The Northern band knew the area, but they were still at the Sun Dance and would be for several days. And how far north would the quest of Gray Mouse take her? That was an open question in itself.

The same thought lay unspoken in the minds of both of these men as they parted.

Will I ever see him again, or is this the last time?

35
»»»

There were times when Gray Mouse regretted her decision. How much easier it would have been now if she had not decided that she must know about her people.

She crouched beneath her robe, which she had spread over a growth of dogwood bush near the stream. Not too close to the stream . . . A flash flood was a common occurrence at this time of year. And not too near one of the giant old cottonwood trees. Their spirit was close to that of Rain Maker, and often attracted his spears of real-fire during the noisy storms of the coming Moon of Thunder.

The sound of the rain pattered on the non-haired side of her buffalo robe. It was much like the sound of rain on a lodge skin. She wondered whether it was raining at Medicine Rock, on the lodge cover of Running Deer. Or on that of Dark Antelope and his parents . . . She counted days . . . The Sun Dance should be ending now. The big lodges would come down and the bands would scatter for the season. She thought of her friend White Rose, and the coming marriage.

No! she told herself fiercely. *Such things are not for me. I have a more important quest.*

Yellow Dog snuggled close to her and whined sympathetically. Or maybe, only because he, too, was uncomfortable in the partial shelter of the robe over their heads. The rain continued to fall.

There were some sunny days, of course, days good for travel. On those days Mouse was filled with the excitement of her quest. There was the challenge of the unknown and the thrill of wondering how it would be to find her own people.

Each time she encountered a village of Growers, or a trader on the trail, she showed her beaded pendant. Some recognized it, at least in a vague way, and pointed to the north. *So,* she thought with satisfaction. *I am headed in the right direction.*

There had been one disconcerting conversation at a Grower town. It was mostly in hand signs. The Grower woman of whom she inquired seemed concerned.

"You travel alone?"

"Yes," Mouse signed casually. "My dog and I."

The woman had clucked her tongue in disapproval. "It is not good."

Gray Mouse tossed her head. "It is the way of the People," she answered confidently. Then it struck her: *But of my people, I do not know!*

She did not say that, in either voice or sign, but inquired further. "What is the danger?"

"Maybe none," the woman answered. "But you know of the Horn People?"

"I have heard."

"Then you know they steal girls sometimes."

"So I have heard. For what purpose?"

The woman shrugged. "Who knows? Wives, maybe. Or to sell . . . And there is their god, Morning Star, who needs a woman sometimes."

Gray Mouse felt a chill of doubt, but tried not to let it show. There *was* such a story . . . Someone of the People . . . Yes, the Southern band, even. Someone had married a woman of the Horn People a generation ago, had he not? So they could not be too dangerous, could they?

"So I have heard," she signed boldly. "But I can take care of myself. I am not afraid of Horn People."

She hefted her ax and glanced at Yellow Dog.

The Grower woman looked at her sadly, which irritated the girl. She turned to mount her horse.

"I must be on the trail," she signed. "I have far to travel."

"May you travel well," the woman answered as Mouse turned the bay northward again.

"Who was that?" asked a man who happened to come out of the earth-covered lodge just then.

His wife shook her head sadly.

"A traveler. A girl . . . Pretty, though."

"Alone?"

"Yes. Sad, is it not?"

"And she goes toward the Horn People?" he asked.

"So she said. I tried to warn her. She would not listen."

"Too bad! Does she not know that this is the year for Morning Star to demand a woman?"

His wife shrugged. "You do not know that for certain, my husband."

"That is true. But the trader who was here was made to think so."

She nodded. "Yes. But traders like to talk, no? Anyway, I did my best to warn her. I am made to think that this one will not listen to anybody. Too bad . . ."

Among the Horn People, the tension was mounting. The Morning Star Priest had made his announcement, and everyone had waited for the vision that would come to some honored warrior. That man would become Wolf Man for the season. Morning Star would guide him to select a virgin bride for the ceremony. The designated girl would be honored and pampered, given the finest of food and garments, and groomed for the morning on which the ceremony would take place. That day was known only to the Morning Star Priest, who followed the wanderings of the stars across the sky. Morning Star would rise blood-red just before dawn on that carefully calculated day, to greet his virgin bride . . .

When the vision came, after many days of waiting, the Horn People had rejoiced. It required only a day for the newly appointed Wolf Man to be anointed by the priest, and to choose the warriors who would accompany him on the quest. His vision had been clear. A virgin would be provided, somewhere to the south.

.   .   .   .   .

Gray Mouse was uneasy that evening. She had camped at a spot on the trail that seemed to be a frequently used camp site for travelers. There were ashes of several night fires, some older than others.

There was also a shortage of fuel. In this area trees were scarce. Especially trees of any size, except for an occasional cottonwood. There were willows, of course, but the willows seemed to grow more like a scrubby brush fringe along the stream bed in this country. Willow made a poor fire, anyway. Mouse had gathered dry buffalo chips to supplement her fuel.

It was nearly dark when she kindled her fire and added the ceremonial pinch of tobacco to honor the spirits of the place. Even as she did so, a strange thought crossed her mind. She had been ill at ease all the time she gathered fuel. Could this be a warning of some danger, an unseen and unheard help from the spirits she now honored? It was an eerie feeling.

There had been evenings before when she had been depressed, lonely, even frightened. But nothing like this. There was a feeling of impending danger, of doom almost.

Yellow Dog seemed to feel it, too. He had been close to her all the time she gathered fuel, nosing around the sandy slopes, poking into brushy thickets. Once, when a distant coyote called, Dog raised his muzzle to answer in a mournful howl.

"Come on," she had snapped at him. "They are not your people."

She could not recall when Yellow Dog had ever behaved this way. She had been glad for his company on the journey. At first she had been irritated that the dog had followed her. He was showing his age, and moved slowly on chilly mornings. She had been afraid that the animal would slow her travel, but it had not been so. In a few days she had decided that it was good to have his company.

It was good tonight. More than ever, she now questioned the wisdom of her mission. It was lonely here, and her thoughts turned to the warmth and security of the lodges of the People. Of the love of Running Deer . . . The warm, brotherly companionship of Dark Antelope . . . *Aiee,* she wished for him to be here just now.

An owl sailed across the starlit sky, and she wondered where there might be a tree big enough for an owl to nest. There was the other thing about owls, too. The People honored this hunter of the night, the messenger. Yet there was, in the back of her mind, the memory that her *own* people feared the silent hunter as a dark thing, a bringer of misfortune. It was a dim memory, poorly defined, but the feeling was strong. A threat of evil . . .

She added a few sticks to make the fire shed a bit more light. Buffalo chips made a smoldering bed of coals. Adequate for cooking, but smoky and giving little illumination. Just now, she would feel better with light. The sticks broke into flame and the circle expanded, pushing back the shadows that kept intruding into her camp and into her mind.

Yellow Dog raised his head, peered out into the darkness, and gave a short, startled *woof* of inquiry. Mouse reached over to pat him.

"It is nothing, Dog," she reassured him. "Some night creature . . ."

But now she realized that the hair was standing on the animal's back. From just behind Dog's ears, all along his spine to the base of his tail, every hair stood erect. A deep growl rumbled in his throat as he took a step or two forward.

"No . . . Stay here . . ." Mouse said softly as she reached for her ax.

Yellow Dog appeared not to hear. In the space of a heartbeat he had leapt forward, barking a challenge into the darkness. The girl watched him disappear into an opening in the willows. She sprang to her feet, calling to the dog.

There was a momentary sound of a scuffle, mixed with the guttural roar of the dog's battle cry. Then a startled yelp of pain, and silence. Mouse stood staring at the black hole through which Yellow Dog had plunged into the darkness. She must go to his aid, but could see nothing beyond the nearest willows. What sort of creature had the dog encountered? A bear? A cougar?

Through the opening in the willows there stepped a tall warrior. He carried a heavy war club, but raised his other hand in the sign for peace. His head was shaven except for a twisted lock of hair on the top, twisted and drawn upward into the shape of a horn. It was painted red, like his shaved scalp.

"Greetings," he signed. "You are honored, Princess of Morning Star."

Mouse gripped her ax and took a fighting stance.

"You will not be harmed," the warrior went on. "Put down the ax."

"Do not come closer," she warned. "My friends will . . ."

The Horn Man chuckled. "I see no friends," he signed. "But do not fear, Princess."

She wondered if she could throw the ax and make it count. She had practiced, but only at a dead tree trunk. Well, this would be little different . . . Her arm rose, the ax lifted, and she aligned it. She did not have a chance to start the throw, because she was grabbed from behind by two, maybe three men. Others came running.

Mouse fought; biting, kicking, scratching, trying to free the hand that held the ax, trying to reach her knife with her other hand. She drew blood on two men, kneed another in the groin, and was finally pinned down by sheer weight of numbers. Someone pulled her hands behind her and tied her wrists.

The first Horn Man stepped to her side. "Do not struggle, Honored One," he signed. "I have told you, you will not be harmed. It will all be explained to you."

She could not answer because her hands were tied. The Horn Men apparently did not understand the tongue of the People, because they did not react at all to the vile things she was saying about them.

36
»» »» »»

The days on the trail were little short of torture for Dark Antelope. Each evening brought the frustration and worry of not knowing.
Where would Mouse spend the night? Was she safe? Was she alive,
even, since she left the last campfire?

He found nearly every one of her camp sites. One he missed entirely, lost the trail, and lost nearly a day in backtracking to look for it.
Another time he pushed his luck too far and tried to travel by the
light of a pale half-moon. That had been a mistake, and lost him much
time and distance.

But his tracking skills were improving. He began to notice small
things that he would not have seen last season. Or even a moon ago,
he realized. His powers of observation were being honed to a fine
edge.

Part of that may have been the fasting. For the first few days he had
been too concerned to eat. Even under the tense circumstances he
noted the results of the fast. He had heard descriptions all his life of
individuals on their vision quests, and the progression of feelings
involved. First the hunger pangs and the spasmodic rumbling and

discomfort of the stomach. That part he had not recognized for what it was. It seemed only a part of the torture he felt.

By the second day he recognized his symptoms for what they were, the effects of his fasting. *Let it be so,* he thought. He could use it to his advantage, because next, as he remembered the stories, would come the clarity of vision, the ability to understand all things. Maybe it would not work that way under these trying circumstances. But if it was so during a vision quest, might not it be the same?

He slept better that night, though he awoke with fragmentary dreams that were only partially remembered. Visions . . . When this was over, he must seek a vision quest. If he survived, of course. Antelope was completely ready to give his life for the safety of Gray Mouse. He did not think of it in such terms, but it was there, assumed to be true. It needed no statement of recognition.

But on the morning when he awoke with the wisps of his sleep-visions still in his head, there was a new feeling. It was a good feeling, an excitement that would have been hard to describe. He seemed to see more clearly. The colors of the dawn were brighter, the sky wider and clearer. His ears were keened to the sounds, the sleepy songs of the night-creatures as they settled in for their rest. These were re-placed by the awakening chorus of those who are active by day.

The sun on his skin, the breeze in his hair, brought sensations he had not experienced before. He realized that under other circumstances, without the worry and concern of his mission, this would be a wonderfully fulfilling experience. Even as it was, it was good. There was a feeling of confidence that regardless of what might happen next, all would be right with the world. This he translated into a sense of expectation. This mission, this quest *would* be brought to a successful ending. In this way he was able to deal with his concern for the safety of Gray Mouse.

His newly acquired skills of observation helped him greatly, if he did not try to push too fast. Usually, he felt that he was one sleep behind on the trail of the woman he sought. On one joyous day, he found the ashes of her campfire while they were still warm. His heart jumped for joy and he hurried on. But the next day it rained, and he lost the trail for a while . . .

Antelope talked to people he encountered, seeking any scrap of information that might be of help. He camped one night with a traveling Arapaho trader and his wife. They had seen a young woman, had talked with her. Antelope questioned them at some length. His use of Arapaho was not fluent, so most of the conversation was in hand signs.

Rather than trying to explain the entire situation in sign talk, he chose to refer to Mouse as "my woman." This brought an unexpected reaction from the trader's wife.

"Ah!" she grunted, laughing. Then, turning to signs, "Your woman has run away to return to her people?"

"Why do you say this, Mother?" Antelope asked. "How do you know?"

"Her pendant, around her neck. A design of people to the north. She asked about them."

This helped to verify his suspicions. He received much the same story from Growers whose towns he passed.

"Yes, that one! She was here . . . Asked about the beaded ornament she wore. People who live that way. North."

He moved on. He had resumed eating, realizing that he must maintain his strength. The sense of confidence remained, as his conversations continued with those who had seen Gray Mouse.

There came a day, however, when his confidence changed to alarm.

"My heart was heavy for her," said a Grower.

"Because she seeks her people?" Antelope asked, puzzled.

"No, no. It is because . . . You know the Horn People?"

"Yes . . . Not I . . . But they are known to my people."

"And of their Morning Star god?"

A wave of concern struck him. The Morning Star Ceremony . . .

"Yes." He was trying to remember . . . The Horn People were said to capture a girl to be given to Morning Star.

"It is told that this is to be their year for Morning Star to ask for a maiden."

"I tried to warn her!" interrupted the wife of the Grower. "But wait! I was made to think she was a maiden. She is your woman?"

"Yes, mine!" Antelope insisted. It was easier to say so.

"Ah! Then there is no problem." The woman smiled. "It must be a virgin, the bride for Morning Star."

Antelope's head whirled in confusion. "But they would not know she is mine!" he blurted. "You were made to think . . ."

"That is true," agreed the woman. "But maybe they will not even find her."

Antelope nodded. "Maybe. But I must hurry now."

He mounted to ride on. Hurry, but not too fast. He must miss nothing. He resolved to begin to fast again to increase his powers of observation. Then he turned back for a moment.

"When was she here? How many sleeps?"

"Two," answered the man.

"No, three, was it not?" his wife answered.

But Antelope was already turning away. Somewhere, he had lost another day, at least.

He watched the buzzards circle, high above the sandy plain. It was a bright, clear day, heavy with the moisture of the morning's dew. One of the great birds half-folded its wings and started downward in a long glide. Another followed. There were several more, riding the warm air without a movement, wings fixed in position as the birds drew circles in the blue. Another dropped to earth.

There must be some large animal dead or dying in the brushy plain there. Some creature drowned by a flash flood along the river? But he saw no signs of flooding, and the rain had been days ago.

Then a terrible possibility occurred to him. He kicked the horse forward, eager to reach the area, yet dreading what he would find. Careful now. He must not destroy any tracks in his hurry. Also, he must cross the small stream, and streams in sandy country are deceptive. He remembered the words of his father, that such streams run upside down. "Their water is beneath the sand," he had said. "The water spirits sometimes reach up to drag down the unwary traveler."

Antelope let the horse pick its way across the stream bed. A false start, another . . . He tried to control his impatience. Finally a lunge, a jump that almost unseated him, and they were across, on more solid footing on the other side.

He glanced at the circling buzzards and turned toward the area that had drawn their attention. He hesitated to dismount until he knew what lay ahead. His heart was beating wildly, full of dread at what he might find. He pushed through the willows and several startled buzzards rose ponderously from their carrion feast.

Her dog! Antelope thought with a mixed sense of relief and further alarm. *Then where is her horse?*

He dismounted, tied the nervous horse, and began to circle, as Beaver Track had taught him. In a short while he had discovered the tracks of several men. He followed them, back toward the stream, pausing to examine a bit of sign occasionally.

By the time the sun stood overhead, Antelope had pieced together a pattern of how it must have happened. He found Mouse's camp, the untended fire now dead and cold. Part of the sticks were not completely burned, so there had been no one to tend the dying fire. He circled . . . Yes, one from that direction, others from over there . . . a scuffle . . .

The dog must have heard or smelled the intruders, and gone to challenge them. A blow from a war club had been his reward. Gray Mouse had fought . . . The sand was disturbed. It had taken several men to subdue her, and . . . *Ah! What is that?* he thought.

Her knife, the little one that she always carried at her waist. He picked it up carefully, examining the weapon. For it had been used as a weapon. Sand was glued to its keen flint edge with the blood of one of her attackers.

Her robe, cast aside when she rose to meet the intruders, lay under a willow. Her weapons had been taken. The horse, too, probably. Yes, they had taken her alive, and had probably used her own horse to carry her.

Antelope returned to his horse, mounted, and rode out to about a bow shot away, to circle for tracks. It did not take long. Five horses, not counting Mouse's bay. He found where one man had stood, holding the horses while the others stalked the camp.

After the abduction they had moved out, heading generally northwest. He followed to their night camp not far away. The ashes were cold, but no more than two days old. A day and a half behind them, then.

At least he had a trail to follow. The captors of Gray Mouse traveled boldly, taking no pains at all to conceal their trail. *They must be in their own country,* Antelope realized. *They do not fear pursuit at all.*

And why should they? his thoughts demanded. *They are many, you are but one.*

He had already conceded one fact. These must be the dreaded Horn People. He tried to remember anything he could that he had ever heard about them. Someone of the People had been captured by

them, married one of their women, did he not? A generation ago . . .
Yes, Strong Bow!

Now what could he remember about that story? He should have given it more attention, but who would know how important it might become?

And in the back of his mind, the question he dared not even think: *how long* until the ceremony for the Morning Star?

37
»»»

Antelope tied his horse and muzzled the animal with a soft buckskin thong around its nose. It was essential that it not cry out to others of its kind in the town below.

He had located what he believed to be the village of the Horn People by a smudge of smoke. It hung over an area just above the river, in a setting that fit the description given him by Growers a day downstream. He then circled to come closer behind a low ridge, where he could watch from concealment.

Now he studied the setting . . . Yes, the large domed structures of a type he had not seen before . . . they fit the descriptions that he had heard. Each of those dwellings, the Growers had said, held several families . . . Maybe fifty people. Antelope was not certain he believed that. However, the domes did appear large enough. *Aiee, to live in the ground!* He shuddered at the thought.

He peered through the sumac thicket. It afforded thin conceal-ment, but would allow him to watch, to get the feel of the village below. There was activity, though not much. The day was growing hot, and people who had been outside were now withdrawing into the earth lodges. Antelope thought about that. His own people would, on a day like this, lift the lodge covers and roll them up around the sides, to allow a breeze through the dwelling. These Horn People seemed to go underground. It must be . . . yes, like a cave, a bit cooler. *Not worth the trade-off, though,* he told himself. To a man of the open prairie the thought of being trapped in an enclosed space was too much. He shuddered, and turned his thoughts to the concerns at hand.

It was not clear which of the lodges below might be the place where Mouse was kept. Actually, Antelope had no clear idea of what he was expecting. Some sign, some clue that would help him. It would do his heart good if he could determine which of the mounds below was the cage that held Gray Mouse. Then it might be that his spirit could reach her more easily.

Was she huddled there in the dark and smoky structure, crying to herself over her fate? He could not imagine Gray Mouse in such an attitude. She would probably meet whatever came with pride and dignity. *That* would be her way.

The last Growers he had visited had given him the lurid details of the Morning Star Ceremony. It had made his heart very heavy. The scaffold, erected over a period of several days, a pole at a time . . . A ritual before dawn, the maiden chosen to be the sacrifice tied to the rack . . . The sacred arrow that would pierce her heart and give her life to the Horn People's god, Morning Star.

Antelope knew that he must stop this horror, or die trying. He had no plan, and the odds looked formidable. But there stuck in his mind something that a woman had said several days before. Something about ". . . she is your woman? . . . then there is no problem . . . it must be a maiden . . ."

In some way, could he convince the Horn People that Mouse was his wife? As he understood their ways, that would make Gray Mouse ineligible for their ghastly ceremony. But *how?*

Evening was approaching when he noticed a flurry of activity around one of the mounded lodges below. Heavily armed warriors, painted ceremonially, took their places at each side of the entrance. Then a man dressed in a flowing cape stepped forward and stood waiting. From his garments and the deference that the others showed him, this appeared to be a holy man. Yes, had not someone spoken of the Morning Star Priest? This must be the one.

Antelope thought for a moment of trying to creep down within range and see if he could kill the priest. The idea was immediately discarded. A childish thought, born of his desperation. But now some-one emerged from the lodge . . . An old woman . . . Another, and then Gray Mouse stepped into the open and straightened to her full height. It was as he had imagined, tall and proud before her captors. She was dressed in fine buckskin garments, with lavish decoration. She was not tied. Somehow she had convinced them . . . Or possi-bly *they* had convinced *her* that there was no danger.

That thought made his blood run cold. He had wondered how it would be possible to carry a fighting, screaming girl up onto a scaffold and tie her into place. In some way, the Horn People must be able to persuade their victim to climb the scaffold to her death *willingly*. The horror of such a thing was almost overwhelming to him.

There were four of the black-garbed women surrounding Gray Mouse now. The thought struck him that maybe the time was *now*. But no, the ceremony was to be at dawn, it was said. There must be priestesses, women assigned to the needs of the captive. Yes, that seemed to fit. The group was walking through the village as if for a stroll. People from other lodges came out to watch. It did not seem to Antelope that this stroll was ceremonial in nature. It might be a prelude . . . *Could the ceremony be at dawn tomorrow?*

He did not know, but the thought sent him running for his horse. He stripped the thong from its muzzle, swung to the saddle, and kicked the animal into a hard run. Straight into the village he rode. He was dimly aware that the priestesses were hurrying the captive inside. He was forced to concentrate, however, on the fact that armed warriors were pouring into his path, raising weapons in a very threat-ening manner. For a time, he expected to feel the stinging blows of arrows at any moment.

He pulled heavily on the reins, bringing the horse to a sliding stop on its haunches. At the same time, he was raising his right palm in the hand sign gesture for peace. He still felt that a hail of arrows might be loosed at any time. His palms were clammy . . . The slightest mis-understanding could be fatal in the space of a heartbeat.

The sweating horse stood trembling, blowing heavily. Antelope sat, hand still raised. Now the priest came forward, the crowd of warriors parting to give him passage.

"Who are you?" the holy man demanded in signs. "Why are you here?"

"Honored One," Antelope signed carefully, "I have traveled far, looking for my woman, who ran away. She is here, in that lodge!"

"You are mistaken," signed the priest. "There is no woman here."

"It is a mistake," agreed Antelope, "but I have seen the woman, as I rode in. Let me tell you of her."

"What is to tell?"

Some of the warriors were becoming restless. Antelope was very uneasy.

"Let me tell, Honored One. I am Antelope, of the Elk-dog People. This woman, I admit, is not of our people."

"Then what is she to you?" demanded the other.

"My wife. Look, she is younger than I, no? I bought her . . . Her people are north, somewhere, maybe. I do not care. She wore a pendant, no? Red, yellow, and black? She left me and ran away. I was made to think she is trying to return to her people. But she belongs to me. I gave eleven horses for her."

He could see that the priest was considering his story. Not completely accepting it, maybe. Antelope hoped that these Horn People were not too familiar with the customs of the People. Some of his story was exaggerated, and more like the customs of Head Splitters.

"Ask her!" he suggested. It could do no harm. It might be that Mouse would understand what was going on and agree . . . *Yes, it is as he says.* That would be good. If, however, she chose to deny what he had told them, it would still strengthen his story. An escaped slave-wife, running away to return to her people, would be expected to lie.

An idea now seemed to occur to the priest. He turned and spoke to some of the others. Two warriors turned toward the lodge where Mouse was confined.

"They will bring the girl out," he signed. "You will ask her. *In hand signs.*"

Antelope was not certain how this would go. Things were happening too quickly. There might be a little while when he would be able to say a few words, which must be chosen carefully.

Now the four priestesses were bringing out the captive, carefully surrounding her, and flanked by the warriors. Mouse looked him straight in the eye, and he was startled to see that she was haughty and aloof. There was recognition, no more. The little procession drew up before him and stopped.

"I have come to help you," he said quickly. "You are my wife . . ."

"Silence!" signed the priest threateningly. "Use signs only!"

Antelope knew that this was a critical time. It must not go wrong.

"Mouse," he signed, slowly and deliberately, "you must tell them you are my wife. Our lives depend on it."

The priest looked annoyed, but did not interrupt.

Mouse stared at him for a moment, then signed calmly. "I will not lie for you, Antelope. These people have honored me."

He had not expected anything like this. "These are not your people," he blurted desperately, aloud.

"But they have made me a princess!"

"Only to kill you!"

The exchange happened quickly, so quickly that the warriors had no chance to stop them. But now they were separated, and the priest warned them, using signs.

"There will be silence! Signs only, or we will kill you both!"

Antelope nodded in understanding.

"It is as I said," he pleaded in signs. "You must believe me."

"You lie," she signed bitterly. "You only want me for your bed." Her eyes flashed defiance.

The thought occurred to him that this was going rather well now. If he could anger her, the reaction would be one which might convince her captors of her slave-wife status.

"Of course," he signed indignantly. "Why else would I give eleven horses for such as you?"

He saw the anger rise, even through the confusion in her face. She did not understand, but this did not slow her rage.

"Son of a dung-eating dog," she began aloud, "what . . ."

Now he held up a hand to stop her. "Hand signs only!" he warned.

There were chuckles among the onlookers, and he decided to push his luck. His charade seemed to be working. Only a little further reinforcement . . . He kneed his horse forward a step and leaned from the saddle toward her. The woman who stood between stepped aside to avoid the horse, and he now looked full into the eyes of the captive. There was still anger and defiance, but he thought that she had never looked so beautiful.

"Forgive me," he whispered. He had taken his braided quirt from the saddle, and now struck her across the shoulders with it. There was probably very little sting through her buckskin dress, but it made a loud pop and she burst into tears.

"How could you?" she cried aloud. Among the People, for anyone to strike another was extremely rare.

"If you will not learn, the whip must teach you!" he signed, even as the warriors moved between them.

The priest spoke a few words and the escort removed Gray Mouse from the scene and back toward the earth lodge. Now the holy man turned back toward Antelope, his face dark.

"Enough!" he signed. "So it is true. You bought her. But important to Morning Star is only whether she has been with a man."

The priest held up a hand. "Yet I do not know whether you tell truth," he reminded. "The girl says you lie. So, if you do, and she is a maiden, we kill you and keep the girl, for Morning Star to honor."

Antelope's heart sank.

"But how . . . ?" he signed.

The priest nodded. "The women will tell us soon. They are examining her now."

38
» » »

Yellow Basket had increasing doubts about the way things were going. *Maybe I am just getting old,* she thought as they hustled the Morning Star Princess back into the lodge. Yet she knew that it was more than that.

Now that she looked back, there must have been doubts in her mind as early as childhood. The first ceremony to Morning Star that she remembered clearly must have been when she was a girl of seven or eight summers. Oddly, she had not thought of that princess as a captive at all. She had been more impressed by the honor that was bestowed on the selected one. The finest of food and drink . . . the sequence of beautiful dresses, lavishly decorated. There were four women whose entire duty for a long time was to see to every slight need or desire of the Morning Star Princess. These women temporarily left their families to accept the honor of becoming the servants of the Princess.

As a little girl, Yellow Basket had longed to be a part of these celebrations. She envisioned herself as one of the priestesses, helping to manage the Morning Star lodge. All the occupants of the lodge, more than forty people in all, had been temporarily evicted. It was an honor, of course. They would stay with relatives in other lodges until after the ceremony.

Most of all, at the time of that first Morning Star Ceremony in her memory, Yellow Basket had envied the Morning Star Princess. The young woman was of a neighboring tribe, a beautiful young woman with a proud demeanor and a friendly smile. She had smiled at Yellow Basket once, when the women had led her outside for the daily exercise. The little girl had been embarrassed by the attention, but thrilled to be noticed. *Maybe,* she thought, *when I grow up I can be as honored as this one.*

It had been confusing when the ceremony took place. Those events were, even now, a blurred memory. The beautiful girl, climbing the painted scaffold, the priest's assistants tying her wrists to the poles . . . *Why is she tied, Mother . . . ? Hush, child . . . So she will not fall.*

There had been a momentary expression of terror on the beautiful face at the last heartbeat, as the priest loosed the sacred arrow. *But the bride must die,* her mother had explained, *so that she may join her husband, Morning Star.*

It had been a shock, but Yellow Basket had been able to accept it. All of the adults seemed to understand, and the ceremony was obviously the most important event in the lives of the Horn People. The village had settled back into the seasonal routine, and the corn grew well.

Several years later, the Morning Star Priest had again announced that this would be the season for the ceremony. The village would wait for a vision to come to one of its warriors, which would reveal where to find the selected maiden. Morning Star would instruct the Wolf Man where to find his bride.

Yellow Basket had wondered about this for a little while, as the village waited for the vision to come. *If it is so great an honor, why is it given to a maiden of another tribe?* she asked herself. She did not speak of this to anyone else, and it was forgotten in the excitement and symbolism when the bride was chosen and brought to the village.

It was a maiden of the Kenzas, the South Wind People. She had been strikingly beautiful, and seemed well suited for her honored position as Morning Star's bride. Yellow Basket, feeling the stirring of excitement in her own young womanhood, had experienced a strange sensuality during the ceremony. It was an arousal that she did not understand, but she now assumed that it must be a part of the entire sequence of life. And the corn grew well.

That was a long time ago. Yellow Basket had married and raised her children. She could not remember how many times Morning Star had demanded a new bride over the years. It was an irregular interval. Only the Morning Star Priest, who watched the movements of the heavenly bodies and charted their positions, could determine when the ceremony must occur. Morning Star, as she understood the story, pursues his wife, Evening Star, across the sky. Sometimes the two are close together, Evening Star in her pale glory, Morning Star red with his passion. But often she runs away, and Morning Star must have a woman. The People, the Horn People, have been chosen to provide this new wife whenever he demands it.

Yellow Basket remained fascinated by the legend, and was greatly honored, after her childbearing years were over, to be selected as one of the priestesses to serve the Morning Star Princess. She had now participated several times. She was the eldest of the four now, and her office carried much prestige. A great deal of the responsibility for the unseen events inside the Morning Star lodge fell to her. The priest was in charge, of course, but the personal care of the Princess was assigned to her . . . Yellow Basket. The girl's hair must be plaited exactly in the traditional fashion. She must be pampered and petted and honored.

Some of those selected had been better than others. There were those who fought the honor. It was possible, if the chosen bride remained reluctant, to administer a ceremonial drink concocted by the priest. That usually calmed the maiden's doubts.

There had been one, a few years back, who had behaved very badly. Things had gone well until the time when the bride must mount the scaffold. The kicking and screaming when the priest's assistants were forced to restrain her had been an embarrassment. The girl had continued to scream and shout in her own tongue until the sacred arrow flew. A few moments afterward, even. The corn had grown well. Moderately well, at least. Maybe that was when Yellow Basket had begun to have doubts again.

Now she looked at the present Morning Star Princess, still flushed with anger. Tears streamed down the girl's face. It had been unfortunate, the arrival of the young warrior who claimed to be her man. It had certainly upset the smooth progression of the ceremonial preparation.

Yellow Basket had rather liked this princess from the first. This one had spirit, and was worthy of Morning Star. Tall, quite pretty in a confident, dignified way. There was a look of eagles in the wide-set eyes, a vision of distance. This would have been a woman who was a good friend and neighbor under other circumstances. The girl had been on a quest of some sort. Yellow Basket had explained to her that *this* was her quest. It must be so. The Wolf Man had been led to her by the vision of Morning Star, had he not?

The old priestess felt just a trifle guilty about interpreting events to match the upcoming ceremony. The girl had been searching, wearing that amulet of the people to the north. Yellow Basket had not asked all about that. There was no need to know. She had nodded, with the implication that yes, this was part of the overall plan. She had allowed the girl to wear the pendant under her dress, because it seemed important to her. No harm, if it would keep her calm.

Then came the young man. It had been a foolhardy thing, for a stranger to ride headlong into a village of the *Pani,* the Horn People. The men might easily have killed him. Maybe it would have been better if they had. But maybe not. There would still have been the problem that they now faced.

The young stranger insisted that this was his wife. He obviously had strong feelings for the girl. And she for him, Yellow Basket thought, though the girl denied it. He *was* quite handsome. If she had known someone like that in her own younger years . . . No matter. The problem was simple. Which one was lying?

It would not have mattered, except that the sequence of the Morning Star Ceremony had already begun. If the young man told the truth, this girl was no virgin. For her to be offered to Morning Star as a bride would be an unforgivable offense. Yellow Basket shuddered to think of the possible punishment that might be inflicted on the village by the wrath of Morning Star.

If the young man were lying, of course, the girl might still be a maiden. It had been assumed so, since the vision of the selected Wolf Man had led to this one. Yet, maybe not. Could this girl have only been in the wrong place, the wrong time? Did the Wolf Man make a mistake?

Yellow Basket had watched the argument outside, as the two principal figures accused each other of lies. It was hard to tell. She had been completely surprised at the command of the Morning Star Priest.

"Take her inside and see if she speaks truth!" he had ordered.

Now Yellow Basket took a deep breath. Here was a terrible responsibility. She glanced again at the proud girl, wiping the tears from her eyes.

If she tells truth, thought Yellow Basket, *she is still a virgin bride for Morning Star.* The man would be killed because he lied. Both would die then, he at the hands of the men who now waited outside, and the girl later on Morning Star's bridal scaffold.

If the examination indicated that the girl was not a maiden, but a wife, she would be useless, even dangerous, for the ceremony. The priest might still decide to kill them both, but who knows the mind of the Morning Star Priest?

Two lives depend on my findings, Yellow Basket thought. *But what will I find?*

"I am to find whether you speak truth," she signed to the girl.

Mouse shook her head, not understanding. "What?" she signed.

Well, let us get it over, thought Yellow Basket. She motioned to the other women.

In the space of a heartbeat the women had seized the girl and pinned her down on one of the bench-like beds. She struggled for a moment, then realized that it was useless. The struggles ceased. *At least her pride does not let her cry out,* thought Yellow Basket. She lifted the buckskin dress and ran a hand gently up the girl's thigh. She did not know what to expect, but there was no question. The girl was telling the truth. Her young man was lying. They had not married.

"What is it?" asked one of the women.

Yellow Basket gave her a scornful sidewise glance. "I tell only the priest," she said.

The women released the bewildered girl, who now signed angrily. "What is happening?"

"Never mind," signed Yellow Basket. "It is nothing."

Her findings solved the problem, of course. The young man would be killed and the ceremonial preparations would go on.

Then a thought came to her. The man must have known about the Morning Star Ceremony, and what it implied. *But the girl does not!*

she thought. The young suitor had been willing to risk his life . . . no, to *give* his life, to try to save her. Ah, that any woman should have so devoted a man! The eyes of Yellow Basket filled with tears. She wiped them away.

She stooped to emerge from the doorway, and straightened to stride across the open space to where the Morning Star Priest waited.

"There has been a mistake," she said, throwing a withering glance at the Wolf Man standing beside the priest. "This man, the stranger here, tells truth. If we gave this woman to Morning Star, we might all be destroyed. The woman is this man's wife, as he said. You should thank him for saving us from a bigger mistake!"

39
»»»

The two rode in grim silence. Antelope had tried repeatedly to initiate conversation, and each time was met with angry words and dark looks.

He did not understand what had happened back there at the village of the Horn People. The old woman had come out of the lodge, spoken to the priest, and a brief argument ensued. There appeared to be angry words between the woman, the priest, and one of the warriors, who seemed to be a leader of some sort. There were gestures toward the lodge and toward Antelope, and at one point he gripped his weapon to fight if needed.

Then suddenly, it was over. The disgruntled priest, with a last disparaging look toward the warrior, turned and began to sign to Antelope.

"Take your woman and go! Do not come back!"

The old woman was bringing Gray Mouse from the lodge. The girl looked angry and confused.

"My woman's horse?" Antelope inquired.

"They are bringing it," the priest signed, his face dark.

Mouse stood, looking from the priest to Antelope and back again.

"What? What is it?" she signed.

There was no answer, and she turned to Antelope.

"What have you done?" she demanded.

"Nothing, Mouse. We are to be allowed to go."

"They have treated me well!" she shouted at him. "Your lies have spoiled it all!"

"Mouse, be still! You do not know . . ."

The priest stepped forward to intervene. "You should silence your woman," he signed. "Here is the horse. Now go!"

A man was approaching, leading the bay. He attempted to help the girl mount, but she pulled away angrily.

"I do not know what you have done, Antelope," she spoke at him, "but I do not like it!"

She dug heels into the flanks of the bay and cantered out of the village, with Antelope close behind.

"Wait!" he called. "You are going the wrong way. The People are to the south!"

"*Your* people," she shouted over her shoulder. "*Mine* are to the north."

She kicked the horse into a hard run before he could answer. It was some time before she drew rein. Both horses were blowing hard and Antelope had begun to fear that the animals would be injured.

"Mouse!" he began. "I must tell you about the Horn People, back there!"

"I know them, Antelope! Better than you. They respected me, honored me. Now that is gone. So I will find my own people. That is what I came to do anyway."

She hurried on, though at a slower pace. *That is good,* thought Antelope. *At least she has not gone completely mad. She saves her horse.*

Realizing the futility of arguing with an angry woman, he rode silently. Once or twice he attempted light conversation unsuccessfully.

"Go on home!" she yelled at him. "I do not need you!"

He was tempted, but could not leave her. At least, not without explaining. No, he could not leave her anyway. He felt the need to support her quest, as one would for a sister or a friend. Yet his feelings for her were much deeper. He saw no alternative but to ride with her, to explain when the chance came. If, of course, he himself could understand what had occurred.

In the hurry to depart, and in Mouse's anger, they had traveled somewhat farther than might be expected. By the time Sun Boy spread his paints across the western sky and prepared for the night, the *Pani* village was far behind them.

The girl chose the camping place, pulling her horse to a stop and swinging down. She said nothing, but began to gather sticks and tinder. Antelope watched for a few moments, and then gathered some fuel himself. He approached cautiously.

"May I share your fire?" he asked.

Mouse looked up, startled. Then their ridiculous plight seemed to dawn on her. She smiled thinly, not quite able to give up her anger.

"Maybe so," she agreed.

He waited. He must not push her too hard. Maybe it would be better not to try to bring it up, but to wait for her to do so.

Mouse had no supplies, so he shared dried meat from his pack, and her attitude warmed a little. She sat staring into the fire, quiet and withdrawn.

"My heart is heavy about your dog," he ventured.

Tears came to her eyes, the first he had seen. "They killed him?" It was really not a question.

"Yes. I found him. I was tracking you."

She was quiet a little longer, and finally spoke. "You hit me."

"Yes. My heart was heavy to do so, Mouse."

"Then *why?*"

"I had told them I bought you. If you belonged to me, maybe they would let me take you."

"But I wanted to stay. Why did you send me away?"

"I . . . I am not sure, Mouse. I told them that you are my wife, so they would not want you. They need a maiden . . ."

"But I *am* . . ."

"Yes. That I do not understand. They must have one who has not been with a man. But you . . ."

"And I have not, Antelope!" Her anger was rising again.

"I know. Or I thought so. But no, that is not important . . . to me. No, this does not sound right."

Her eyes were flashing now.

"Wait, Mouse. You know *why* they seek a maiden?"

"Yes. To be their Morning Star Princess. I had been chosen!"

"Yes. But do you know the ceremony?"

"Not yet. It would have been told to me!"

"But too late. Mouse, they *kill* the Princess so that she becomes their Morning Star's bride!"

"That is not true!" she snapped.

"Yes, yes, it is. You were being prepared for that. The Growers back there told me."

She was silent, and he waited. He had not understood the sequence of events. The priest had said that the girl would be examined, the old woman had returned and announced that Antelope's lie was truth. The Morning Star Princess was not a maiden, but a wife, and therefore unfit to be the bride of Morning Star. But why would the woman lie?

Slowly, a suspicion began to dawn on him. Women often have an empathy for other women. Might it not be so in this? There must be those, even among the Horn People, who regretted the sacrifice of another woman on the altar of Morning Star. Given the opportunity, might not such a woman use the chance to save the life of a captive girl?

"Mouse," he spoke carefully, "had the old woman been kind to you?"

"Of course. They all had! It was as I said. I was honored."

"Yes, I know. But that one, the oldest. She was a leader of the others, no?"

"Yes . . ."

"And the most kind?"

"What are you asking, Antelope?"

"I am made to think," he said slowly, "that *she* saved your life. Mine, too, maybe."

"I do not understand."

"Nor do I. But . . . Mouse, when I struck you . . ."

He saw her anger rise. "I have not forgotten that, Antelope," she vowed.

"That was to show that you were mine," he explained.

"But men of the People do not strike their wives!"

"That is true. But many others do. Head Splitters . . . I thought that it would make the Horn People think that you *are* my wife and let you go free."

She was silent for a little while, and finally spoke. "It is true? They kill the Morning Star Princess?"

"Yes. I had to hurry to find you, before . . ."

"You might have been killed, Antelope."

"But I was not. Nor were you."

Now her tears started again. "What can I say?" she mumbled.

He placed an arm around her and drew her close. Soon she drew back, dried her tears, and smiled at him.

"So it is over," he stated. "I am forgiven?"

"Of course, Antelope. I am made to think that I have been very foolish."

His heart beat faster. "But it is good now," he told her. "Let us return to the People, and . . ."

"No!" she stated emphatically.

"What? But you said . . ."

"I said you are forgiven . . ." She smiled. "For striking with the whip, saving my life. But this changes nothing. I must find my people!"

Aiee, he thought. *This is where it started.* He remained quiet for a little while, absently poking at the fire. It was apparent that he had lost. Even though he had managed to save their lives, he had lost Gray Mouse to the call of her heritage.

She pulled the pendant from between her breasts and let it dangle outside the dress where it should be, displayed as a part of her identity.

"Those who made this are my people," she told him. "I have talked to those who know them. My own people are to the north, and I can find them . . . learn who I am. Do you not understand this, Antelope?"

"Yes," he said slowly. "Not really, Mouse. But I am made to think that you must do this. That I understand."

"It is good," she said, pleased.

"Yet there is something that I must do, too," he said thoughtfully, staring into the fire.

"A quest, Antelope?"

"Maybe. Yes, a quest. That is true."

"Tell me of yours, Antelope! You will start back in the morning?"

"No . . . On my quest, I am made to think that I must help you on yours."

40
»» »» »»

They sat on their horses overlooking a cluster of lodges along the stream. Gray Mouse's heart beat faster.

"My people," she murmured softly.

In the days since they had left the village of the Horn People, everything had seemed to go well. Travel was easy, and the weather continued to be fine. It had taken her a few days to overcome her anger at Dark Antelope for interrupting the marvelous pampering that she had enjoyed as the Morning Star Princess. She had been so completely absorbed in the ceremonial pageantry that she found it hard to believe that the final act would have been her own death.

It was three days before the situation became really clear in her mind. She had ridden glumly, in silence most of the time. It was as if she knew that Antelope spoke truth, but that she was unable to accept it. He had wisely refrained from conversation, except for that necessary for travel and camp and care of the horses. Her anger at the entire situation seemed to descend on Antelope, where it lay smoldering. He had suggested that she might have been drugged to alter her thinking. It would not have been hard to administer some potion in the form of the ceremonial food and drink that she had been given.

Such spells were known. Even such a suggestion had angered her. But maybe that was part of the spell.

She had awakened one morning with her mind clear. She had thought that it was so all along, but *aiee!* The colors of the sunrise, the songs of the birds, the feel of the morning air on her skin, all seemed like a wonderful new experience. She could remember the events of the past days, but dimly, without detail.

She looked over at Antelope, rising sleepily from his robes. With regret, she realized how ungrateful she had been. Most men would have abandoned her, she thought, in response to such treatment. And she had not even thanked him.

"Antelope," she had said impulsively, "you saved my life."

He had looked at her, puzzled. He had *tried* to tell her. "Maybe so," he said simply.

Mouse was too embarrassed to speak of it further, so the awkward silence continued. Even in the joy of being alive, she found it difficult to share, to speak of her new insights into the situation. She had been afraid, she now realized, that Antelope might misunderstand the change in her. He might expect that her return to normalcy would mean that she would abandon her quest. So, rather than face such further misunderstanding, she remained quiet. She did try to behave in a more kindly manner toward him, and he seemed to appreciate that.

They had stopped often to talk with Growers about the people she sought. That was easier as they penetrated into the north country. The pendant that she wore was easily recognized now. Her quest was nearly over.

Then came the day. They showed the pendant and hand-signed their usual question, to receive the long-awaited answer.

"Yes! They are in summer camp, over there."

"Where? How far?"

"Half a day. Follow the river. You will see their camp. Fifteen, twenty lodges."

So at last, here they sat overlooking the camp of her people.

"My people."

It seemed that her entire life had looked forward to this moment. She glanced at her companion. Antelope sat on his horse, studying the scene below. She wondered what he might be thinking. In fact, Mouse was not certain what to think herself. She had concentrated so long on the quest that she had overlooked the obvious. *Now that I have found them, what do I do next?* she thought, in a sort of panic.

Antelope brought her back to reality. "Are you ready to go down?"

"What? Oh, yes . . ."

The horses picked their way down the steep trail, shifting their balance, following the turns and slopes by instinct as the riders gave free rein to do so. As they neared level ground at the bottom of the slope, a number of dogs rushed out, barking an alarm or a greeting. Mouse thought for a moment of her own Yellow Dog . . . She could hardly remember a time without him.

A tall warrior stepped into the trail in front of them, and another joined him. They were armed, but it seemed only a formality. Mouse had the impression that she and Antelope had been under observation for some time, and were probably considered harmless.

"Greetings," signed Antelope. "We have sought your people . . . the people of this woman."

"How are you called?" asked the warrior.

"I am Dark Antelope, of the Elk-dog People. This is Gray Mouse, one of yours."

Mouse lifted her pendant, which met with smiles and instant recognition. There was also a flurry of talk in an unfamiliar tongue. Not completely so. The syllables had a familiar sound and cadence, but no meaning. She was startled. Somehow, she must have had the idea that she would understand their language, but it was not so. This was a meaningless babble.

"Wait!" she signed. "I do not understand!"

The talk stopped for a moment, and then the tall warrior began to sign.

"How is it," he asked, "that you say you are one of us, but do not know our tongue?"

She nodded eagerly. "Our band . . . my parents . . . died from the spotted sickness. I was small. I grew up with Elk-dog People. Now I have come home."

The warriors nodded, only half interested.

Antelope reentered the conversation. "We would pay our respects to your leader," he signed. "And how are you called?"

"I am Looking Wolf," signed the tall one. "This is Killer of Owls." The other man nodded and pointed to a nearby tree. There hung three dead owl carcasses, with flies buzzing lazily around them. A slight shift in the breeze brought a whiff of decaying flesh. Mouse tried not to react. Now she saw that the one called Killer of Owls wore a necklace of owl feet. She had almost forgotten her dread of the owl when she had been a child.

Now the taller man, Looking Wolf, was signing again. "We have no problems with evil spirits when we have Owl Killer here," he boasted. "Come, I will take you to our chief."

They wound their way through the camp, with people gathering to stare as they passed. Mouse glanced at Antelope.

"They dishonor *Kookooskoos,* the messenger," she whispered.

"It is their way," Antelope said calmly. "No problem of ours."

The little party stopped in front of one of the larger lodges, and Mouse and Antelope dismounted. A distinguished-looking older man sat leaning on a willow backrest, smoking. He did not rise. Looking Wolf was talking rapidly, and the chief nodded, looking over the newcomers. Then he began to sign.

"Wolf, here, has told me what you have said. You were of the band who went south?"

"Yes, yes," Mouse signed. "You know of them?"

"Yes, I remember well. Wait!" He paused and spoke to Looking Wolf, who turned and hurried away. The chief began to sign again. "There is a woman here of that band," he explained. "We will see if you can talk to her."

Mouse nodded eagerly. "It is good," she signed. "I am called Gray Mouse. Do you know my name?"

"No, no, daughter. I was not of that band. And you were small, no?"

"Yes, Uncle," she agreed. "That is true."

"Who is this?" he signed, indicating Antelope. "Your husband?"

Mouse hesitated, and Antelope moved to help her.

"Her almost-brother, Uncle," he signed. "I hope to be her husband."

The old man chuckled. "It is good!"

Mouse was looking at the ornament around the neck of the chief. She was almost certain that the shiny black claws were those of a bear. And the robe, thrown over the backrest . . . She had assumed that it was a buffalo robe, but *no!* It, too, was *bear.*

"Antelope, they kill bears!" she whispered.

"It is their way," Antelope said calmly.

"What is it?" signed the chief.

"Nothing, Uncle. We were admiring your robe," Antelope signed.

"Yes," nodded the chief, stroking the thick brown fur. "A nice fur, no?"

Now Looking Wolf had returned, and spoke briefly to the chief, who nodded.

"I will take you to the woman of your own band," Wolf signed. "Come!"

They thanked the chief and hurried after their escort. The day was growing short.

The old woman sat beneath a small tree, rocking back and forth and singing softly to herself. A younger woman stood beside her. "This is her daughter's lodge," explained Looking Wolf. "Sometimes the mother . . . you will see."

"Grandmother," signed Mouse, "I would ask you of my people."

The woman appeared confused, and the daughter spoke to her, apparently explaining Mouse's inability to speak their language. The woman nodded, and motioned for Mouse to go ahead.

"You were with the band that went south, Grandmother?"

Only now did she notice that the woman's face was deeply pitted with the tracks of the *poch*. On an impulse, Mouse pushed back her hair to show one of the deeper marks on her own skin. The woman's expression brightened.

"You were there?" she signed.

"Yes, yes!" Mouse responded eagerly.

"I remember you!" the woman stated. "Yes! Your husband died too, just before mine. But how is it that you cannot speak, Rabbit Woman?"

Despair swept over Gray Mouse. She had actually found someone who had been there, but whose mind was gone. The woman thought that Mouse was someone else, a friend who may have died. This could tell her nothing. Mouse lifted her pendant.

"Do you know of this?" she signed.

"Yes, yes. Many times. Very pretty. It is good."

"I am sorry," the daughter signed. "Some days are better. You were there?"

"Yes," Mouse signed, tears streaming. "I was too small to remember much. My parents died. Your father?"

"Yes. Nearly the whole band. There are three, maybe four lodges, north of here. You could find them."

"How far?"

"Two or three sleeps, maybe. But stay tonight. Here, I have stew. Bear . . ."

Bear meat. To the People, to eat the flesh of the bear, who often walks on two legs, would be close to cannibalism. Mouse knew that their allies, the Head Splitters, hunted bear on occasion, and relished the meat. Now these people, too.

"Thank you," she signed. "But my almost-brother, here, cannot. His people do not eat bears. And I will honor his customs this time."

"I understand. You will stay?"

"Yes . . . Thank you. We will camp by the stream there."

"It is good," the young woman signed.

Gray Mouse lay sleepless for a long time. She could hear the slow breathing of Antelope beyond the fire. It was good that he slept, because she could not.

She had not known what to expect, but surely not this. Maybe she had hoped for a relative to welcome back the lost sister with a warm embrace. Instead, there was only a mild curiosity . . . "Oh, yes, *that* band . . ."

An owl floated across the star-filled sky. *Be careful,* Kookooskoos, she thought. *You are in danger here. Aiee!* She had known, but had not fully thought this through. These people not only killed owls, but bears, and ate the flesh. *Do they eat owls, too?* she wondered.

Kookooskoos, the messenger . . . Wait . . . Could the owl that had just soared across overhead have been bringing a message to *her?*

As if in answer came the distant cry, the owl's hollow rendition of his own name. But *what* message?

She stared at the Real-star, and at the Seven Hunters making their nightly circle around it. At least that was the same.

Maybe that thought was the thing that caused her other thoughts to begin to fall into place. Whatever the cause, by the time the first pale yellow smudge could be seen against the eastern horizon, she was certain.

Dark Antelope stirred, and looked across the ashes of their dead fire into her eyes. He smiled.

"Antelope," she said, "let us go home. Shall we ask Grandmother when we can marry? It is pleasant in the Moon of Falling Leaves, no?"

And it was good . . .

GENEALOGY

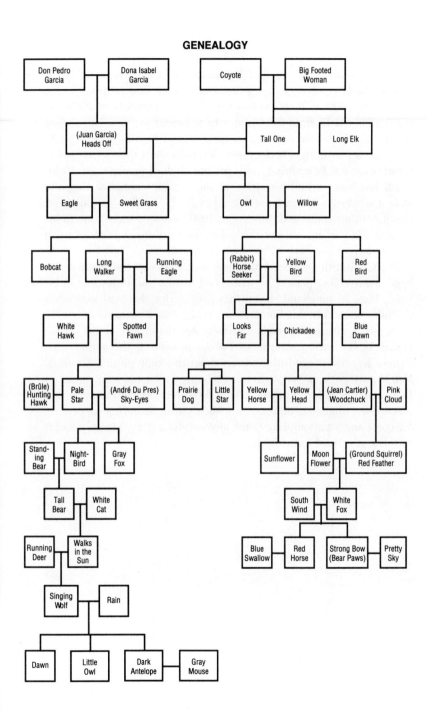

Don Coldsmith was born in Iola, Kansas, in 1926. He served as a World War II combat medic in the South Pacific and returned to his native state, where he graduated from Baker University in 1949 and received his M.D. from the University of Kansas in 1958. He worked at several jobs before entering medical school: he was YMCA Youth Director, a gunsmith, a taxidermist, and for a short time a Congregational preacher. In addition to his private medical practice, Dr. Coldsmith has been a staff physician at the Health Center of Emporia State University, where he still teaches in the English Department. He discontinued medical pursuits in 1990 to devote more time to his writing. He and his wife of thirty-four years, Edna, operate a small cattle ranch. They have raised five daughters.

Dr. Coldsmith produced the first ten novels in the Spanish Bit Saga in a five-year period; he writes and revises the stories first in his head, then in longhand. From this manuscript the final version is skillfully created by his longtime assistant, Ann Bowman.

Of his decision to create, or re-create, the world of the Plains Indian in the early centuries of European contact, the author says: "There has been very little written about this time period. I wanted also to portray these people as human beings, men and women, rather than as stereotyped 'Indians.' As I have researched the time and place, the indigenous cultures, it's been a truly inspiring experience for me. I am not attempting to tell anyone else's story. My only goal is to tell *a* story and tell it fairly."